F
Buffie, Margaret.
Out of focus

Out of Focus

by Margaret Buffie

KCP Fiction

An Imprint of Kids Can Press

KCP Fiction is an imprint of Kids Can Press
Text © 2006 Margaret Buffie

Kids Can Press acknowledges the financial support of the Government of Ontario, through
the Ontario Media Development Corporation's Ontario Book Initiative; the Ontario Arts
Council; the Canada Council for the Arts; and the Government of Canada, through the
BPIDP, for our publishing activity.

Published in Canada by
Kids Can Press Ltd.
29 Birch Avenue
Toronto, ON M4V 1E2

Published in the U.S by
Kids Can Press Ltd.
2250 Military Road
Tonawanda, NY 14150

www.kidscanpress.com

Edited by Charis Wahl
Cover and interior designed by Céleste Gagnon Smale
Cover photo of negative © iStockphoto.com/Driftwood. Cover photo of woman
© Mel Curtis/PhotoDisc. Cover photo of trees courtesy of Céleste Gagnon Smale.
Printed and bound in Canada

CM 06 0 9 8 7 6 5 4 3 2 1
CM PA 06 0 9 8 7 6 5 4 3 2 1

Library and Archives Canada Cataloguing in Publication

Buffie, Margaret
        Out of focus / Margaret Buffie.

ISBN-13: 978-1-55337-955-3 (bound) ISBN-10: 1-55337-955-1 (bound)
ISBN-13: 978-1-55337-956-0 (pbk.) ISBN-10: 1-55337-956-X (pbk.)

1. Alcoholism—Juvenile fiction. I. Title.

PS8553.U453O98 2006   jC813'.54   C2005-906821-3

Kids Can Press is a **LOrUS**™ Entertainment company

To Susan — who knows why

Chapter One

When I photograph, what I'm really doing
is seeking answers to things.

Wynn Bullock, photographer

I have to begin somewhere, so I may as well start at
the End of Life as We Knew It. My mother's — Celia's —
wedding day.

The ceremony was to start at three o'clock. If I didn't
wake her up by noon, she'd never make it. So I dumped the
last three Aspirins out of the bottle, sent my brother, Ally,
and kid sister, Jojo, to the corner drugstore to buy more,
poured a mug of day-old coffee and headed for Celia's room.

When I accidentally on purpose banged the side of her
bed, a muffled groan came from the lump under the flowered
duvet. I bumped the bed again — harder. I'd heard her stum-
ble in, but I'd left her alone then. I wasn't up for a screeching fight at two in the morning — but I'd stayed awake for
a long time simmering. What had happened? Why was she
drinking again? Where was Mario Fonti, her slave-dog hus-
band-to-be?

Celia hadn't had a drink in over four months. She'd
solemnly promised me she'd never touch booze again. And I
had believed her. Almost.

Now, we had passed stage one — that groan meant Celia
was more or less alive. Soon we'd be into the *I'm-dying*
stage, followed by the *Kill-me-and-put-me-out-of-my-misery*
stage, building to the *Just-give-me-the-damn-coffee-and-leave-
me-to-die* finale.

I put the mug — double sugar — on the bedside table along with the Aspirins, pulled the blind down a ways and let it go. It spun to the top of the window with a satisfying clatter. Dusty light streamed in. I twitched back the duvet to uncover a bone-white face. Thin fingers dragged the duvet up again.

"Oh God, I'm dying." She could actually string a few words together. Stage two. *Check.*

"Wake *up.*" I gave the mattress a thump with my hip.

"Go away, you little shit. I really *am* dying."

"You're getting married today, remember?"

Silence. The duvet went down and the face rose like the dead, mascara smeared, eyes bulging.

"No!" it wailed, before falling back. "The pain. My skull ... cracked open. Please. Kill me. I'm gonna die anyway."

Stage three. *Check.* "Look at the birdie!" My camera was around my neck as usual, so I snapped off a shot.

"God, not *now*, Bernie! I'm at death's ... dark ... door."

"Coffee and Aspirins right beside you," I said. "Get *up*. If you fall asleep again, that dark door can slam shut behind you, for all I care."

"Wait, Bernie, don't leave. I've gotta talk to you. Where are the kids?"

I sighed. "Buying drugs on the street corner. Get up, Celia!"

"Oh no ... oh God, what have I *done*?"

Celia pulled herself to a half-sitting position, white T-shirt askew, short pale hair on end, and reached for the pills and coffee. Her hands were shaking, and the black liquid dribbled across the duvet like engine oil. Her eyes were glazed with misery, her mouth slack.

"I — I've got to tell you — just wait," she said, gulping down the pills. But as soon as the acid and coffee hit her stomach, she leaped out of bed, staggered against the wall, lunged for the bathroom and threw up. *Yes.* Served her right.

She'd *sworn* she'd never touch another drink. At the wedding, Celia's friend Lucy would recognize that bleary face for what it was. So would Ally and Jojo. But would lovesick pathetic Mario? Not likely. Schmuck.

Our living room and kitchen doorways were at right angles, and I was standing in front of them like an escaped juvie trying to decide which way to run when the toilet flushed and Celia stumbled toward me, her new silk housecoat floating around her thin legs. It was inside out ... like her stomach. She held up both arms, ready to hug me — guilt always made Celia *huggy* — but I stepped aside. That's when she saw the living room. She frowned ... then it dawned on her.

Behind us, the apartment door banged open. The kids burst in and stopped dead. I raised the camera and took a quick shot. Allister, as always, looked worried, while Jojo just stood there, mouth open, like her mama, waiting to see whether she should stay or make a beeline to the bedroom the three of us shared and hide under the blankets.

"Oh. My. God," Celia said in her husky voice, waving one hand listlessly at the paper streamers and decorated card table. They'd looked so perky and downright cheerful last night, but in the morning's glare now seemed wilted and pathetic. I took a snap of her shocked face.

"There," I said. "Now we have a picture of your hen party for your wedding scrapbook. And wasn't it *fab*?"

I should have known better. Experience is a good teacher, but only if you actually *listen* to it. Mine has taught me to be very careful, as there are always nasty things lurking in the shadows ready to run right over you. But I'd got to know Mario and I figured he loved Celia, and she seemed to be behaving, so I'd given in to Jojo's begging and arranged the party. Lucy said it would be a good-luck gesture for the whole family. Yeah. Sure it would.

I'd asked Mario to get Celia to the apartment at exactly

nine o'clock. I hadn't explained why, but Mario had smiled a knowing smile and promised not to be late. Mario is like that. Punctual. Reliable. Eager to please. Poor old goof. I felt sorry for him. He was nuts about Celia and pathetically working to win over us kids. Which was okay by me. I mean, if your mother's going to marry someone, it may as well be a guy with a grocery store, right? We were never short of food now, which made a nice change from boxed macaroni and chicken wieners.

But last night, nine o'clock came and went, and neither of them showed up. Or phoned. I called Mario's cell twice but it was turned off. At about ten thirty, I sent the kids to bed and ordered Lucy to go home.

"Nothing's happened, Lucy," I said. "He has his cell phone. Besides, someone would have called with bad news by now." Experience had taught me lots about missing mothers, too.

"But I know Mario. He would have called just out of courtesy," she said.

"Luce, where my mother is concerned, there are no courtesies, remember?"

She did. She left.

Please, God, don't let Celia screw this up, I'd prayed as I'd stuffed food back in the fridge. I sat on the living room couch in the dark to wait it out, but fell asleep — to be woken around two, drooling into a pillow, by a key fumbling at the lock, the door banging open and slurred swearing. So *that* was it. Mario had dropped Celia off and she'd headed to the nearest bar. This was great. Just *perfect*. But soon it would be Mario's problem, not just mine. So ... welcome home, Bride of Frankenstein-Fonti.

Now, Celia stared at the decorations and whispered, "This was for me?"

"No. It was for Mother Teresa, but she died, so we called it off."

"It's okay, Mommy," Ally piped up. "We don't mind. Do we, Bernie? You and Mario got busy, right, Mom? Getting ready for today, right?"

Jojo's bottom lip trembled. She was still sad about the ruined party, and now she was sensing the beginning of a fight.

I shrugged like I *didn't* want to slap my mother silly. "Let it go, Celia."

"How long did you guys wait up?" She wasn't looking at us. Celia never did when she was feeling guilty.

"What difference does it make? The kids were tired, so they went to bed — and Lucy had to get up early to arrange the flowers at Mario's, so I sent her home."

"Oh God, Lucy was here, too? I am *so sorry*, Berns." She finally let her glance slide over the kids. "I'm sorry, Ally, Jojo. I feel like such a —"

"Hey, kids. Time's a-wasting," I said. Her apologies are always so *wet*. "Your wedding clothes are all laid out. Go get washed."

Their faces lit up as they escaped down the hall to our room.

"Bernie," Celia said, "please, *please* don't be mad. Look, I'm really sorry about last night. If you'd only warned me —"

She was hard on my heels as I stalked into the kitchenette. "No big deal, okay? What time do you have to be ready?"

"But it *is* a big deal." She slumped dramatically onto a chair and threw her head back. Celia should've gone into acting. She could bring on the waterworks at the drop of a gold stud earring. Right on cue, two crocodile beauties rolled from her eyes.

"Okay," I said between clenched teeth, "it was a *semi*-big deal. Feel better? Where did you get to last night anyway?"

She shook her head helplessly, her eyes on the ceiling,

as if looking for inspiration in the cobwebbed cracks in the old plaster.

Fine. I'd take this one step at a time. "Was Mario with you?"

Another dismal shake.

"So you went on a binge alone," I said. "*Lovely*."

Celia sat upright, sighed and rubbed her eyes. "We got back here about eight thirty and ... I don't know what happened, Bernie, but when I looked at him, sitting there behind the wheel of that damn delivery truck of his, smiling at me with such ... *kindness* — suddenly it came at me. Like a bolt of lightning."

"What did?"

"What I had to do."

My throat tightened. "*Had* to do? Celia, you didn't!"

"I did, Bernie. I did. I told him it wouldn't work."

"Ah, jeez, Celia! What'd you do that for? What'd he say?"

Celia rubbed her cupped hands up and down her arms. "He — he tried to talk me out of it, but not *urgently*, you know? He's just so *nice*. But I let it all out. I *had* to. Finally he believed me. Said to call him in the morning if I changed my mind. Otherwise, he'd start calling people at noon. Then he drove away." She glanced at the kitchen clock. "I guess it's done now. Finished."

I'd been keeping a tight lid on my anger for hours. Now it blew off like an overheated pressure cooker. "Are you *nuts*? Are you completely *crazy*?" I shouted.

"I — I couldn't —"

"Where did you end up last night?" I hissed.

"I was upset, Bernie. I walked over to the coffee shop to calm down. I was going to come home right after. *Honest*. But a couple of friends from my old job came in just as I was leaving." She sighed and slumped lower in her chair. "I told them I'd just canceled my wedding — and they asked me to a club for a quick drink. I didn't intend to stay long. But I was ... worked up, Bernie, I needed to unwind. I needed to think."

"So you did some deep *thinking*?" I sneered.

"Don't get snarky at me, Bernice Dodd. I *did* do serious thinking."

"And?"

"It wouldn't have worked. You warned me not to marry him and you were right."

"I said that two months ago, when you got engaged! But you said Mario was right for you! I wanted you to tell him about your drinking. But you said that was all in the past. And look, less than four months and you're at it *again*!"

"No, no, last night was a one-off! Honest. People do stuff like that when their world is falling apart, Bernie. I'll be fine — *really* ..."

"You were so *sure* Mario was the guy for you. Third time lucky, you kept saying. Did you even *think* about the kids? They were finally going to have a decent place to live, a new school, a dad they might actually like! A dad who didn't shout all the time or smack their mother around, or up and leave or —"

"Don't! Don't you dare start —" Celia ground out.

"We were *finally* going to get out of this dump! Call Mario and fix this. Fix it!"

"It won't work, Bernie," she said in a hollow voice. "I don't love Mario."

Love? Why was she yattering on about love? Like she had any idea what *that* was.

I opened my mouth to shout louder, when the phone rang.

"Don't answer it!" Celia cried as we both made a grab for the cordless receiver, but I wrenched it away, giving her a push for good measure. She collapsed onto the chair, sobbing like the bad actress she is.

"What!" I shouted into the phone.

"Bernice? Honey? It's me — Lucy. What's going on? I'm at Mario's. He says the wedding is *off*." Lucy tends to squeak when she's upset.

My eyes burned, but I refused to give in to stupid tears. "Yeah, Luce. It's off. Celia needs time to think," I said. "Actually to *drink*."

"Oh no, she's not!" Lucy wailed. "Do you need me? Does *she* need me?"

I stared at my mother, slumped in the chair, head in hands. I grabbed my camera and took a quick shot. She looked up at me with her soulful cat eyes. A sliver of pity slid into me, but I pulled it out before it could pierce a sympathy vein. A few years ago, I would have hugged her, told her everything would be okay. But not now. Not anymore. This was the absolute end of Put-Up-with-Anything Bernice Dodd.

"Hey, Celia. You wanna tell Lucy why you've copped out?" I held out the receiver.

Celia shook her head.

"Listen, Lucy," I said into the phone, "I'll call you later, okay? I gotta talk to the kids. They don't know yet."

Lucy's voice was a whisper now. "Mario's very upset, as you can imagine, so I'll stay with him for a while. I'll drop by for dinner with a pizza. Don't worry, Bernie. It'll all work out."

"Will it? I won't hold my breath," I said in a dead voice.

When I hung up, Celia mumbled into her hands, "What are we going to *do*?"

I just stared at her. There were no words.

"I don't even have my job anymore," she moaned. "They've hired someone else. Mr. Todd has been good about the rent, but I promised to pay it off the day we moved out. God! — that was supposed to be next week, when we got back from the honeymoon! Oh, Berns, I think we're in a real mess."

"You *think*?" I shouted.

"Do you think Mario would —"

"Oh no! You're *not* going to ask that poor guy for one red cent, Celia. I'll figure something out."

She nodded, staring at her feet. She was used to me fixing things. Feeding the kids. Doing the laundry. Cleaning this dump. Until Mario came along. He'd made sure our shelves were stocked and had even hired a woman to clean the place every few weeks when I told him how hard it was to keep things up, go to school and take care of the kids.

Now all that was gone — because Celia had looked at his van and his *niceness* and decided she didn't want any part of him. *Now* I had to face never-ending dust bunnies, cockroaches, a vanishing mother and nighttime escapes from angry landlords. Rock on, Celia.

I left her moaning at the ceiling and walked down the hall, camera tightly in hand, trying to decide how to break the news to Jojo and Ally.

And that's when it came to me with absolute certainty. We *could not* go back to the way things were. I had to get these kids to a safe place. Nothing was ever going to change if I didn't change it.

Chapter Two

While photographs may not lie,
liars may photograph.

Lewis Hine, photographer

Jojo cried like her heart would break. Ally just stared at me like a fawn whose mother'd been downed by a bullet. Then he nodded and started sorting his pencils into neat piles.

Jojo sniffled. "I guess I won't get to wear my bridesmaid dress, right?"

"No. Not today, kiddo," I said.

"But will we still get to live at Mario's house?"

"No. Sorry, Jo."

"But he'll still visit and we'll see him lots, right?" She wiped her eyes and looked at me, full of hope.

I didn't want to burst all her balloons all at once, but why prolong the torture? I swallowed hard. "I don't think he'll be around here much, but he'll still be Lucy's friend like before. Maybe we'll see him at her place."

"That won't be any *gooood*." She fell onto her pillow, sobbing.

I patted her back and said to Ally, "You should rest, too. There's tons of sandwiches in the fridge for later. If Mom leaves, call Lucy's cell phone, okay?"

He nodded, and in a small voice said, "I guess I'll still have to see that Sean guy every day, now that we're not moving, huh?" He glanced over his shoulder, the tight spot between his eyebrows white with tension.

This was killing me. "I'll think of something, Ally. I promise." I ran my hand down the back of his head. My own had started to throb. I was getting headaches a lot lately — like a giant's fingers gripping my skull.

Ally had been happy about the wedding — as happy as Ally ever got — especially when he found out we were leaving this apartment and the bully down the hall. A lot of his strange little ways had eased off when Mario came into our lives. I'd had high hopes for Ally becoming a regular kid. Now, he was obsessively counting and recounting his colored pencils. Square one again.

Jojo, of course, had been ecstatic, especially about her new ankle-length teal-blue chiffon dress with its thirteen black buttons, its black sash and matching black velvet shoes. I'd even found her a tiny black velvet purse for her wrist. She'd worn the shoes so often — even to bed the past week — they'd become a bit worse for wear. I'd steamed them yesterday to make them presentable. The only good thing about Celia's meltdown was that I wouldn't have to wear *my* hideous dress — matching teal blue with twenty-two black velvet buttons and black velvet sash. It could now molder in the back of my cupboard with the low-heeled ugly velvet shoes. I didn't like dresses at the best of times, but that thing was definitely Bridesmaid of Frankenstein-Fonti.

I tried to cheer Jojo up. "Hey," I said, sitting on the bed, "think about it. It could be worse. We could be in a huge, wet, prehistoric jungle with no food or water, being tracked by kid-eating dinosaurs."

"You've said that one before," Jojo muttered. "And it *is* worse than that."

"Not if you're dinosaurs with no kids to eat," I offered. "You'd starve."

Jojo hiccuped. "That's dumb." She rolled over on her stomach.

"Yeah, I know. Sorry. You were up late, Jo. Why don't you have a little nap? Hey, what do you call a sleeping dinosaur?"

She mumbled into her pillow, "Dunno."

"A dino-snore!" Then I laughed like it was the best joke ever.

Ally gave me a look of disgust. Jojo thought about it, then said, "I like that one, Bernie."

"Me, too. Listen, Lucy's coming over later — with pizza."

"Ham and pineapple?" she asked in a froggy voice.

"You know it!" I said, grabbing a knitted afghan. She was asleep before I finished tucking it around her.

"You'll stay by her for a bit, okay, Ally? I gotta think."

He had moved on to counting erasers, sketchbooks, sets of colored paper Mario had bought him. Ally's always counted things — peas, candies, pencils, stairs — anything, really. And for a long time, if different foods touched on his plate, he'd panic. I finally put everything on separate plates. When he started tying and retying his shoelaces a dozen times a day, I got him sneakers with Velcro. But then he just switched to making sure the stove was turned off or that no one had left a hair dryer plugged in or the door unlocked before we went to sleep at night. He'd get out of bed a dozen times to check. Celia said it was a phase, that he'd outgrow it. But I knew growing had nothing to do with it. This kid was an oddball.

"You okay?" I asked.

Another nod, followed by an annoyed *tsk* and more counting, keeping his world in order.

I walked into the living room and fell on the couch. Cardboard boxes lined the walls, ready to go to Mario's. We'd have to unpack the stupid things now. Why did Celia agree to marry him in the first place? I mean, when she'd announced she was going to marry Mario Fonti, Grocer

Extraordinaire, I'd instantly felt sorry for the poor guy. He had no idea what he was getting himself into.

Well, *now* he knew.

Mario was Celia's latest desperate attempt to find someone to take care of us. Dad took off when I was twelve and a half and Ally was seven. We hadn't seen a whole lot of him even before that — he'd been a photojournalist, the kind that went to dangerous places to take pictures of wars, famine and disasters. But out of the blue, when I was almost nine, he quit and bought a photo studio here in Winnipeg. That only lasted a few years. Sometimes I've wondered if he needed disasters — even if he had to make *himself* one.

It had been fun having him home at first. He and Celia had lots of friends and parties. But after he lost the studio to bill collectors, things went crooked. They usually had a bottle of wine with dinner — but soon they added a second, then another — and before long, dinners weren't a whole lot of fun. Mostly they turned into ugly arguments.

Ally and I'd slide away to our rooms. But once, out of nowhere, right in front of us, Dad threw a glass of wine in Celia's face. He tried to laugh it off, but Celia looked at him like he'd turned into a snake before her very eyes. I guess he had, really.

After that, he started pushing her around when he'd had too much. Not hitting, just pushing. One night, he pushed her so hard she fell off her chair and banged her head on the side of the counter. I ran at him, punching. Dad was a big guy and when his hand connected, it packed a wallop, let me tell you. I landed against the wall.

The next morning, he offered to buy me a pair of sneakers I'd been begging for, but I just said, "I don't want them. 'Cause every time I'd look at them, I'd feel sick. Like *you* should when you look at Mom."

He stared at me like I'd grown a second set of eyes, but

a few days later, he announced that he'd joined Alcoholics Anonymous, where people with drinking problems could get better. He began freelancing for a newspaper and photographed weddings and parties on weekends. After a few months, he started taking me along to help with the equipment. Things seemed better. No wine. Celia seemed happier. I relaxed a bit.

Dad made part of the basement into a darkroom. Soon he let me help develop his pictures. While we worked, he and I would talk about photography — sometimes about the way he saw the world through his camera lens. He said he could see things other people missed just using their eyes. He said if you wanted to catch the essence of people — see what was *really* going on inside them — you had to use black-and-white film. He always carried an extra camera loaded with it.

"Send the shutter deep into their souls," he said. "Color shots are like sunglasses, reflecting back social masks — not people's real essences."

I wasn't sure what he meant until I watched the images surface in the chemical baths — people on buses, in restaurants, on the street as well as at weddings, bar mitzvahs and other events. Then I understood. Without the mask of color, faces gave away whether they were tired, lost, happy, sad, mean, kind, sly, angry. Sometimes it was like magic, other times it was plain scary, when the camera caught people's secret thoughts and exposed what they figured no one else could see. Would Dad ever risk taking his own picture in black and white? What would I see in it? What would he see?

Whatever. He seemed a lot happier. Maybe things would stay better, I thought. Naive, that was me.

Dad is one of those guys people immediately take to — tall and handsome, with a pile of coffee-colored hair, a short beard and a slow, easy smile. At weddings, I saw how he would become like one of the family almost immediately. And, of course, he got free drinks. In his first few months of AA, he only drank cola, but then he started having a few beers during the receptions. Then a few more. One night, a good-looking woman from the wedding party told me there was a cab — already paid for — waiting for me, and she'd see that my daddy got home safely.

I may have been only twelve, but I wasn't stupid. Celia wasn't stupid either. When she saw me alone in the cab, she knew.

Ally crept into my room when the shouting started during the night. I gave him my earphones, turned up the volume and put in my swimming earplugs. The fight went on for a long time. The next day was a Saturday, so I snuck Ally out to the mini-pool at the end of our block before they got up. I told him a lot of knock-knock jokes — neither of us laughed. We stayed until noon.

When we got home, Lucy was there, with red eyes and a shaky smile. She said in a strange bright voice that there'd been an accident. Celia was fine, she was in the hospital — but only for a day or so — and Dad had gone to visit his family in Newfoundland. Then she took Ally and me to her place and gave us ice cream and cake before dinner. Now *that* would make any kid suspicious.

When Celia came home, the left side of her face was swollen and purple, and there was a chip out of one front tooth. She was kind of hunched over — I found out later she had two cracked ribs.

In my desk drawer, I discovered an envelope with two black-and-white photos inside. Of my father. In one, he had his sunglasses on, looking straight at the camera. In the second, he'd taken off the glasses. It looked like someone had drained the life right out of his eyes. On the back, he'd written "Always use black and white to see the truth. Sorry, kid." I flushed them both down the toilet.

I *tried* to remember the quiet talks in his car, the times we worked side by side in the darkroom, but it didn't tell me why he drank. Or why he hurt Celia. And it didn't stop me hating him for leaving, for not *trying*.

Celia wandered through the house like a ghost. Didn't seem to know we were there. Soon, she started sleeping past the time we left for school. I'd try to get Ally breakfast and some kind of lunch to take with him, but we were late a lot, and usually had to run to catch the bus.

A month or so after Dad left, Ally's teacher sent a letter home, asking Celia to come in for a visit.

When she got back, she shouted, "Can you believe it? That ... that *woman* had the *nerve* to ask me if I'd like Ally put in the breakfast program — *and* did I need help planning his lunches — he often shows up without one and has to take bits and pieces from his friends. Aren't you feeding him, Bernice?"

I gaped at her. "You're blaming me? If you don't like the way he's being looked after, get out of the damn bed once in a while and do it yourself!"

She'd actually looked surprised. It was almost laughable. Two nights later, she told us that Lucy had got her a job as a receptionist at a small-stage theater — Lucy was a costume designer for the main stage. Celia said she was sorry for neglecting us, but she was fine now. We celebrated with a Salisbury House burgers and chips feast. Then we played cards and laughed a lot.

She seemed to like her new job and Ally got breakfast and lunch. Things improved.

Dad sent us a postcard now and again of lighthouses or views of the sea. I asked Celia once or twice when — *if* — he was coming back home. But she said she didn't know, so I stopped asking. Then one Sunday, out of the blue, he called. After Celia hung up, she said in a tight voice that he'd met an old girlfriend and wanted a divorce. That it was for the best. I could tell she needed to cry, so I took Ally to the living room and put on a video. Then I lay on the floor, trying to decide what I felt. Sad, I suppose — the times we'd spent together working in the darkroom would never happen again. And guilty, for not missing him more. Sometimes I'd forgotten him for days on end. But, mostly, I was relieved. Now Celia would be safe.

Imagine my surprise when, for my thirteenth birthday, I got a present all the way from Newfoundland. It was one of Dad's better automatic cameras, with two rolls of black-and-white film and a small booklet explaining how the camera worked. And two more snapshots. Both in color. One was just of him — smiling, but wearing sunglasses. In the other, he still had them on, but his arm was around a small, chubby woman with big hair. She was smiling, her eyes a bright blue, her hand in the air as if waving at me. She looked so happy.

I shoved the camera and the pictures to the back of the closet. The color film and the sunglasses said it all. He knew — and I knew — he hadn't changed. And I felt sorry for the smiling woman.

Things leveled out a bit until Celia met Sebastian Mantras, a local actor, at the theater. Seb also taught a couple of courses at the university downtown. He was a six-foot-two bag of bones with a large orange nose, enormous ears and frizzy brown hair and beard. He threw his long, flat hands around when he talked. Which was a lot. And mostly about him. He always said other people talked a load of crap, but he clearly never listened to himself. I figured if he flapped those ears and hands at the same time, he could get liftoff, hover above the rest of us and look down his nose without having to engage in crap conversations.

A few months after Celia met him, we moved into his warehouse loft in Market Square. I thought it was a pit, but Celia said it was very arty. She and I tried to clean it up, but

Seb was always in the way — preparing his next audition, strutting splay-footed up and down the living room quacking like a demented mallard and asking us to please, *please* give him some *space*. How about a one-way ticket to Mars?

As you might have guessed, Seb was ... *intense*. Not at all interested in Ally or me, but the less attention he paid us the better. He gave me the creeps. Yet Celia was smiling more — which completely baffled me. What she had to smile about, living with the Ego on Stilts, was beyond me. Until, that is, she announced she was expecting a baby.

Chapter Three

The brave ones were shooting the enemy,
the crazy ones were shooting film.

Anonymous

Overnight, Seb got all glum and sour faced. He said Celia had become pregnant on purpose — that he'd told her he didn't want kids. I don't know what he thought Ally and I were, but I guess we didn't count.

As the weeks went by, just in case Celia didn't understand how ticked off he was, Seb picked up the pace, growling about how hard done by he felt. I knew that it was only a matter of time before he started acting like Dad, so I hunkered down and waited.

I'm still not sure why, but after Celia told us she was having the baby, I dug out Dad's camera and started taking pictures. Maybe I was hoping to send him shots of Celia looking round and happy, or Ally looking healthy and carefree. Maybe I wanted to show him what he was missing. Yeah, sure. Pathetic really, because Celia wasn't happy. And Ally was still wetting the bed most nights. Maybe I figured the camera would see something I was missing — maybe a way out of this new mess.

Joanne — Jojo — came home from the hospital wrapped in a white gossamer coverlet, looking like a crumpled peach rose. I had about eight shots left on the roll and I took five of her right away. Ally was always lugging her around, a sublime glow on his thin face. Even Celia smiled when she looked at them together. Jojo had chubby cheeks and dark eyes and a shock of black hair that stood out around her head like a night mist. She smelled like milk and soap and warm vanilla. And, unlike her miserable jerk of a father, Jojo was a smiler. The thing is, she's never changed. It drives me crazy at times, but mostly it keeps *me* from going crazy.

I finished the roll with shots of Ally — him playing goo-goo eyes with a grinning toothless Jojo, doing his homework beside her crib and lying on the floor reading, Jojo in her car seat by his head.

When I got the film developed, I saw again what Dad meant by finding the *real* person in black and white. The first few were of Celia — near the end of her term. Her tummy was round, her legs and arms like sticks, her face gaunt, her cat eyes uneasy ... distant. My lighting was a mess — one overexposed, another under — but I hadn't finished reading the manual when I shot them.

The next couple were better. One was a group shot taken at dinner when Lucy was over. Seb had a hot white light running down one side of his face, the other in deep shadow. His eyes were narrow, mouth pulled in like it was sewn shut. If *only*. Celia looked tense and exhausted, while Lucy looked like she always does, a bit scatty, flyaway brown hair, clothes a little snug on her plump frame, warm smiley eyes. Ally had that tight little frown between his eyebrows — the frown that never left his face, even when he was smiling at the baby — and, of course, Jojo looked pleased with herself. I reloaded my camera later, but put it away. I didn't want more Life-with-Seb reminders.

At first he seemed to like the baby, preening and telling his friends how he'd produced his own little character for his own little play. But when he finally got a decent part in a *real* play, Jojo's crying interfered with his "creative energy," so he spent even more time away. And when he deigned to drop in, he'd start right in carping at Celia.

Sebastian didn't hit Celia. No, he was more subtle. He used *words* to hurt her, pushing his face into hers and telling her how she was getting scrawny and losing her looks, how she couldn't cook if her life depended on it, how, if she was a *real* mother, she'd be able to keep that kid from screaming. I got into a few fights with him, but soon figured out it only made things worse for Celia. So I pushed my anger down, when what I really wanted to do was push his face into one of Jojo's steaming diapers.

I thought Celia would fight back. I *told* her to fight back, but she made me promise to keep my mouth shut and she'd handle him. Then she did nothing.

Soon after Jojo's first birthday, Seb landed an acting job in Toronto, saying he'd send for us when he was settled.

As he was leaving, I called, "Break a leg!"

He smiled awkwardly and said, "Thanks, Bernie."

"No," I shouted. "I mean it. Break a leg. Fall under a bus and break both legs!" I raised my camera and snapped off a shot, the flash lighting up the doorway out, not *him*.

He looked at Celia and said, "See? That's why I'm leaving. She's a *nut*. You're a nut. And that kid Ally is *completely* nuts."

Celia stood in front of us and said with a curled lip, "And you can't act your way out of a paper bag, you pathetic, arrogant little worm. A bus would be too good for you."

When the door slammed behind him, we cheered.

Chapter Four

*I wanted to show the thing that
had to be corrected:
I wanted to show the things that
had to be appreciated.*

Lewis Hine, photographer

Seb the Creep sent child support for Jojo for about two months, then the checks stopped. Around the same time, he sold the loft from under us. So, after some frantic searching, we found a three-bedroom apartment close to downtown.

Celia looked pretty washed out and dejected — I'd have been doing cartwheels if I was her. After supper one day, she asked me to babysit so she could go clubbing with friends from the theater. I figured it would do her good. She went out the next night, too. And the next. Soon, she was hardly ever home after supper. In the mornings, she walked like she was on eggshells and always with a look that said "Make a noise and I'll have to kill myself," so I knew she was having hangovers like Dad used to have. Then one Saturday night, she didn't come home at all.

The next day I called Lucy to see if Celia was there. Lucy came right over and wanted to call the police; but I refused. "She went to a party. She's probably just not feeling good. She'll come home later." I had no idea if this was true. But I didn't want police around.

Lucy said, "Bernie, what's going on? I've hardly seen Celia since she met this group of friends. We used to meet for lunch halfway between the theaters and now she's too busy. And she's never home anymore when I phone."

So I told her how Celia spent most nights clubbing. Lucy sucked in a sharp breath but didn't say a word. She stayed with us all day and made us supper. While we were eating a Safeway roast chicken with mashed potatoes, Celia showed up looking like she had a bad case of the flu. When Lucy tried to talk to her, Celia told her to bug off and went straight to bed. Only she didn't say "bug." The next day she was back at work.

About that time, I started taking a photography course at school. I did assignment shots in both color and black and white — the neighborhood, my family and Lucy, pigeons on my windowsill, cats in the alley, homeless people, tattooed gang members, Mr. Patak's family from the corner store. My teacher gave me really good marks, and I was the only student he lent his personal cameras to.

During the following year, Celia's vanishing acts continued — sometimes lasting days at a time — and the empty wine bottles mounted up at home, too. The day the theater fired her, I started calling her Celia.

"I'm your mom!" she said.

"When you stop being a drunk, I'll call you Mom."

She looked like she wanted to smack me. Instead she got dressed in jeans, a turtleneck and a leather jacket and headed for the door.

"'Night, Celia!" I called out sweetly. "See you in a week or two!"

Of course she didn't come home that night. After school the next day, I picked up Jojo at the day-care center and took one of my photos to our local copy shop to have it enlarged. It was a black and white of Celia taken at breakfast before a shower and a thick layer of makeup had resuscitated her. She looked a hundred years old — hair matted, bags under heavy-lidded eyes, bony face, sagging mouth.

After I put the kids to bed, I taped the photo to the wall across from the front door. "No pity this time, Celia. I'm all done with pity." I left the hall light on and went to bed.

The next morning, I found the print crumpled in the garbage. Celia eyed me over her coffee cup, as if deciding what poison to put in my cereal, but she came home from work early that night.

I'd won. But not for long. A stack of overdue bills arrived, warnings attached, including a threatening note from our landlord, a nice guy who was finally fed up with Celia's excuses. The next day, she borrowed money from Lucy without telling her why, packed our clothes and we did a runner. We stayed with one of her friends for two days. Both nights they went out. I stayed home with the kids.

I lost count of how many times we moved after that — old apartments, rooms in houses ... the kinds of places without doors on the cupboards or seats on the toilets — whatever we could find. Celia took any work she could get — waiting tables, sales — you name it. But within weeks, sometimes days, she'd get herself fired for not turning up.

Just before my sixteenth birthday we'd been booted out of an attic apartment that oozed with a smell like dirty socks. Lucy took us in — she lived in a tiny two-bedroom house in the west end — until we found a cramped apartment downtown. At least it had wood floors and no holes in the walls.

The day we moved into it, I was too busy unpacking, trying to keep track of the kids and how many bugs lived in the kitchen cupboards and figuring out how we'd get by on the few groceries we got from Lucy (Celia's last credit card was in bits in a pizza joint wastebasket) to notice the head of steam Celia was building up. While I was making our beds, she vanished — I swear, right from the middle of the room.

She was supposed to be starting a new job the next day — clerking in a nearby secondhand store, but she didn't come home that night. The next morning I called Lucy, who prowled the bars and called Celia's so-called friends until she found her and dragged her home. Celia was blind drunk and mad as hell. Lucy, who never gets mad, screeched at her and dragged her into the bedroom. Loud voices went back and forth for a long time, then quieter talking, and finally Lucy crept out, whispering that Celia was asleep.

That night Lucy and I had a long talk before she called the Sunhaven rehab center, where a cousin of hers worked, and booked Celia in. She paid a couple of months' rent on the apartment and took us kids to her place until Celia was ready to come home.

About a week after Celia was released, washed out and loaded down with bags of remorse, Lucy arrived on our doorstep with a buddy of hers, Mario Fonti. Lucy had tried to set Mario and Celia up once before, but it hadn't happened because Celia was searching for the bottom of a bottomless wine bottle every night. But after Sunhaven, I guess Lucy figured it would be good for Celia to have a new love interest. So she led poor old Mario to the slaughter.

She forced Celia into a dress, brushed her hair until it shone like spun sugar, applied enough makeup to give the transparent skin a faint glow and marched her and Mario off to the theater where Lucy's costumes were being used in a production of *To Kill a Mockingbird*.

It was nice to have a few hours without Celia apologizing for everything she'd ever done to us in the past five years. That's one of the things they make recovering alcoholics do — apologize. I don't think they realize how people like Celia can turn it into a marathon of self-pity. Jojo and Ally were just happy to have her back. As for me, I'd only get excited if and when I saw a sober spell last longer than five minutes.

After Seb, I figured Celia would never date again — never mind decide to marry — and certainly *not* someone like Mario. He was short and wiry with thinning black hair, bright eyes and a big nose. But the energy that radiated off him made him appealing in an exhausting kind of way. He could get pretty in-your-face at times, but he was so *nice* you couldn't get too irritated. No fashion plate was Mario — short-sleeved shirts, black pants, black sneakers — except when he came to pick up Celia for dinner or the theater. Then he looked like a minor Mafia wiseguy. But *nice*.

We ate regular meals, and the kids were happier. Celia stayed sober. Yeah ... it was pretty okay.

From the minute he looked at Celia, I knew poor old Mario was *doomed*. Lucy could see it, too. At first she seemed happy, but then I caught her looking at Mario as if she couldn't decide if she'd handed him his lucky break or a letter bomb. A few weeks after Celia and Mario started dating, Celia got a job at his friend's clothing shop. She seemed to like it there. She seemed to like Mario. Lucy stopped looking so edgy. Even I believed it. For about five minutes.

Now Celia had no job, no Mario and no future. Which meant that if I didn't do something fast, she'd hit the bottle again.

Chapter Five

Photography is like life ...
What does it mean? I don't know —
but you get an impression,
a feeling ... walking through the street,
walking through the park,
walking through life.

Leonard Freed, photographer

The phone rang. I grabbed it before it could wake up Jojo.

"Bernie?" Lucy's voice was strained. "Mario and I are almost done canceling everything. We've phoned guests, stopped the food and the liquor, but we can't find the invoices for the bakery or the florist. Go ask Celia where the invoices are and get her to call me on my cell."

"I don't want to ask her anything," I growled. "She's asleep. I might just smother her with a pillow instead."

"Okay — wait — they were in the living room desk. I think we labeled the box when we packed it. Look for me, will you, honey? We have to get this done."

I put the phone down and pushed boxes around until I found one marked "LR, Desk & Music." Inside was our meager supply of CDs, tapes, a few bitten pencils, capless pens, paper clips, old letters, bills and — I picked up a long clear-plastic folder stuffed with papers. Tucked in the back was an envelope addressed to Celia Dodd from McDullum, Wall and Todd, Barristers and Solicitors, Stellar, Lake of the Woods, Ontario. On the other side, through the plastic, was an official-looking thing that read "Last Will and Testament of Charlotte Jane Munsey." Who the heck was Charlotte Jane Munsey?

I could hear Lucy's tinny voice calling from the phone, so I put the curious package aside and searched the box until I came up with a file marked "Wedding."

"Lucy? I got them." I gave her the information and before she could hang up, I said, "Do you know anyone called Charlotte Munsey?"

"Not offhand. Why?"

"It's okay. See you later on."

I slid back up on the couch and opened the package. I glanced through the will first. The word "niece," followed by Celia's name, jumped out at me, so I read the whole thing carefully. I didn't understand all the words, but I got the gist pretty quickly. Then I stared at nothing for a long time, my mind trying to take it all in. I opened the letter from the lawyers and read it. Then I read it again.

Charlotte Munsey, I found out, was Celia's aunt. My grandmother Lydia's sister. Lydia had died when I was a baby. Charlotte had died just a year and two months ago. And she'd left Celia something in her will — Black Spruce Lodge on Black Spruce Lake in northwestern Ontario, and approximately five hundred dollars a month. The lawyer, Bernard McDullum, said he had been a long-time friend of the deceased and told Celia to contact him to discuss what she might do with the property.

I looked at the date on the letter. Also a little over a year ago. That meant that Celia had known she owned a lodge on a lake about a four-hour drive from Winnipeg (according to Mr. McDullum) — and had owned it for months. And had been getting five hundred dollars a month — money she'd never told me about, money she'd probably spent on booze.

Fury and excitement took turns in my head. I had to think. I went into the kitchen, grabbed a cold drink, pressed the can to my temple for a minute and read everything again as I drank. Then I marched into Celia's bedroom and shook her awake.

"Whufh?"

"Wake up. We've got to talk."

"Oh ... please, not now, Bernie. I'm not changing my mind."

"Sit up, Celia. And listen to me! I mean it!"

With a slit-eyed glare, she sat up. Her fine hair stood up like a kitten's, her face puffy, her eyelids dull red.

"You are a drunk," I said between my teeth. "You are a drunk and a devious, vile, lying bitch."

"What the hell are you talking about, Bernie? I haven't lied —"

"You've had a way for this family to get out of these lousy dumps we've been living in and you kept it all a secret."

"I still don't know what you're going on about."

I waved the will at her. "This. Your Aunt Charlotte's will!"

She leaned back on her pillows. "Oh. *That.*"

"Yes. That! You've got ... no, *we've* got a lake lodge. A house. Land. And five hundred dollars a month. And you never told me."

"Why would I tell you? I knew how you'd react. Just like this. *Badgering* me."

My heart lurched in my chest. "God, you haven't sold it, have you?"

"I wish. No, I haven't sold it. Go *away*. We'll talk later."

"We'll talk now!" I shouted. "We have money coming in every month and you use it for booze, I bet!"

She tried to laugh, but it came out as a snort. "Five hundred dollars is peanuts, Bernie. We eat it up. Literally. Where do you think the food came from when I wasn't working?"

I gave that some quick thought. She'd been out of work a lot and we always had food — not great food, but enough — most of the time.

"Whatever. But you *didn't* sell the lodge and spend the money?"

She snorted again. "I've tried to get rid of that thing for a year. God knows what it must look like. My grandparents built it years ago and Charlotte took over when they died. It's been up for sale for a year, and no one who got a good look at it put in an offer. I've talked to the agent. Even he more or less calls it a dump."

There was no way it could be that bad. "I didn't even know you had an Aunt Charlotte."

"Who cares? She was a miserable old bag."

"An old bag who left you a big gift in her will! What else haven't you told me? What else have you been hiding? Why didn't we move there?"

She sat up again, rubbing her temples. "Go away, Bernie. Just go *away*!"

"Answer the questions and I will!" I wouldn't, but that was beside the point.

She sighed. "I called the lawyer after I got the letter. He said it would need a lot of work and money to make the place livable for a young family. I had no money. I had three kids. I was out of work a lot. And —"

"And you were clubbing every night with your friends," I sneered, tucking my hands inside my jeans pockets to keep them from shaking.

She ignored that. "I told the lawyer to get a real estate agent on it — and every now and again, I check in. No one wants the place. Least of all me. But when it sells — and I keep lowering the price, so someone is bound to be dumb enough to buy it — we'll have money to live on for a while. Satisfied?"

"No way," I snarled, "and I've decided to do something about it."

"And what would that be?" she said, her lip curled.

It was now or never. I had to scare her good.

I cleared my throat. "We're already packed, so we're going to load the car and we're going to drive to your Aunt Charlotte's place — the place you *own* — and we're going to run the lodge as a bed and breakfast. We will also open the little attached store the lawyer talks about."

She stared at me for a long time in silence, then she started to hoot, holding her head in case it rolled off. "Ooo, ooo, aaah ... good one, Bernie. Nice try."

"I mean it, Celia."

"Don't be ridiculous. Where would we get the start-up money?"

"We'll go to the bank in Stellar and get a loan. I bet that lawyer, Mr. McDullum, would help. We'll get some summer bookings and use that money to stock the store. The letter says that the campers on the lake have really missed having a place to get milk and bread. We'd have instant customers."

She looked at me like I was the dumbest kid on earth. "All pie-in-the-sky nonsense. It'll never work. Grow up, Bernie!"

"Why won't it work? Your Aunt Charlotte ran it for years and years."

"*That's* debatable. McDullum told me she was seventy-something when she died and hadn't run it as a lodge or store for ages. She became some kind of hermit. I'm not surprised — my mother said she was always weird. They couldn't stand each other."

"How do *you* know?"

"My mother pulled no punches where Charlotte was concerned — especially after she asked Charlotte to come and take care of her when she was dying. I was almost nine months pregnant with you and sick a lot, so we really needed help. All we got from Charlotte was a firm *no*. Miserable old thing."

"So you and Dad never met her?"

"She couldn't be bothered to come when my mother needed her, but she managed to show up at the funeral. Came by bus."

"What did she look like?"

"Long string bean in a black coat and ancient green felt hat. You were only a few months old. She marched right up, peered into your carry-cot and said, 'Poor Lydia. She'll miss out on controlling this one, won't she?' Then she touched your forehead like the bad fairy and whispered, 'Be strong.' Ridiculous old bat!"

"So, *did* your mother control you?"

She twisted her shoulders as if shaking off hands. "We didn't always get along. But she was dead, for crying out loud! Her own *sister*."

"Was your dad dead by then?"

Celia said, "Don't slip-slide around this preposterous notion of going there, okay? I'm not going anywhere."

I stared at her long and hard. "Well, I'm not staying in *this* dump one more week, Celia, and neither are the kids. I'm not going to watch Ally get more and more scared and more and more ... *strange*. We owe two months' rent. I can't support us on my part-time job at the Dairy Whip. And *you* can't hold a job longer than a few weeks."

"That's not fair. I quit my job. I was getting married. Remember?"

"And you won't change your mind about Mario?"

"No."

"Then we have no choice."

She sneered. "Read my lips. We are not going *anywhere*. Lucy will help us."

My voice came out low and even between my teeth. "We aren't asking her for any more handouts. We're moving! And if you don't agree" — I swallowed hard — "I'll call Child Services and ask if the kids can live with Lucy. And if the social workers say no, then I'm going to have them put into foster care."

She threw back the covers. "You little bitch! Don't you *dare* threaten me!"

I was lying through my teeth but she had to believe the threat was real. I stood over her. "I'm the oldest of three kids with a wino for a mother. I've had it, Celia. This is it! You're an unfit mother and I can prove it."

"You will *not*, you — !" She reached out to grab me, but I moved back fast.

"Better start packing, Celia. *Now*. Or I'll make that call. I swear to God I will."

"Oh no you won't!" she cried.

"Oh. Yes. I. Will. And if you go and get drunk before we leave, I'll call Social Services, crying like a beaten puppy. I'll tell them you hit us when you're drunk and that you bring strange men home all the time. That'll get things rolling."

She gasped, "I've never —"

"We're getting out of here. With or without you! You've got one hour to decide, Celia. One hour!"

I ran down the hall, the will and letter in hand, slammed out of the apartment and stomped down the stairs. At the bottom, I was blocked by Sean the Bully's dad, talking loudly to the caretaker. The giant slug took up the whole staircase, so I shoved past him. His squashy unshaved face and piggy eyes glared at me.

"Hey! Who the hell you think yer pushin'!" He grabbed my T-shirt from the back.

"Take it easy there, Pat," muttered the caretaker, edging back into his open doorway.

I turned and shouted in Sean's dad's face. "Get your slimy hands off me, you creep!" I twisted out of his grip when he tried to get a better hold.

"Why, you little —" He lunged, but I was already through the door.

As it swung shut, I shouted, "Child abuser! I'll get the cops on you!" and I ran down the shady side of the building and out into the searing sun.

I wanted to hit somebody. I wanted to head-butt Sean's dad's fat stomach. But I'm not a complete idiot. Bouncing on the balls of my feet, I looked left, then right. Except for a few cars, the street was quiet. Why wasn't it raining? It should be raining. *Buckets.*

The downtown streets were like griddle tops in a fast-food restaurant, but I think best when I'm on the move. I started walking — thinking and walking — down Sargent, past Padak's grocery, past Vietnamese, Portuguese and Greek restaurants, the German meat market and dusty furniture store squeezed between apartment buildings — all the way to Mattern's chocolate shop, my feet burning inside my sneakers. I stared at myself in Mattern's big window. Heavy shoulder-length dark brown hair with straight bangs, pale face, red T-shirt, all overlaid on glass bins of jelly beans.

I grimaced at the reflection, took a shot of me taking a shot. The back of my neck was sweltering and my head was pounding. I dug an elastic out of my jeans pocket and tied my hair into a loose ponytail before traipsing back the way I came. At our apartment, I veered off toward a small park half a block away. It was deserted except for a young mother sitting on a bench in the shade, watching her little boy coast slowly down a slide, his bare legs sticking to the hot plastic. But he looked happy, and she was smiling and talking to him in a low, sweet voice.

I found my own bench in the shade, sat and took three deep breaths, like Lucy had taught me. She takes yoga every Tuesday night. Offered to take me, but I told her I didn't want to become a human pretzel. Actually I'd like to have gone, but I couldn't leave the kids.

An old woman, a dog and a girl about my age came toward me along the gravel path, the dog walking slowly in the heat, his tongue hanging out. The girl was carrying a peat flat holding a dozen marigold plants. As they got closer,

I could hear them talking intently, laughing, completely in tune.

I wanted to be that girl. Off to plant sunshine in her window box with her grandmother. Happy. Loved. No hope of that from my mother. No grandmothers, either. I didn't know any of my grandparents. Dad's lived in Newfoundland. They sent Christmas presents and birthday money, but that was it. As for Celia's parents, they were a mystery. She never talked about her dad — I assumed he was dead — and her mother, Lydia, was certainly dead.

But, now it turned out I had a Great-Aunt Charlotte — who had died only a year ago. Lydia had told Celia that Charlotte was weird. That they couldn't stand each other. How was Charlotte weird? Why had they hated each other? And if that was so, why had Aunt Charlotte left the lodge to her despised sister's daughter?

Maybe I'd find out a bit more when we got to the lodge — *if* we got to the lodge. No! No ifs. I was going to win this one. For the kids, if not for me. Surely even Celia could be won over by fresh air, clear water, a safe place for Jojo and Ally. Free rent. And if not? Then wham! I'd threaten her again with losing her kids and I'd make it stick.

Chapter Six

When is the present?
When did the past end and
the present occur, and when
does the future start?

David Hockney, artist

I opened the door to our building cautiously and let out a wooph of relief. Sean's dad was gone. I climbed the sticky linoleum stairs. The hall, drizzled with graffiti, was hot and smelled of mold and fried onions. Behind a door, a kid screeched, followed by a loud slap and louder bellowing. Sean and his dad. Sean took the hatred that lived in his house and turned it on Ally, who lived in terror of going out our door alone. I'd bellied Sean against the wall a few times, threatening him with gruesome images of what I'd do to him if he bothered Ally again, but it went in one thick ear and out the other. He had a jail cell waiting for him down the line, and I didn't want my little brother to be one of his first crime victims.

I tiptoed past their apartment and eased myself into ours. Silence greeted me, the kind that whispers no one's home. Uh-oh. I walked down the hall, checking rooms just to be sure. All I found was an empty wine bottle sitting on the kitchen table.

Where was Celia? At Mario's? No way. With Lucy? I looked out the window. Our car was gone. I grabbed the portable phone and dialed Lucy's number. The answering machine came on.

"Lucy? Me. Celia's gone somewhere in the car with the

kids. She's been drinking. Call me!"

I stood in the middle of the kitchen, thinking hard. That bottle hadn't been there this morning. Where had she got it from? *Get serious, Bernie. You haven't checked her regular hiding places for ages.*

She had to be on her way to Lucy's. She always turned to Lucy when she needed help.

I jumped when the phone rang. "Lucy? Have you heard from her?"

"She's here." Lucy's voice was low and strained. "The kids are okay, Bernie. Celia's fine, too. She's — uh — had a bit of an accident. Went through a stop sign. No one was hurt, Bernie. They're all fine."

"She's drunk, isn't she?"

"She's okay — a bit dazed," Lucy said. "And the kids aren't hurt. She and the other driver exchanged insurance information, so she didn't have to report it to the police."

I shouted, "But the point is, she's drunk!"

Lucy's voice quavered. "The — uh — other driver didn't notice. It will be okay."

"It's not okay, Lucy!" I cried. "She could have killed Ally and Jojo!"

"Bernie. She knows what she did and what could have happened. She's lucky she —"

"Got away with it? Well, we'll see about that!"

"Bernie. Calm down. Catch a bus and come over. I'll drive you all back home. Your mom's car's definitely a write-off."

I felt like throwing up.

"Bernie?" Celia's voice came on the line. "I'm so sorry, Bernie." She began to cry.

"Go to *hell*!" I shouted and hung up.

My head was ready to burst off my shoulders. I wouldn't — couldn't — go over there. I never wanted to see her again. She was now officially worse than Dad. She was the

Ultimate, the Incomparably Supreme, the *Mount Everest* of losers, and I hated her.

The phone rang again. "What!"

A small voice said, "Bernie? It's me. Ally. Can you come now? Please, Bernie?"

"I'll be right there."

I grubbed through my backpack until I found enough change for the bus and ran for it. I stared out its dusty windows at the heat shimmering off the cars that edged by in rush-hour traffic, my backpack hot against my spine, my camera over my shoulder. I bet those people all had cool drinks and swimming pools and happy families waiting for *them*.

The door of Lucy's small brick and stucco house opened as soon as my foot hit the front step. Lucy was in a striped sundress and bare feet. The hall smelled of cigarettes and coffee.

"She's a wreck," Lucy whispered. "Try not to be too hard on her."

I shook my head. "They call people like you enablers, you know that, Lucy? I read it in the stuff she brought home from rehab. You always cover for her. She's a wino, Lucy. And now she could've killed the kids. She'll never change. Don't you get it?"

I moved to push past, but Lucy grabbed my arm. "I think she's so horrified by what might have happened today that —"

"Forget it, Luce! It ain't gonna happen."

"I — I'll go make us some iced tea," Lucy said. "Just don't say anything until I get there. And don't yell. It won't take me a second."

That was Lucy all over. Tea and sympathy. Sympathy and excuses. My sympathy was stone-cold dead. Six feet under. I walked into the tiny living room. Ally and Jojo were kneeling at the coffee table — Ally doing a puzzle, Jojo putting stickers in a book. Celia was curled up at one end of the couch. Her face was gray. She blinked at me and then at the cigarette in her hand.

"So this is it, huh, Celia?" I said calmly. "You've finally reached the end."

She looked at me, startled. "The end of what?"

"Of dragging us down into that hole you live in. Well, *we're* getting out. Ally, Jojo, me. I won't give you another chance to kill them."

She began to cry, her head down — dry hacking sobs. I felt nothing. I was steel. I was brick. I was Antarctic ice.

Jojo threw herself at Celia's legs. Celia patted her back. "I'm okay now, sweetie. You go find Lucy, okay?" But Jojo stayed. Celia looked up at me through swollen eyes. "I'm so sorry, Bernie. I was so upset about the wedding. And you — you upset me this afternoon and then when you left, I —"

"Huh! That's right, Celia. Blame the wedding — which *you* canceled. And, sure — while you're at it, blame me. Why would running a stop sign while drunk be your fault?"

She cried, "I didn't mean that. You're not listening —"

Lucy set a tray on the clear side of the coffee table. She glared at us, then said cheerfully, "Hey, kids! I got a new carton of ripple ice cream. Wanna make floats?"

Ally looked at me and I nodded. Jojo was already halfway to the kitchen. Lucy followed them. I crossed my arms. I could feel the tightness in my shoulders and neck. A new headache wouldn't be far behind.

"You were drunk, Celia. Is there anything more to say?"

She blew her nose into a wad of tissues. "Okay — I had a bit of wine to calm down. But I wasn't drunk. I was distracted by Jojo, who —"

I laughed — or tried to. It sounded high and off-center, but I kept it up for a while just to block out her words.

"You're too much. Nothing is *ever* your fault, is it?"

Celia sat up, bare toes touching the floor. "This accident was no one's fault but mine. I know what I did and I won't ever forget it. I love those kids. I would never harm them. I —"

"Are you *hearing* yourself? You *would* harm them. You almost *did* harm them. It's always about *you*, isn't it?" I lifted the camera and clicked off three shots. "You. You. And you!"

"Damn it, Bernie, can't you give me something here? This has been a day from hell. I only had one or two glasses. I wasn't —"

She reached for her iced tea, but I swiped it off the table. "Shut up! You're a liar, Celia! You could make the national team. You could win Liar of the Century! *You were drunk!*"

"Okay — I had maybe more than one or two glasses. I did. But I will never risk the lives of my family again. This accident has woken me up. Believe me, Bernie. Please give me one more chance."

"If you mean that, you'll agree to move to Aunt Charlotte's place with me and the kids," I said. "We're going with or without you."

Lucy stood in the doorway. "The kids are in the yard. They don't need to hear you two arguing. What happened? Who spilled the tea?"

"Bernie slapped it out of my hand," Celia said, mouth drooping, like a kid who's just been bullied.

"Better than slapping your stupid drunken face!" I shouted.

Celia opened her mouth, but Lucy bellowed, "That's it! Enough!"

Celia and I stared. Lucy never shouts. Her plump neck was flushed, her hands trembling. "This day has been hard on all of us, not just you two, *okay*? Bernie, sit down! No, Celia, not another word!"

I sat. Celia shut her mouth.

"Now. Neither of you talk unless I say you can. Not one word. I mean it!"

We sat in silence for one full minute. Celia slumped back, tucking her feet under her. She sucked on her cigarette. Good. Carcinogens. I rubbed the sides of my sore neck.

Lucy said, "Okay, Celia — you go first."

"She's not going to let up on the stupid idea of moving to Stellar," Celia growled. "I also told Lucy about your childish threats of going to Social Services, Bernie."

"Okay, Celia," Lucy said judicially, "it's Bernie's turn now."

"It isn't Stellar," I said quickly. "It's fifteen miles away from Stellar. And it isn't a childish threat. I will have the kids taken away."

"But why so extreme?" Lucy asked. "Why not stay here and work things out?"

Was she being deliberately dense? "Come on, Lucy!"

"I told you — I won't take another drink," Celia cried. "I mean it. I won't!"

I stood up. "Yeah, well, tell that to someone who hasn't heard it a thousand times. We either go to the lodge as a family or you face Social Services — and the police."

Lucy stared. "The police?"

I poked the air with my finger. "If Celia doesn't agree to my deal, I'll let the cops know she was driving drunk, with kids in the car. And then they'll ask you, Lucy. And you won't lie!"

The silence of the room was as heavy and dark as hot molasses. The doorbell cut through it. A Pizza Place minivan was humming at the curb.

"Well," Lucy said, "come on — let's all eat something. Then we can get this straightened out with some civilized discussion."

Civilized? Where had she *been*?

Celia and I picked at our pizza slices. Ally ate a bit, looking worried each time one of us spoke. Jojo ate a lot, with bulging cheeks and greasy fingers.

Afterward, Lucy told Ally to go to the living room with Jojo and pick a DVD. Then she set out mugs, poured coffee and slapped a pad of paper on the kitchen table.

"Okay," she said. "Let's discuss this sensibly. What are the pros and cons of the move Bernie proposes?"

I knew immediately which side *she* was on when she listed the cons right off: a run-down business, too far from Winnipeg, no car to get there, no money, no nearby schools ...

"Yeah," interrupted Celia, "what about school? You three have to go to school." I was surprised she didn't shout "Aha!" after it.

"A school bus picks up kids all along the highway. There are good schools in Stellar," I said.

"How do you know?" Celia demanded.

"It's in the lawyer's letter. Didn't you *read* it?"

She bared her teeth and reached for another cigarette. So did Lucy, and she didn't even smoke anymore.

"Oh, Bernie," Lucy said, putting the cigarette back, "why so *drastic*?"

I listed the pros. "We owe two months' rent, so we'll be evicted soon. This lodge of Aunt Charlotte's is rent free — with fresh air and land all around. The lodge is a way to make money. Celia has no job, and school's finished in a week. And most important, things have to change. Celia says she won't drink anymore. So why not make a completely new start?"

They stared at each other. Then Lucy said in a thoughtful tone, "You know, Celia, this *might* possibly work — just until you get back on track. Just for the summer, like."

Celia lurched to her feet, gathered up the kids — who

protested at missing the end of *Shrek 2, again* — and ordered Lucy to call us a cab, but Lucy insisted on driving us. The ride passed in silence. After dropping us off, she drove away without even a good night. Celia and I didn't speak as we trudged up the stairs. I couldn't. My head hurt so much it threatened to crack open like an egg. I didn't care if we all fell off the face of the earth.

We were in bed before sundown.

The following morning, Lucy came over and told Celia that things *had* to be sorted. They talked and talked at me. With Lucy's careful urging — it could be seen as a break, a holiday, if you will — Celia grudgingly agreed.

"But only until the damn place is sold," she snarled.

I was smart enough to merely nod solemnly — but then I just *had* to run to my room and dance a little jig.

Chapter Seven

A mad, keen photographer needs to
get out in the world ...
and make mistakes.

Sam Abell, photographer

"Mommy!" wailed Jojo. "How much longer?"

Celia had been white-knuckling the steering wheel of Lucy's car for three and a half hours. It was raining and traffic on the Trans-Canada Highway was heavy. Good thing our windshield wipers were on high, slapping away, because an eighteen-wheeler had just roared past, drenching us in gray water.

Lucy had loaned Celia her car, which she rarely drove. She said we could have it until Celia bought another one. While we packed it that morning, I took quite a few pictures of Lucy as she went to and from the car with luggage. I think I was collecting the memory of her, so I could feel her near me even though we'd be miles apart.

I looked at the map resting on my knees. "Not much longer now," I said cheerfully. "We're close. Keep your eyes peeled for a sign that says Black Spruce Lake."

"Ooo, neato-beato," sang Jojo.

I looked over my shoulder. Ally had been silent and ashen-faced the entire trip, except for two emergency stops so he could throw up on the side of the road. I'd had to wash his hands and face over and over again with wet wipes I'd tucked in our car bag. Now he peered listlessly out the window, his hands clenched in his lap.

Getting him out of the apartment had not been easy. Most of our furniture was junk and we'd left it behind. But Ally got attached to things in a desperate way, and he'd gone wide-eyed and stiff when I'd told him he couldn't take his small bed. So Lucy and I'd tied it to the frame of the roof rack, the mattress wrapped in plastic. That settled him for a while, but then he started unpacking and repacking his stuff. I'd finally tied the bags shut and dragged them — and him — to the car. To keep him in one spot, I gave him the job of counting the boxes and bags we carried out, yelling out each number so he wouldn't get mixed up.

Now, turning in my seat, I took a shot of him. He looked at me. Suddenly, I didn't want to have this film developed. I didn't want to see that look in his eyes again. I didn't want to feel the pain of loss, looking at Lucy helping us move away. I wanted the future, not the past. I snapped open the camera, pulled out the film, opened the window and threw it into the rain.

A narrow sign loomed ahead through the thunking swish of the windshield wipers. "Black Spruce Lake — next right!" I said. "Hey, guys! We're almost there!"

A minute later, Celia pulled over to the shoulder and turned onto a narrow gravel road.

"It says half a mile along here straight ahead, then hang another right," I said.

I didn't expect an answer. She wasn't talking to me. Hadn't been for days.

The car lurched down a rocky incline, past an old sign that had gangly black trees painted like arthritic fingers across it and the distant echo of what looked like "Black Spruce Lodge" in faint letters below. We were at such a steep angle, I figured Ally's mattress would arrive ahead of us if Celia slammed on the brakes.

We passed a well-used side road, its rustic sign reading

"Black Spruce Campers Assoc. Boat Launch and Parking" and, a little farther on, an overgrown drive and the sign "Lower Point — Private Road."

We continued along a lane so narrow that wet branches slapped the car and sprayed water over the windows — downhill all the way. Jojo loved it, but Ally was deadly quiet. Before long we lurched to a stop at a wide gate. Peeling paint spelled out "Black Spruce Lodge. No Admittance. Private Property! Keep Out! Trespassers will be" — the last bit had rotted away, but we got the point.

"Is this it?" shouted Jojo. She stuck her head between Celia's and mine. "Are we here? Where's our house? I don't see it."

I climbed out into a light drizzle. "I guess it's down that track. I'll open the gate." I put my camera strap around my neck and threw my rain poncho over my head.

Celia sat, arms around the steering wheel, staring out the window.

A big chain was wrapped around the post with a solid lock on it.

"We'll have to walk. Grab your raincoats, you guys." Then to Celia's stiff profile I said, "I hope the lawyer left the house keys where he said he would. Hope he got the phone and electricity hooked up."

Mr. McDullum had been surprised to hear from a kid, but I'd explained that my mother was too busy arranging our move, and he'd reluctantly told me what needed to be done. As we'd talked, he'd warmed up a bit. Seemed to think we were going to live there for the summer, fixing the place so it would sell. He said it needed a bit of work, but that a good cleaning, some paint and the odd repair would make it more presentable to buyers. I agreed brightly, keeping my real plans to myself.

"Should be able to get that done by the end of summer," he said. "Meanwhile, I'll set up a temporary account in the bank here in Stellar and deposit your monthly check there. You'll just need to pick up your passbook at our office."

Before we hung up, he told me to call any time if I had questions. He might be good for arranging a loan, but I didn't want to push my luck yet.

"Are you coming?" I asked Celia, leaning into the open passenger door.

That cold-as-death look didn't scare me anymore.

"Suit yourself," I said. "Come on, kids, let's go see our new home!"

Ally held my hand in a death grip, while Jojo splashed ahead through shallow puddles, chattering away. The car door crunched open behind us and slammed with a wet thunk. We edged past the chained gate and down the narrow roadway surrounded by leggy poplars and tall white pines.

To our right was the glimmer of water, to our left, a narrow road disappeared through an overgrown cavern of foliage past another sign, "Lodge Parking." I wanted to stop and take a couple of snaps, but my film was lying somewhere in a ditch, so I kept going, my socks squelching in my sneakers.

The road took a sharp right. Jojo shouted, "Come see! Hurry up!"

Ally's hand tightened in mine. His face was so pale, the veins in his temples stood out like fine blue wires. But some of Jojo's excitement had got to him — he strained forward, pulling me along.

And suddenly there it was, behind a row of spruce — a hulking monstrosity of logs the color of dark coffee.

My heart dropped. I'd pictured a white clapboard building with a big garage and a picnic table under a shady tree. Maybe run down, maybe in need of paint, but a *home*.

"Uh-oh," I said.

From behind me, a loud intake of breath. As if the same puppeteer was pulling our strings, Celia and I walked side by side to the only door we could see. There was a long row of main-floor windows running from the right-hand corner of the wall to the door frame. High above was a scattering of second-story windows. To the left of the door was a single large window, covered in old advertisement stickers — Stubby Root Beer, Black Cat Cigarettes and a green-bottled drink called Hi-Lo. The roof seemed miles above.

I turned over rocks near the door until I uncovered three keys in a plastic bag. The screening in the outside door was almost all holes, but the inside door looked solid. The second key turned the lock with a dull grating sound, and the door screeched open. Jojo's hair brushed my hand as she ran in. Ally hung on to my other one for dear life. Or maybe I was clinging to his.

The building was dim and cold, and it smelled of damp wood. There was a long dark area to our right, its windows covered by green curtains strewn with felt bulrushes and misshapen mallards in full flight. I could make out a half dozen wooden tables, with chairs turned upside down on them.

To our left was an arched opening with a small counter halfway across it. Behind that, lit by gray light from the large grimy window, was a square room. Around its walls ran rows of shelves — dusty boxes, tins and bottles scattered across them. The store. *Supermarket* it was not.

Straight ahead were two doors side by side. Jojo ran through the left-hand one and back out again, calling, "Kitchen, Bernie, Mommy," before darting through the right-hand door. We heard a loud yelp and she reappeared. "It's all dark in there and something small ran across the floor!"

I took off my poncho and camera, and put them on the counter, walked to the door, felt around and found a light switch. A dozen old-fashioned electric candles glowed, revealing a cavernous log room with lumps of furniture under white drop cloths. I imagined them rearing up — and the four of us screaming through the back door. But they stayed where they were, quietly huddled and eerily silent.

On the blackened log walls were deer, bear and moose heads and a dozen or so animal skins — red fox, silver wolf, black bear, even a skunk — all covered in dusty plastic. I shuddered. By this time, Ally had my right hand again, his grip almost cracking my knuckles.

Celia wound her way through the hulking shapes and snapped up three window shades. A screened veranda flashed behind her just before the air was choked with a mini dust storm. She sneezed. I sneezed. She glared at me. I glared back.

"We'll find a motel and head home tomorrow," she said.

If I'd been her, I'd have picked that moment, too. The stink of dirt, moldy fur and mothballs filled the air.

"We have nowhere to go," I said, trying to sound tough and unshakable.

Celia scowled. "We'll *find* somewhere."

"Yeah? I bet Stellar has a Dairy Whip that needs a server." I sneezed again and wiped my nose with the back of my hand. "You take that job, okay? I'm through serving ice cream to snarly people with whiny kids."

"But you're willing to serve snarly people with whiny kids in *this* dump?"

I didn't have an answer for that. Luckily, Jojo, who'd disappeared up some stairs behind a log partition, thundered back down again shouting, "There's loads and loads of bedrooms up here! It's so greeeeat!"

"Ally won't do well here," Celia said, ignoring her. "He needs to make friends in a regular neighborhood. He —"

I gave her The Look. She shut up. But Ally was no longer holding my hand. He was standing nose pressed against a dingy glass display case full of bugs and butterflies, mouth open, eyes wide. "Hey, Bernie," he said, "do you think these all came from around here?"

"Probably. You could start your own collection, huh?"

"Could I? I wouldn't kill them, but I could collect them, right?"

I smiled at him. "Right. You could put them in jars with holes punched in the lids."

"Yeah! And see if they eat leaves and things. And I'd be able to see if they matched the ones in here, right?"

"Right!"

He gazed longingly at the insects, all neatly laid out and labeled. Celia looked as if she'd like to hang me between the leering moose head and the snarling bear.

I said, "Look, Celia, we're here now, right? We can fix this place up just enough to make it sell — and get a good price. It's a dead loss as it stands, that's what Mr. McDullum said on the phone. And like Lucy said — we can look at it as a free holiday. Somewhere to live 'til we figure out what to do."

She didn't look convinced.

"It's the end of the road, Celia," I said.

She chewed her lip. "We'll give it a few days. I need time to think."

That was good enough for me. I'd got her through the door. With a bit more time, I could figure out a way to keep her here.

Chapter Eight

To me the face — the eyes,
the expression of the mouth —
is the thing that reflects character.
It is the only part of the body that permits us
to see the inner person!

Philippe Halsman, photographer

I had a hard time getting to sleep that night. Celia and I had barely spoken as we unpacked the car. When she went out to gather the final load of odds and ends, I sneaked into the big bedroom she'd chosen for her and Jojo and rummaged through everything, hoping against hope that she hadn't brought any booze. But *dream on, Bernice Dodd*. There were four bottles of cheap wine in one box and two in another. I scoured the place — in the dust under the bed, inside the old dresser drawers, even the tops of the log beams. She hadn't had time to find good hiding places, and I was an expert at locating stash. I was pretty sure I'd found it all. I ran downstairs, unscrewed the caps, and poured the wine down the kitchen sink. Ally watched in horror.

"Mom's gonna be really mad at you, Berns."

"Mad about what?" Celia stood in the door, arms loaded with pillows and toilet paper.

She didn't need an answer — the room smelled like a winery. She looked at me, her mouth opening and closing like a shocked guppy.

"What are *you* looking at?" I growled. "I'm just keeping your promise for you!"

"It's only a couple of bottles, for crying out loud! I wasn't going to *open* them. They're for when Lucy comes."

"Sure, they're for Lucy! You're pathetic." I stomped past her and up the stairs.

After we'd roughly cleaned out our chosen rooms, Celia and I managed to get dinner organized, sniping at each other like gunfighters trading shots around saloon doors.

The gloomy kitchen had a greasy commercial stove with eight heavy cooking rings and two ovens, a wood cookstove, two fridges, a crusted old freezer that sizzled when I plugged it in and loads of cupboards. In the middle of the worn linoleum floor was a work table with a sticky wooden top. After I scrubbed it, Ally and I dragged chairs in from the room with the duck curtains and laid the table with paper plates for the ham sandwiches Lucy had made. The cupboards were littered with evidence of generations of mice. Neither Celia nor I would eat off anything until it had been washed with bleach and boiling water. It was the only thing we'd agreed on since we arrived.

Ally ate a bit, but Jojo wolfed down two sandwiches and a bag of chips. Afterward, they ran off to explore, with strict warnings to stay in the house.

"Could be rabid skunks or foxes out there," Celia muttered, drinking the last of the coffee. "Or weird survivalist types ready to cut off our heads."

"More likely they'd fall in the water," I said brightly.

"Oh, shut up, Bernice. Look what you've landed us in! This place is falling apart! It stinks of mold!"

"It's not that bad," I lied. "We could —"

She swept her arm through the air. "*Look* at it, Bernie! My mother always said Charlotte would ruin the place — and she did!"

"Why would she say that? Why did they hate each other?"

She shrugged. "How would I know? I already told you I only met Charlotte once. And that was enough. She lived here with her parents until they died, then took over. That's all I know."

"Did you know your grandparents?"

"No. They died before I was born — drowned. Mother said it was late in the fall, the water was freezing, a flash storm came up and tipped their canoe. They were wearing heavy hunting boots and woolens and couldn't get to shore. Charlotte was in her late thirties. Mother was a lot younger. Soon after the accident, Mother married and moved to Winnipeg."

"But Lydia must have owned half, right?"

Celia shrugged. "According to my mother, Charlotte made her sign over her share of the lodge — for next to nothing — and told Lydia never to darken her door again."

"Why?"

She lit a cigarette. "I have no idea. Charlotte was a nasty piece of work. My mother said she was jealous of her marriage and her baby." She snorted softly, lost in thought, then sighed and said, "Anyway, I *do* know —" She stopped and looked at me. Jeez. We were having an *actual* conversation. I guess it surprised both of us.

"What?" I asked, trying not to look too interested.

She pushed her chair back. "All I know for sure is that my mother would hate us being here. And she'd have a point. Look around. Even scrubbed down, this couldn't pass health regulations! The logs are probably rotten — the roof could cave in any minute. The mice probably have hantavirus, and I bet the wood ticks are teeming with Lyme disease. We could die out here and no one would know."

"Hey, Lucy would come and clear out our bodies in a few weeks."

She stood up and leaned over me. "Don't think you're fooling me, Bernice Dodd. Now find a vacuum! Once this place is cleaned up, we're *out of here*!"

"Oh yeah? That's what *you* think!" I shouted, and

stomped away. Don't let anyone tell you I'm not loaded with clever comebacks.

I found a vacuum in a cupboard under the stairs and decided to clean our upstairs bedrooms first. When I'd looked earlier, I'd noticed that four of them, besides the two we'd chosen — one for Celia and Jojo, one for me and Ally — had newish mattresses covered in thick plastic protectors. Not bad. I'd also found a huge linen closet full of sheets, pillows and blankets and smelling of cedar — and no sign of mice. As I vacuumed, I rapped the logs in each room with my knuckles. Seemed solid. If we scrubbed them, painted the floors and supplied the guest rooms with good linen, decent towels and the best antique furniture in the old place, there was no reason why we couldn't get things up and running in a few weeks. It would be great ... okay ... it would be *decent*. I bet some guests liked things pretty basic — like fishermen. And once I had the bookings, Celia would have no choice but to honor them. I'd drive into Stellar in a few days and put an ad in the paper. It would work. It had to.

But now, lying in the pitch blackness, smelling the musty old wood around me, it all came crashing down. Celia hated Charlotte for deserting her mother when she was sick, and now she hated her decaying house. Thinking logically, how could we *ever* get this beast of a place working? Touched in the head, that was me. *Nuts.*

I argued with myself for a long time — sorting out the reasons I could give Celia — and me — for staying permanently. But in the end, the best I could come up with was the desperate "What else can we do? Where else can we go, for crying out loud?" argument.

I tossed and turned, I flapped the covers, I ground the back of my head into my lumpy pillow, but I couldn't relax. For one thing, it was so *dark*. And so *quiet* — except for weird croaks and peeps that made the silence even creepier. Prickly with heat and frustration, I got out of bed and headed to the kitchen with my flashlight. I turned on the kitchen light, poured myself a big glass of milk, drank it down and looked around.

Opening a narrow door beside the fridge, I expected a broom cupboard but found a small office. The windows were bare, letting in pools of pale moonlight. I tried to find a light switch but no luck, just an old coal-oil lamp on the desk — and no matches. One window faced the water, and the other one had thick pine boughs pressed against it.

Apart from the desk, two filing cabinets and some sagging shelves, the little space was crammed with fishing rods, broken chairs, a couple of rattan plant stands, badminton rackets, woven baskets — even a moth-eaten deer head. My flashlight bounced off sprung traps that gripped gray tufts of long-dead mice. Yuck.

Inside the stiff desk drawers was more junk — pencil stubs, pens, elastic bands, coins, a ring of keys and a couple of black ledger books. I took the keys and put them in my pocket.

I'd check the ledgers in a few days. Right now, I was in an exploring mood. Directly across the kitchen from the office was another door. Was this the broom closet? Locked, but the first key worked. The hinges groaned. I felt around the corner, found a switch and clicked on an overhead light. Another room. The windowless walls were lined with corkboard. The air had an underlying hint of chemicals. Best of all, no sign of mice. Three shallow plastic trays sat by a double porcelain sink in the Arborite counter that ran in a U around the room. Lots of cupboards above and below. And one large wooden filing cabinet.

Above the sink and on the far corkboard were pinned a number of black-and-white photos. A small table held something that looked like an inverted camera on a pole. A film enlarger.

It was a darkroom! Charlotte had had a darkroom! This

was too good to be true! Had Aunt Charlotte been a photographer? If so, how strange was that? She was Celia's aunt, not Dad's.

The prints were mostly nature subjects — a pale mauve mocassin flower, raindrops pock-marking water around a cluster of flat leaves holding a single perfect water lily, an etched dragonfly perched on a small pointed stick. The rest were animal shots — a sharp-nosed fox looking down from a high rock, a squirrel alert on a branch, a beaver placidly sitting on his lodge. The shots were good, but studied, cool, uninvolved. Professional.

Pinned up on a narrow strip of corkboard above the counter were four completely different shots — all faces ... actually *parts* of faces. The first was a close-up of a man's eyes, with the peak of a ball cap throwing dark brows and squinting eyes into deep shadow; the second, an old woman's solemn eyes set in soft wrinkled lids. When I looked closer, something was reflected back at me in the softly blurred irises — a sad awareness of some kind — as if she was grieving. The third was the lower half of a face, chin resting on a folded hand, one knobby finger across part of her unsmiling mouth. On the hand was a cameo ring that had flopped to one side because it was too big. Looked like the finger had worn that ring for a very long time. The last picture was also an old woman's eyes, but the wrinkles weren't as heavy, the irises were a little lighter, and I saw humor and warmth in their clear depths.

I looked at the nature prints and back at the faces. Had Aunt Charlotte taken both sets? Couldn't have. One was so distanced, and the other up close and ... intimate. But who else could it be? I shrugged. Did I really care? I had a darkroom. I rubbed my hands with glee.

The filing cabinet was loaded with photo files. I peeked in a few. Again, mostly nature prints. Clearly, Charlotte had had a lot of time on her hands. I would look at those when I wasn't so sleepy. The cupboards and drawers were full of chemicals for developing, packages of paper, even rolls of film in containers — mostly black and white. Yes!

In a narrow cupboard was a tall brown box. I lifted it down and peeled off a layer of tape so the flaps would open. Inside were two brown files stuffed with photos. On the top one was written "Early Years." It was packed with gray-toned snapshots. The same four people appeared in many — a tall balding man, a small skinny woman with a mass of dark hair, and two girls. According to the writing on the back — my great-grandparents, great-aunt Charlotte and grandmother Lydia.

In a few, one of the girls looked in her early teens, the other a toddler in her mother's arms. Later, the older girl — probably Charlotte — looked to be in her twenties, Lydia around ten. They didn't look much alike, except for their dark hair.

Charlotte was tall like her dad, with a narrow nose, hooded eyes and long heavy hair with thick bangs cut straight across. My hand went up to my forehead. Just like mine. Weird.

Lydia was petite like her mother, with a small nose, full pouty lips and fine hair brushed off her forehead above large slanted eyes. Most of the shots had been taken on the veranda steps, the family posing self-consciously. Probably got a guest to take a new one each year.

It felt strange staring at people I'd never met, yet recognized and, in a bizarre way, felt connected to. Especially Charlotte. She always stood slightly apart from the family, whereas Lydia was always tucked under one or other of the parents' arms. Charlotte seemed so ungainly and awkward — her face closed, her eyes shadowed. Lydia looked a lot like Celia. Is that why I didn't like the look of my grandmother's smug little face?

I put the file to one side and opened the second, marked

"William." Only one picture had that name written on it. I could see why. Every photo in my hand was of the same guy. Clearly an artist. There were lots of outdoor shots of him in bright sunlight bent over a sketchbook, pencil in hand, or sitting on a small stool balanced on a rock or in deep grass — usually working with a long paintbrush on a canvas. There was one of him stretched out under a tree, cigarette in his mouth, eyes half closed, lost in thought. He wore a white T-shirt under a short-sleeved open shirt, baggy pants spattered with paint and dirty running shoes. He was stocky, with floppy blond hair, a wide face and a slightly flattened nose. Deep lines ran past his mouth, giving him a world-weary look.

The most interesting shots were three indoor close-ups in what looked like candlelight or firelight. He was gazing at the photographer with such longing, it made me uncomfortable. Either he was acting — or he was looking at someone he loved.

Charlotte?

If she was the photographer, then boy, they had been smitten big time.

What had happened to William? Had he been a guest she'd fallen in love with who'd simply moved on? Probably. I put the file back in the box. Maybe this guy was the reason Charlotte had never married. I'd never know, but it did make me feel as if I'd seen a completely different Charlotte. She obviously had had feelings after all, despite what Celia and her mother thought.

I yawned. I was getting really sleepy, but first I'd check a few drawers and cupboards on the way out. I opened the cupboard closest to the door and — eureka! Cameras! The shelves were littered with them, as well as tripods and other equipment. Some of the cameras I didn't recognize. Most were really old and probably useless. Two in front I knew right away — one a 35 mm Pentax, just like Dad's favorite, the other a 35 mm Leica M4. Dad told me he'd bought his Pentax in the late eighties. I knew the Leica was older because my photography teacher had one. He'd said, "This is what I call the grab-shooters' camera — for poets who never want to miss the moment. Perfect exposure is never as important as catching that shot."

He'd let me use the Leica a few times. It was specially made for quick, candid shots. I held Charlotte's with deep reverence, my heart singing. It had no built-in light meter, so I figured that Charlotte must've had a manual one somewhere — then I'd get to work.

With *both* cameras, I could take any picture I wanted. This was *fantastic*. I loaded the Leica with black-and-white film, slung its soft strap over my head and across my chest and let it fall gently against my hip with a perfectly weighted thump. *Heaven*. I left the Pentax on the counter for another day. I'd store Dad's camera with it.

I opened a few drawers. Better and better. A Gossen Luna-Pro meter lay in state in an otherwise empty drawer beside a brown leather case. I strung the case and meter onto the camera strap. I was ready.

"Thanks, Aunt Charlotte," I whispered.

Chapter Nine

*Avoid making a commotion, just as you
wouldn't stir up the water before fishing.*

Henri Cartier-Bresson, photographer

I woke up in bright light to the loudest, noisiest, most irritating racket I'd ever heard. In the city, there'd been the low growl of cars, the blare of a horn and the distant coo of pigeons. But here, the birds were more annoying than Saturday night boom boxes in the park.

I was about to wriggle deeper into my sleeping bag when something light and fast ran across my legs. A small gray thing skittered along the floor and vanished into a hole the size of my fingernail. I was up and out of the bag in two seconds flat.

Ally muttered but didn't wake up.

No way was I going back to bed now. After pulling on some clothes, I stuck my feet into my damp sneakers, grabbed my new camera and crept down the hall to the bathroom.

Yesterday, the cold water tap had spit out a thin stream of yellow water, but not a drop from the hot. The toilet was working at least, so we didn't have to use the tall, narrow outhouse that stood behind a stand of spruce at the back of the lodge. Not so far, anyway. I checked my watch. Six thirty, for crying out loud! I knew the others wouldn't be up for at least an hour. I should go back to bed. But there was that mouse.

Maybe I'd walk around the property and get a feel for the place, take some photos. I splashed cold water on my face, pulled my hair into a ponytail, ran down the stairs and wound my way through the hulking furniture in the living room to the veranda. It was full of rattan tables, straw chairs with sun-washed floral covers and shabby throw rugs. The floor let out creaks and muffled cracks, but I didn't fall through, which kind of perked me up. I pushed open the screen door and walked onto a stone landing.

Wow. Blackout. Or more accurately *gray*-out. There wasn't a speck of lake showing. All that was visible was a short stretch of wet grass and flagstone path. A solid wall of fog hid everything else, except for a few misty pine branches sticking out here and there. I shivered, went back through the house and grabbed my rain poncho, wrapped it around my waist, sat on the bottom step and listened to the birds calling behind the mist.

Propping my chin in my hands, I took a few deep breaths. So this was fresh air, huh? Moist and sweet and piney pitched. No exhaust, no hot asphalt, no stink of rotting garbage. I took a couple more deep breaths. I needed plenty of oxygen to keep fighting Celia. I tried to empty my mind and pay attention to the stillness and peace. Slowly the sun reached the tops of the trees, peeked over and lightly warmed my head. The fog swirled and stretched thinner. I thought of Great-Aunt Charlotte. How many misty mornings had she seen in her lifetime? Had she been happy here? What had she really been like? *Was* she a nasty piece of work, like Celia said? I laughed out loud. That would definitely be the pot calling the kettle black.

I leaned back against the step, enjoying the solitude. Before long, I could make out some fuzzy buildings near the shore. Wait. What was that? A dark shape swam through the fog toward me. Before I could run inside, the shape became a man. He was tall, with thick gold hair that glittered with beads of moisture, and he moved with a loose-hipped grace that made my heart do a little flip. He wore jeans, bare feet in deck shoes and a black T-shirt under a black-and-white flannel shirt. He smiled and lifted a hand in greeting. Something in my chest melted and sank through my body right to my knees. I would have taken a photo but my bones had turned to mush.

"Hi!" he said. "I was out in my canoe and heard someone laugh. Thought I was imagining it. But look what I found. A pretty girl."

I don't know if I smiled or just stared at him like I'd been hit with a stun gun, but he seemed to think whatever I was doing was just fine.

He stuck out his hand. I don't remember lifting mine, but I must have because when I looked at it, it was tucked in his. His forearm was covered in fine golden hair. I'm pretty sure I stopped breathing.

"You camping out here?" he asked, stepping back, hands on hips. "I don't want to come on the heavy" — he smiled gently, just to show me he wasn't threatening — "but this is actually private property. If you kids are camping —"

I found my voice and croaked, "It's — uh — mine ... my mother's — ours. My Great-Aunt Charlotte left it to us."

A slight frown flickered across his face. "I understood that Charlotte Munsey's family was selling the place."

"Why? Want to buy it?" Celia's voice came from behind me.

He looked up and smiled. "Oh. Hello. Alas, I couldn't afford it. But I'd like to buy a small cottage on the lake one day. I'm renting a place down the shore." He pointed to his right. "Called Lower Point. I was out for a pre-coffee paddle and —"

"I've just made coffee. Would you like some, er ...?" Celia asked. I turned and glared at her. She was wearing the silk housecoat, her hands wrapped around a steaming mug.

"Tony Lafferty," he said. "Coffee sounds good." He winked at me. "You coming, little one?"

I shook my head. I couldn't watch Celia behave like a geriatric flirt. I wrapped my arms around my knees and glowered across the now-wide expanse of sparkling water. A few minutes later, when Celia's fake tinkly laughter filtered through the veranda windows, I marched around the side of the house and banged through the back door.

I stood in the kitchen eating bread and peanut butter, glad I couldn't hear her irritating voice anymore. To distract myself, I opened cupboards. The shelves were loaded with enormous cast-iron frying pans, pots, metal coffee percolators and piles of old-fashioned china. I'd been to a teahouse with Lucy that had china like this. Why couldn't we do the same thing? Celia actually was a great cook when she put her mind to it. Lucy, on the sly, had given me a cookbook on muffins and quick breads for the B and B. I felt a flutter of excitement. Maybe it *could* work.

"We're hungry, Bernie." Ally walked in, eyes puffed from sleep, little sister trailing groggily behind.

Pushing the camera to the small of my back, I set about scrambling eggs while Ally made toast in an old flip-down toaster. They were just starting to eat when Celia walked in laughing, her head dramatically thrown back. Tony Lafferty followed, gazed around with interest and winked at me again in the process. Celia hugged Jojo and Ally, murmuring motherly things to them. I tried not to gag.

"But you don't have any juice!" she cried. Turning to me, she put on a gently scolding face. "I've told you before, Bernie. They need their orange juice. Vitamin C. *Every* day!" She sailed over to the fridge and searched inside. I reached around her shoulder and grabbed two juice boxes off the door rack, stuck a straw into each and plunked them beside the kids.

"Would you like one, Mr. Lafferty?" I asked brightly. "I'm afraid we only have pink grapefruit and apple. They don't like orange juice."

"No, I'm fine," he said, trying not to smile.

Celia insisted Tony have more coffee and they sat at the table. Celia fussed over the kids. Jojo looked pleased. Ally just looked baffled. I ate the remaining eggs out of the frying pan. Tony caught my eye, and suddenly the crusty eggs tasted like heaven. I could hardly hold back a silly grin. He had Celia's number.

Celia rolled her eyes. "Sit down and eat, sweetie. Honestly, Tony, bringing up a teenager is *not* easy."

I snorted and put the pan in the sink. "I need the car keys," I said.

"Why?"

"I have something to do."

"What?"

"I'm going to put an ad in the Stellar paper."

She frowned. "An ad? For what?"

"For the bed and breakfast. I'll say we'll be up and running by the beginning of August. Maybe we'll catch some late holiday people."

She looked at Tony and tried to smile, but only managed to bare her teeth. "We've already discussed this, Bernie. We're going to sell the place once we clean it up a bit. I've been telling Tony —"

"The keys?" I said, holding out my hand. I had no intention of going to Stellar yet, but it felt so good to see her lips go that thin.

Celia raised her eyebrows. "Tony, you can talk until you're blue in the face, but teenage girls never listen. This place needs a face-lift and then maybe, with a lot of luck — and hard work — we can get it off our hands. But try to convince a stubborn kid —"

I sneered. "Hard work. A new experience for you, Celia."

"You can't drive on that highway alone, Bernie. With your restricted license you're on probation for a year and need a licensed driver with you. And we haven't discussed *any* ad in *any* paper. Go and put on some work clothes, we've got lots of cleaning to do before this place will be habitable —"

"Forget it," I said, to stir things up even more. "I'll hitch a lift."

"Bernice Dodd! Stop right where you are!"

I walked out the back door with her voice following. She wouldn't follow, though. My mother's act never included exerting herself. I'd go for a nice little walk and come back later. I was halfway down the path when she caught up and grabbed my arm. Well, that was a new one for the Book of Celia.

"Don't you ever embarrass me like that again!" she said fiercely.

Now it made sense. "Embarrass you? Oh please, Celia. Get over it! 'I've told you before, Bernie,'" I mimicked her. "'They need their orange juice. *Vitamin C. Every* day.' Give me a break! You do a good enough job of embarrassing *yourself*!" I shook her hand off and walked away.

"Bernie!" she shouted. "You are not hitching into town! Get back here!"

Dropping the lens protector on the old camera, I turned, quickly focused and clicked off a couple of shots.

"What are you doing? Put that camera down! You aren't going anywhere!"

I just grinned at her.

Her eyes narrowed to slits. "You did that whole scene in there on purpose! Just to get at me."

I shrugged.

"Come on, Bernie. I'm *trying*, okay?"

"You are? News to me."

"Well, I am. But you have to meet me halfway."

"Halfway to *where*?"

"Bernie, let's work together, not against each other. Can't we try?"

"Will you drive with me to Stellar soon to put the ad in the paper?"

"Bernice! We are *not* going to run this dump as a B and B. We agreed we'd fix it up and then *sell*, and that's exactly what we'll do!"

"Listen, Celia, we can bring in some money while we fix it up. Open the store. Get a few guests. *Then* sell it as a real business. It'll sell a lot faster and for more money." Then I hit her with the big one. "Besides, what else do we have to do? Where else do we have to go? Think about it, Celia."

She rubbed her neck. "Look, this place needs a ton of work and *money*. Let's see how much — if any — the bank will loan us. But I'll keep what you say in mind."

I stared at her. "Seriously?"

She let out a huge sigh. "Yes. Seriously."

"You'd better mean that, Celia."

"Just let me think. We'll talk later."

"And you'll actually listen to my ideas? Not just wave them away?"

"Yes ... I promise."

"Okay." But my inside voice said, *I'm not changing my mind, Celia*.

"Are you coming back with me?"

"No, I'm going for a walk."

She looked at me suspiciously, but I marched away. I'd just reached a bend in the path when I heard her shout, "And stay away from that damn highway!"

Chapter Ten

You have to be ready for luck.

Neil Leifer, photographer

So, did I win that round? Maybe. But, let's face it, I had to win *every* round. Yet somehow I didn't feel as sure about everything. *Would* it be better to sell the place after we'd cleaned it and slapped on some paint? And if it did sell — if that's what I really wanted — how long would it be before the money was gone and we were back to crappy apartments and Celia's nights out? Something in my gut told me that this place was our only chance at normal life.

That made me laugh. *Normal*? Celia and me running a store — *and* a bed and breakfast in a run-down lodge? *That* wasn't normal, for crying out loud — that was *deranged*. I walked around the chained post into the shadowy coolness of overhanging trees. The car sat where we'd left it, streaked with dirt and scattered with seeds like soft brown caterpillars.

When I came to the "Lower Point — Private Road" sign, I stopped. Tony's place. What was it like? A rustic cabin of mellow varnished logs? Tweed couches and plaid woolen throws? Pillows piled up in front of a roaring fire? I cringed — partly because he was so good-looking but mostly because my mother had just flirted with him. It was disgusting. She was years older than him and would end up making a fool of herself. *Again.*

The heavy foliage was wet and shiny along the narrow lane. A cloud of mosquitoes attacked. I batted at them and veered toward the sunny road beyond the campers' parking sign. It was wide and well worn, with tall grass, purple clover and flat pink roses frothing along its shallow ditches. I'd barely started down it when a minivan passed, heading away from the lake. A pile of kids had their faces pressed against a side window. The van tooted its horn, and the driver, a woman with bright red hair, waved. I waved back. The wind from the van sucked away the last of the mosquitoes.

Fifteen minutes along the road, I saw a long white cottage set back and facing the lake. To one side of it, the lake shone through clumps of birch trees, the wind ruffling the surface, light sparkling off the waves. A gray log fence enclosed the property. Behind the house was a huge, carefully tended flower and vegetable garden that ran right up to the road. The house beyond looked old, but it was everything the lodge was not.

I crossed my arms on the top fence rail, breathing in the sweetness of flowers and the earthy scent of tomato leaves. After checking the light meter, I decided to take a shot of the garden, filling the lens with leaves and shadows and sprays of sunlight. Just as I pressed the button, a man walked into my viewfinder. I advanced the film, clicked again, then let the camera rest on my hip. The man, carrying a garden hoe, continued straight toward me, between a row of corn stalks. He wore a light-colored shirt, a ball cap and faded jeans. The hair under his cap was salt and pepper. His face was sharp featured, mouth downturned, deep lines creasing narrow cheeks, eyes hidden behind aviator sunglasses.

"Can I help you?"

"Nah, it's okay," I said. "We just moved into the old lodge. I'm figuring out where everything is. Nice garden."

"Thanks. You're at the lodge? Renting?"

"No. It was my Great-Aunt Charlotte's. I'm Bernice Dodd. Bernie."

"Didn't think we'd ever see you folks around here. Heard you were selling."

The back door to the house opened and an old woman walked out. "Hellooo!" she called. "Are you lost?"

"No, Ma," the man called back. "This is Bernice Dodd. Charlotte's niece's girl. Her family just moved into the lodge."

"Dodd? Really? Charlotte's family? Well, goodness, how *about* that!"

The woman wore jean overalls and a short-sleeved cotton shirt with scattered pink flowers. I was itching to take another shot but figured she'd think it was rude.

When she got to the fence, she grinned at me. Her hair was pulled back into a pale reddish knot, but the loose fluffy hair that framed her lined face was snowy white — and what a face!

"So you're Charlotte's grand-niece?"

I nodded.

"And how many are over there? Mom, Dad and kids?"

"Ma ..." the man said, a warning in his voice, but she flapped her hand at him.

"Just my mom and my little brother and sister. And me."

She looked at me closely. "You have a lot of Charlotte in you. Same hair, same eyes. Got time for iced tea?"

I shrugged. "Sure, I guess."

"Follow me. Name again?" she asked over her shoulder as I trailed behind.

"Bernice ... Bernie."

"I'm Ruby Broom," she said. "You can call me Ruby. I don't hold with the Mrs. Broom thing. Everyone calls me Ruby. This is my son, John. You can call him *Mister* Broom. No one calls him John unless he gives them permission. And that" — she pointed at a body lying in a hammock tied between two trees — "is my grandson, John Junior — Jack."

A hand lifted out of the depths of the hammock. John Broom gave it a push with his hoe and tipped the contents. The boy who bounced quickly to his feet was taller than me, with taut stringy muscles. He wore long shorts in a tie-dyed pattern of red and purple and a loose red shirt. On his feet were unlaced sneakers. His hair was flaming orange with black roots. He had a pile of earrings in each ear and a single ring in one nostril. His eyes were heavily lashed and so dark they looked black. The rest of his face was angular, with a full mouth and short nose. He bowed with a sweep of his long arm.

"A girl! I was just lying here dreaming that a girl would come and lift me out of my summer doldrums. The forest gods are usually very stingy, but hey! when you wish upon a pine cone, your dreams *can* come true."

His grandmother shook her finger at him. "Get inside and pour us some iced tea. And bring out those gingersnaps I made yesterday."

He saluted and clattered through the screen door. Ruby waved at a cluster of white Adirondack chairs under a vine-covered pergola. "We could sit on the dock, but the sun's getting hot. Nice and shady here."

I sat on one of the padded chairs, suddenly shy. When Mr. Broom took off his sunglasses, his eyes were as dark as his son's. Ruby's were small amber beads, with thick pale lashes. Freckles crowded her wrinkled face and neck and ran down her arms, where they joined clusters of age spots on rough-skinned hands with square fingernails. She wore a gold band on her left hand.

"So tell me, Bernie," she said, "what are the four of you doing here? Summer vacation? Permanent? What?"

"Mother ..." warned Mr. Broom again.

"We're hoping to run it as a store and a B and B." I tried not to sound defensive. She was asking too many questions too fast.

Mr. Broom shook his head. Disapproval radiated off him, as if I'd announced we were turning the old place into a biker bar. Then a small jolt ran through me: I was looking at the narrowed eyes under the baseball cap hanging in Charlotte's darkroom. I looked closely at Ruby. She smiled. She was the old woman with the smiling eyes on the corkboard! These people were probably Charlotte's friends — and victims. Wait ... was the other woman on the corkboard Charlotte? If so, who took *her* picture?

I heard Ruby say, "Goodness, that place needs tons of work. Are you up to it?"

I shifted uncomfortably. I hoped she wouldn't talk to Celia too soon. One local agreeing with her would have us steaming back to Winnipeg in a flash.

"We think we can get it running by the beginning of August," I said. "Maybe people will want to stay for getaway weekends in September and October, too."

"Mmm. I don't know about that. We always closed early September. Can your mom cook?" Ruby asked.

"Uh — she used to — she hasn't been well. But she's better now ... and I'll help."

"Sell," Mr. Broom said firmly. "It's not a place for a woman with kids and no man around to do the heavy work."

No man around? What century did he live in, for crying out loud?

Ruby shot him a disapproving look. "What John means is that it takes a lot to run a place like that, Bernice. Booking, accounting, ordering supplies for both store and guests. Bed making, toilet scrubbing, cooking, general cleaning. You'd best have the septic field checked out, too. Charlotte was using the outhouse for the last few years. Pipes froze in the winter — she couldn't heat that big place just for her. But when you have customers, it's a whole new ball game. They can be very picky — especially when it comes to food, heat and bathrooms."

"Did you work at a hotel or something?"

She gave me a big smile. "I was your Great-Aunt Charlotte's chief cook and bottle washer for as long as she ran it. We were great friends. I know that place like the back of my hand."

"It's kind of a mess now," I said. *Under*statement of the year.

Ruby's face stiffened. "Charlotte closed the place down about eight years before she died. She had emphysema — her lungs were shot from smoking — and she didn't have the breath to run up and down those stairs looking after people. When she was alone, she wouldn't let me do much for her. Stubborn. Said I'd done enough for too many years — on too little pay."

"That's true enough," Mr. Broom muttered. "Always took advantage of you."

Ruby's cheeks pinked. "She was my *friend*, John." She glanced at me. "The last few years, she puttered around the place — fishing, taking her photographs, smoking like a chimney, hardly eating. I made sure she had a few good meals a week, but she hardly used the kitchen that last year."

I nodded. "It's really dirty."

"I should have cleaned it, but John wouldn't let me."

"You were sick, too, Ma," he growled.

She nodded. "Breast cancer. But I'm doing real well now."

Not knowing what to say, I changed the subject. "But I really like the place. Once we get rid of the mice —"

Mr. Broom snorted. "Least of your worries —" But his mother interrupted, "You've got your work cut out for you, Bernice. But if you need help of any kind, I can —"

Mr. Broom leaned forward and stared hard at his mother. "No, you won't, Ruby Broom. You're seventy-three years old. You do too much around here as it is. You won't let me get you a house cleaner, so there's no way you're going to be someone else's. Besides, these folks won't be here long. Guaranteed." Mr. Broom was sizing me up — and I wasn't getting an A rating. Probably a D minus. D for Dumb.

Jack pushed open the screen door, carrying a tray. "My grandma is the best cook in northwestern Ontario. Try a gingersnap and you'll see what I mean." He set the tray down: four tall glasses of amber liquid along with four cookies swimming in the middle of a big plate.

"Only four left?" Ruby squealed.

"Sorry, Gran. But they're Dad's favorite."

Mr. Broom tipped his cap onto the back of his head and, for the first time, a flicker of a smile crossed his face. "Don't you blame me, kid. You're the resident stomach."

Ruby just shook her head. "About the lodge, Bernie. Are you sure your mom isn't getting it ready to sell?"

I lied through my teeth. "I don't think so."

"In that case, my advice would be to concentrate on the store and worry about the B and B later. Put a big notice on the campers' sign and another one up on the highway. There are at least three lakes nearby that need a store. Get in bread, milk, pop, canned and packaged goods like beans, spaghetti sauce, pizza and pancake mixes, syrups and cereals — also soaps and shampoos. I can make you a list."

"Ma ... leave the girl alone," Mr. Broom said.

"I'm just offering a bit of —" Ruby began, but I interrupted her by taking a quick gulp before standing up and saying, "Thanks for the tea, but I've got to get back. Thanks for the advice, too."

Her grandson leaped to his feet. "Hey, Bernie Dodd. Why don't we walk back to your place along the shore? Give you a guided tour?"

"Sure. We just got here yesterday. I haven't seen much of anything yet."

"Well, let's fix that. And speaking of fixing, you can

check the place over for Bernie and her mom, right, Dad? Let them know how things stand? Those docks are in bad shape, but what about the building?"

Mr. Broom muttered, "Show Bernie the shoreline walk, that'll do for now. They'll soon figure out that selling is the only way to go."

My heart sank. I'd have to keep him away from Celia.

"Come on, Bernie," Jack said, leading the way around the side of the house.

"Thanks again," I said to Ruby, who replied, "I'll bring that list by soon, Bernice. You'll need it. I used to stock the store. I can tell your mom where to pick up the best deals. And don't you worry, John'll come, too, see what needs fixing."

Her son snorted again, already heading back to the garden.

Chapter Eleven

*Photography, alone of the arts,
seems perfected to serve the desire
humans have for a moment —
this very moment — to stay.*

Sam Abell, photographer

I followed Jack down a rocky path where two wide docks slid out over the water. A long aluminum boat rocked gently on one side of the shorter dock, and a metal barge with huge pontoons sat unmoving on the other side. At the longer dock was a small prop plane. Yellow. With green stripes.

Jack said, "My dad builds and repairs cottages and docks — he uses the plane to get to remote lakes. We also have a small marina — repairing motors, selling gas."

He pointed at a boathouse on the far side with a slanted ramp leading up to a garage-sized opening. Gas prices were listed above the door, an old-fashioned bell with a pull rope hanging beside it.

"Does your mom work with your dad?" I asked.

"My mom died when I was born. Leukemia — found out when she was expecting me," he said. "Dad and Gran are my only family since Granddad died. About five years ago. He was a great guy."

Once again I had no idea what to say. Besides, he talked so matter-of-factly, I wasn't sure he wanted sympathy.

He continued, "Anyway, Dad's between jobs now. He could be designing and building cabins twenty-four hours a day, but he only takes jobs that interest him. I help sometimes, but he mainly works alone. I take care of the marina.

Gran helps out, if I'm not around. So Dad'll have time to check the lodge over for you." He headed quickly down a rough path along the shoreline.

"But we can't pay your dad. Not yet, anyway," I said, puffing after him.

"Oh, don't worry, Gran will figure it all out later."

Suddenly a huge animal growled, leaped out of the bushes and attacked Jack. I yelled and ran behind a tree.

"Badger!" Jack shouted. "Down! Can't you see we have company?"

The huge German shepherd dropped his paws from Jack's shoulders and bounded over to me. I scrunched farther behind the tree.

"Badger. Sit!" The dog sat. Jack laughed. "You can come out now."

As I edged out, Badger crawled toward me on his belly, whining and grinning.

"He's apologizing. You can pat him. Don't be afraid. He's a pussycat."

"If he's a pussycat, I'm a werewolf," I muttered, barely touching the top of the monster's head before skittering past.

Badger loped beside us the rest of the way, except for taking off now and again to chase something. He banged against me by accident a couple of times and almost knocked me over. Soon we were both panting from the heat.

When I finally accepted the fact that the beast wasn't going to bite my leg off, I said, "Your dad's kind of growly, isn't he?"

"Growly in a good way." Jack's voice was edgy. "He's a great dad. Straight-talking. Hides nothing. Same as Gran. He's only giving you his best advice."

"Sorry. But, one person's good advice can be another person's Waterloo."

"Huh?"

"Nothing. Forget it."

He shrugged. "Is your dad coming or what?"

"Not coming." Jack looked like he might be about to get nosy, so I added, "Your Gran seems pretty okay with us being here. She's nice. I like her. Talks a lot, huh?"

He stopped and I bumped into him. "Yeah, okay, so she talks a lot sometimes. That's because she's got things to say." Then he grinned and said, "Not like me. I just talk. Drives the old man nuts!"

To prove it, he sat down on a fallen log and told me all about the lake — how long it was, how many cottages were on it, how great the fishing was (mostly pickerel, bass and jack) and how sometimes it was boring to live here and other times it was great.

"I guess you'll be busing into Stellar to school?" he asked. "Like me."

"Guess so. Haven't registered yet." I didn't add that I *could* be back in Winnipeg before school started.

"So what's with the camera? You like taking pictures?"

"Yeah."

"Taken many since you got here?"

"A few. It's the one thing I really like to do."

When I glanced over, he wasn't looking at me, but at my camera. "That's Charlotte's. I recognize the strap. You know anything about a Leica? It's not just any camera, you know."

I bristled. "I found it in the darkroom at the lodge. And yeah, I know how it works. My dad's a photographer. Lives in Newfoundland now. I worked with him — even helped him develop film. And I took photography at school, used my teacher's Leica quite a lot."

"So, was Charlotte your dad's aunt, or your mom's?"

"Mom's. Weird, eh? My dad and Great-Aunt Charlotte should have been related but they're not — and my mother's never had a second's interest in photography. Did you know Charlotte well?"

He nodded. "Yeah, she taught me a lot about film. I used her cameras. That one" — he pointed at it — "well, never mind. She taught me how to develop film, and I did it for her after she got sick."

"What was she like?"

"She was great. Funny, in a dry sort of way."

"So you liked her."

"Didn't I just say that? She could be cranky at times, but she was a good person, and really passionate about photoraphy. I used to bring over dinners Gran made a few times a week when Charlotte got sick. She'd always make a pot of tea for us and, after she ate, we'd look at her latest photography magazine or I'd work in the darkroom — and she'd give advice. She really liked seeing what I'd been doing, you know, with her cameras. She said I had a good eye. That's what she called it if I took shots she thought were good." He scowled at my camera. "I'm saving for one like that."

"She promise this one to you?" I asked on a hunch.

He stood up. "Don't worry about it."

He walked quickly down the path. I followed, the camera banging on my hip. Winding up and over rocks, near the water one minute, ten feet away the next, we came to a wall of bushes, cut through a break onto a well-worn path and emerged into a field of tall grass and shrubs leading down to a wide sandy shore. Straight ahead, surrounded by heavy underbrush, crouched two huge boathouses with sagging roofs. To our left stood the lodge on the sloping crest, to our right, a row of docks. They were linked by a platform of wooden slats that hugged the shore — four wide piers sticking out like gapped teeth. Two of the "teeth" were tipped and twisted, but the middle two were fairly straight.

Seeing my grimace, Jack said, "Those docks were made the old way. Log cribs — like open-bottomed boxes filled with rocks. The docks are built on top. But as they age, the nails loosen and the docks lift and twist during freeze-up.

Most docks have metal underpinnings now."

Great. Skewed docks. Crumbling boathouses. The far one leaned out over the water as if working up its courage to dive in face first. And the lodge — sitting serenely in the hot sun — was, no doubt, chock-full of mice and dry rot.

I sat on the grass, wrapped my arms around my knees and put my chin on them. Jack plunked himself down beside me.

"What's up?"

"We can't do this."

"Do what?"

"Stay here. Your dad's right. Celia's right. It's crazy. We'll have to sell it and go back to Winnipeg. Then it'll just start all over again. It'll never end."

"Who's Celia? What'll start all over again? What'll never end?"

I never cry. But I was close to it.

An unfamiliar feeling of loyalty — or maybe embarrassment — made me say, "Celia's my mother. She doesn't have a job. We'll *have* to sell this place. It's crazy to think we can make it a business."

I tried not to remember the bug-infested apartments; the nights waiting for Celia to creep in, full of slurred, pathetic excuses; Ally's growing weirdness; no money. As I looked over the sparkling water, suddenly I wanted to live here more than anything I'd ever wanted in my life. And, as usual, what I wanted wasn't going to happen.

Chapter Twelve

I want to be receptive to an image coming together.

Keith Lazelle, photographer

—

"So why *can't* you just give it a try?"

I waved my arms in the air. "Look around, Jack! Two of those docks think they're double-jointed, the boathouses are older than the pyramids, the lodge is filthy — mice running amok. The plumbing doesn't work half the year at least, apparently, and hey — good news! — we're completely, utterly flat broke!"

"So ... *what* ... you're afraid of a little hard work, is that what you're telling me?" He rolled his eyes in mock disdain.

I just stared. Then a huge bubble of laughter burst out of me. I laughed until I got the hiccups, which made him laugh, which made the dog slide between us whimpering, which set us off even more. I couldn't remember the last time I'd laughed 'til I hurt.

When he got his breath, Jack said, "Because if you're afraid of work, then sure, sell the place and run away. But I bet my grandma's already busy making up a list for you. That means she thinks it's got potential."

"You really think so?"

"Worth a try, but your mom's the one you have to convince. What made you decide to come here in the first place?"

"It's a long story." I stood up. "Another time, maybe."

A faint stirring of hope riffled through me. If Ruby Broom believed the place could make a living ... maybe, just *maybe*, we could do it. She said to open the store first.

Hope died as fast as it had risen. *No money, ergo no stock, ergo no store.*

"You'd better get your mother ready for Gran," Jack said. "Ruby Broom believes in hard work."

"It's not the *work*. It's the *money*. I have to be realistic. Being broke is a major reality check."

"Before you turn back into *Ms.* Despair, let me show you something."

He led me to the first boathouse. Inside, the big doors over the water were half rotted, but two narrow walkways on either side had new boards in them. Streaks of light quivered across still black water. Canoes — two green canvas and two of varnished wood — hung on racks above it. A small red one was on its side at the end of the walkway nearest us. On the far side, half a dozen old outboard motors were hitched to wooden frames along the wall. Six sets of paddles and two sets of oars with oarlocks hung above them. The place smelled of ancient wood, water weeds and oil. Everything was splashed with whitish gray glop.

A bird flew out from the rafters and slipped through a gap in the wide door. The source of the glop, no doubt. Faint peeping came from the beams. Another bird dive-bombed us and swirled out the same hole. Then another. I snapped off a few shots.

Jack made a face. "Swallows aren't worth photographing."

"Says who?"

"Says me. They fly, eat and poop, and take over boathouses. You'll have to plug up the gaps and tie strips of rag on the bottom of the doors to scare them off."

"What's the point? These places will soon be submerged piles of rotting fish food anyway."

He shrugged. "Dad and I keep the roofs and walkways mended to protect the canoes and boats. The other boathouse is bigger. There are four more canoes, all fiberglass, and three aluminum boats. The newest aluminum boat and motor are already in the water. I — uh — well, I use them to go fishing."

"You go fishing in *our* boat? Don't you have enough boats of your own?"

His face stiffened. "If I didn't use your motor, it would have seized up by now. But, hey, I won't touch it."

"I hate fish — so knock yourself out." Wanting to break the tension in the air, I added, "Those plain wooden canoes look like they're honey coated."

It worked. He crossed his arms over his chest and grinned. "This is what I wanted to show you. Dad told me these old canoes are valuable, so out of curiosity, I went on the Internet one day and found out that collectors will pay as much as two thousand dollars for an antique Peterborough like this."

Was he putting me on? He wasn't. "No kidding! Really?"

"I'd hate to see those two go, but Dad knows of at least three people on the lake who would pay that, or more."

"Can we sell the other canoes and boats, too?" I asked.

He shook his head, his earrings flashing in a slash of sunlight cutting through a small window. "Bernie, Bernie, *Berneeeece*. Why would you sell off the biggest draw? This is a lake lodge. People come to fish, canoe, have *fun*. All this equipment would cost a *ton* to replace. Most of the motors are too old to fix, but you might get some money for them from collectors. I'm sure Dad would loan you a couple of rebuilt ones for the summer, but eventually you'll have to buy more."

"Can you sell one of the honey canoes?"

"I'll call around, get their juices going. We'll sell one for sure, I bet, and maybe the second one later, when you need to. Okay?"

I slapped him on the back. He pretended to stagger against the wall. "The sooner the better!" I cried. "I need ammunition and I need it fast!"

A few minutes later, I watched him walk through the bushes back to the trail, Badger at his heels. Things had suddenly gone from impossible back to ... well ... *maybe*. I could live with that for a while. I was about to walk up the front steps when Ally appeared from under them, cobwebs in his hair, a smudge of dirt on his forehead and a big smile on his face.

"Ally, where have you *been*?"

He held up a jar. A large-bodied spider with long hairy legs sat spread-eagled at the bottom. "Look!" he exclaimed. "A dock spider. I caught her by that diving board. With a big fat egg pouch on her!"

"Ugh and double ugh!" I exclaimed, peering at the thing. "Dock spider? You mean it *eats* docks? Not people *on* docks, right?"

He giggled. "She's big, huh? They have a mean bite, but they're fast and always get out of the way of people. There's a ton of bug books in the house. I'm gonna keep this spider for just a bit and then take her back. Then I'm going to collect some black bugs with long antennae I just saw under the cottage."

I told him to hold up the jar and took a shot of him and the spider.

When we walked into the kitchen, Celia was at the table wreathed in cigarette smoke. Jojo sat in the evil fog eating SpaghettiOs. I was tempted to take a photograph, but didn't. How was I going to tell Celia about the canoes? I had to be careful. Any money in the bank could be an excuse to leave ... or shop for booze. Still, she had to know sometime.

But she spoke first. "So, you finally decided to come home. I hope you didn't hitch into Stellar. If you did, I'll just cancel the ad."

"If you must know," I snapped, "I was visiting some people along the campers' road. John, Jack and Ruby Broom."

She laughed. "*Broom*? What a name!"

"Dodd isn't exactly up there with the Royal House of

Windsor," I sneered, doling out a bowlful of canned spaghetti for Ally. I started eating out of the pot, but my hands were
trembling and my stomach rebelled. I slammed it back onto
the stove. Might as well go for it.

"*Anyway*," I said, "this Ruby used to work for Aunt
Charlotte. She was her cook and did the ordering for the
store and the lodge. I guess Charlotte did the office stuff and
looked after the guests and the store customers. Ruby said
the store was a good business. Busy. The only one for three
lakes around."

"So?" Celia looked at me with half-closed eyes.

"So, we could do worse than run the store."

"Bernie, you are relentless. Tony agrees that the place
is a junk pile. And, he *said* you wouldn't give up."

"It's a good idea, Celia. Besides, I have some good
news."

"And what would that be?" She looked at Jojo and said,
"Jojo, honey, wipe your mouth with your napkin, not the
back of your hand."

She handed her a paper napkin. Her hand was shaking
as much as mine. If she was kept busy ... maybe, just maybe,
she'd stay sober long enough to find out that we might be
onto a good thing. I looked around at the grime and dirt. A
good thing? Who was I kidding?

"So? What's the good news? Believe me — I could do
with some."

Something told me to hold back. "Ah, well, we've got
two boathouses full of canoes and boats. Jack says guests
come to fish and go canoeing, so, of course, boats are a big
attraction."

"That's the good news? Boats and canoes? Yeah, sure.
More than enough attraction to make up for staying in this
moth-eaten hole."

She was probably right about that. It *was* pathetic. But I
swallowed down any agreement. "Ruby Broom says she

worked for Charlotte for a long time. She says this place did *really* well." A lie. I had no idea if a thousand people came every year or five.

What was I doing, for crying out loud? Setting myself up to spend *more* time with Celia, that's what. More sniping. More arguing. More worrying. Okay, the worrying part never went away. But is this what I really wanted? I amazed myself — the answer was yes.

She lowered her voice. "You can see how ridiculous this is, Bernie. Tony said —"

I cut her off. I knew what she was going to say and I needed to divert her. "What does Tony do for a living?"

"He's a writer."

"How old is he?"

She gave me a sharp look. "How do I know? Aah ... I get it. You think he's too young for me ... supposing I'm interested, that is?"

"He must be in his twenties."

"He's near thirty, I'm certain of that," she said, lighting up another smoke. "I don't think he's terribly interested in little girls, though, Bernie. I suspect he's a man who prefers women." She blew a billow of smoke over the table. "As for women, I'd say he's strictly a wham-bam-thank-you-ma'am kinda guy."

My cheeks burned. I stood up. "And you're known for your good judgment when it comes to men, aren't you? Did you give him the struggling single mother routine? Poor brave Celia. Her husband left her and she's spent the last few years sacrificing her life for her kids. Isn't that the story that won over Mario? Think this guy will fall for it? I don't think so. So maybe you told him you've always wanted to be a writer — that you're sure you have a story in you — because you know what life is really all about. Heart-wrenching loss. All that loving and *giving* — especially to your wonderful children."

She stood up, kicking her chair back. "That's an ugly thing to say, Bernice Dodd. But believe me, no guy will ever look at you twice as long as you're such a spiteful, nasty child!"

"Hit a nerve, did I, Celia?" I snarled. "So you *were* giving him the poor-little-me routine. I bet you invented a whole new version of your life, batting your eyelashes and sighing through it all. Hey, while you're at it, why don't you blow that smoke right into Jojo's lungs and ruin them, too. Then you can really play the caring mother!"

With that, I stormed out into the hot sun.

Chapter Thirteen

*When you use a camera, not as a machine
but as an extension of your heart, you
become one with your subject.*

Anonymous

Jojo ran out of the house behind me. "Hey, Bernie, where you going? Can I come?"

"No," I said over my shoulder. "Later maybe. I'm *busy*."

"Why can't I come?" she cried. "Pleeease?"

"NO!" I shouted. "Later!"

I ran along the back path. I hated myself for yelling at her, I hated myself for saying those awful things to Celia — and I *hated* Celia for making me say them.

I came to a stop at the sign to Tony's place and, before I could give myself time to think, walked down it. The road was well worn, but narrow. Soon I came to a small clearing where a sports car sat under a tarp. I lifted a corner. Red. Shiny. Vintage.

I kept going, past a small outbuilding, then an old outhouse with a rusting metal moon nailed above the door and finally onto a rocky ledge at the same level as a green roof and an attached deck with lawn chairs, a small table and a barbecue grouped in the middle. A short bridge crossed the narrow space between the rock and the deck. Tony was sitting at the table working at a laptop, head bent, fingers tapping away.

Crouching down, I snapped off three pictures. Tony looked up and waved.

"Hey! Hi there, beautiful. I was just going to get myself

a drink. Want some hard lemonade?"

He reached down into a cooler and pulled out two dripping bottles. I had no idea what hard lemonade was, but I nodded and crossed the little bridge. He was wearing turquoise swimming trunks, his skin a golden brown, the muscles soft but defined. His hair was even blonder in the sun. Why couldn't I breathe?

Tony handed me one of the small bottles of cloudy yellowish liquid. His fingers were short and rough-skinned, and I noticed he bit his nails. His forearms were sifted with freckles and fine silvery hair. I sat down on a lawn chair and took a sip. It was tart, cold ... and wonderful.

"It's got a bit of rum in it. Am I being wicked giving it to you?" He grinned and his teeth were crooked and white and utterly perfect.

"It's okay," I mumbled, finally finding my voice. "I'm used to it." I was lying, of course. I'd sworn never to take a drop of alcohol.

But this was different. I drank half of it in one swallow.

Tony laughed. "Hey! Take it easy. That stuff's pretty potent."

I shrugged and, because the alcohol was warming my blood, I smiled, too, and said, "So, are you writing the great Canadian novel?"

"Trying to. I've taken a year off work." He looked across the shimmering lake and then back at me, his eyes sad. "It's lonely here, but it's a good place to work. I — uh — got divorced last year. Married too young. You know there's an old song that goes something like 'I'll go my way by myself.' Well, that's me. By myself."

I sighed. Poor guy. "Is that the one that ends 'I did it my way'?"

He laughed. "No, that's a different song — different theme."

"Oh." I shifted uncomfortably. *Idiot.* "So, um, what did you do before this?"

He said, "Oh, this and that. Mostly journalism. A couple of documentary scripts. I needed time to see if I could do this ... actually finish a novel."

"What's it about?"

He leaned back in his chair. "Writers often say if we talk about our work it takes away its energy. But its working title is The Stone Door."

I swallowed more of my drink and said, "Mmm. Interesting. I have two novels I've finished."

He looked amazed. "Really?"

"Yeah, but they're crap."

"Does your mother know?"

"God, no! And please don't tell her."

"What are they about?"

I raised an eyebrow and he laughed.

"Okay — what are their titles?"

"I called the first one The Back Door and the other one I called The Trap Door, and I have a third one I'm working on called The Revolving Door."

He slapped his leg and hooted.

I grinned.

"What's up between you and your mom?" he asked. "None of my business, but how did she ever decide to come to Black Spruce Lodge? She's clearly not up for the challenge. Not like you. I think you like challenges."

That threw me off a bit. Did I like challenges? Did he mean *him*? I took a sip of my drink. I was loose, yet in total control. I stretched my legs out, examined my sneakers and said, "I guess I do. I used gentle persuasion to get Celia here. I'm good at persuasion. Don't admit to blackmail."

He laughed, then looked at me for a long time. My cheeks burned. Slowly, languorously, he got up and, taking both my hands, lifted me to my feet. He was so close I could smell his skin — a warm biscuity scent mixed with coconut oil. His chin had a fine shadow of golden bristles. My bones melted.

He transferred his hands to my shoulders and gently moved me back a step. "You have violet eyes. I've never actually met anyone with violet eyes. With that dark hair, it's quite a combination."

I said whatever popped into my head. "Like peanut butter and jelly."

He laughed, reached around and gave my ponytail a little tug. "You're funny. I like that. You'd better go home now — before I do something I'll regret."

He turned me around and gave me a gentle push. I stumbled along the rocky plateau, feeling confused, frightened and excited. Just before I reached the edge of the wooded area, I turned back, certain he would be watching me leave. But he was sitting at the table, head down, typing on his laptop.

Chapter Fourteen

Simply look with perceptive eyes
at the world about you, and trust to
your own reactions and convictions.

Ansel Adams, photographer

That night I sat by the screened window in my bedroom listening to Ally's soft breathing and watching the moon glint
off the calm water. Things had happened after I left Tony —
things that had allowed hope to float again. But it was a
twisting sort of hope, filled with anxiety and unsettled
excitement.

I'd stumbled home from his place in a daze, still feeling
his hands on my shoulders. It was like some pathetic
Harlequin romance. It couldn't be real. It couldn't have
happened.

As I walked into the kitchen, five sets of eyes looked at
me across the table and I landed back in the real world with
a thump. Jojo and Ally were standing beside Jack, who sat at
the table. Ruby sat on his other side. Jojo was staring at
Jack's orange hair as if he'd just landed from Saturn. Ally
waved at me, before concentrating on a piece of paper on the
table. Jack gave me a raised eyebrow and a thumbs-up.

Celia, leaning against one of the fridges and smoking a
cigarette, was clearly irritated, but trying not to show it. She
waved the cigarette at the table. "Ruby's been telling me
we've landed in a gold mine. If we can raise the cash to start
the store." She added that bit with a roll of her eyes.

Ruby nodded benignly and tapped the notebook with one
finger. Uh-oh, Ruby's *list*. "Yep. You'd only need a few

thousand, and Bob's your uncle."

"We don't have an Uncle Bob," Ally said absently. He was busy concentrating on what Jack was drawing — a long thin bug with even longer antennae. I noticed Jack's hands, long and slender with square nails. Ally whispered in his ear and they consulted over the drawing.

"We also don't have a few thousand dollars," Celia said. "So I think we'll just spruce the place up and sell it, but thanks anyway, Mrs. Broom."

Jack looked at me with a question in his eyes — hadn't I told Celia about the canoes? I shrugged and looked away.

Ruby shook her head. "Call me *Ruby*, please. This place won't sell without lots of work, Celia — we know that for a fact. The real estate agent sent a few prospects to me to try and convince them. But all of them want a place that's ready to go — with a liquor license for the restaurant and an off-license store as well. Licensing rules are pretty stringent here. You have to get a place up and running before the liquor board will even consider one."

Celia suddenly looked interested. "You mean if we got this place going, they might allow us a liquor license — and that would bring in a lot of cash?"

Celia living in a liquor store? I'd have to make sure *that* didn't happen.

Ruby said, "Yes, but it's unlikely you'd get one. Besides, you'd make a nice living just on the store. Believe me, I *know* — and of course, there's the income from the campers' parking lot and boat stalls. For years now they've been paying a quarter of what you could charge them."

"We own the campers' parking lot and docks?" Celia looked like a cat ready to pounce on a mouse. "Where does that money go now?"

"Why, to Charlotte's lawyer. Uses it to pay the taxes on the place. He gives John a small amount to keep the camper docks in good repair. Not enough, but John never thinks about things like that. And I guess you get the rest. Didn't you know this?"

"I just cash the checks," Celia sneered. "And a pitiful amount it is. Are you on our land, too?"

Ruby frowned. "No. It's common shared land. We own ours, you own yours — but we pay our land taxes together."

Celia looked back, speculatively. "So, I could raise the rent on those spaces."

"I wouldn't do that yet," Ruby said firmly. "You don't want to alienate prospective shoppers. Get the folks dependent on the store, then raise the rates. They know they've been getting a deal for years."

I held my breath. Celia was thinking seriously about the potential. Finally she said, "Well, thank you for all this, but I have to be practical. I have no cash —"

"You do now," Jack said.

My heart did a double flip. Celia looked at him like he was the bug in his sketch. "*Excuse me*?"

"I have a check in my pocket for twenty-five hundred dollars, made out to Bernice Dodd. Sorry, I couldn't remember your first name, Mrs. Dodd. I told the guy I'd let him know if and when he could pick up the canoe and decide which one he wanted. I said I'd have to double-check with the owner — you — but he was so excited he insisted on writing the check right away. Didn't even postdate it!"

"A canoe?" Celia's voice was sharp. "Twenty-five hundred dollars? What are you talking about?"

I was stunned. "No kidding! You sold it?"

Jack grinned. "Two other guys were interested but don't have the cash right now. A dentist down in the third bay was drooling at the thought of owning one."

Celia demanded, "What are you talking about? *What* canoe! You sold something of mine without asking?"

"In one of our boathouses are two old wood canoes in perfect condition," I said. "Jack says they're collectors' pieces. He told me he could raise at least two thousand for one. And he got twenty-five hundred!"

She stared at Jack. He grinned back at her. "You can easily sell the other one, too. If you stay, I hope you stock up on licorice pipes. I love them."

I could hear the wheels grinding in Celia's head — *Take the money and leave this hell hole* making the loudest noise, followed by sounds of a store full of clinking wine bottles. I held my breath.

"Use that money to stock the store with basics. I'm sure the bank will lend you the rest," Ruby said. "Get a good business going and you'll make a handsome profit on this place. Easy enough to get a business license. Just apply at the civic office in Stellar. I can take you, if you like. Or your lawyer can apply for you."

That stopped the wheels in mid-gear.

"So whaddya think, Celia?" I asked. "Sounds like a good idea to me."

"I'm sure it does to you, Bernie," she said tartly. She gazed around the room. "There are so many repairs to do. I tried to open my bedroom window this morning and it came apart in my hands."

"Not hard to fix that," a voice said from the doorway.

Leaning against the door frame was a tall, lean figure.

"This is my son, John Broom. John ... Celia Dodd, Bernice's mom," Ruby said. "John'll help you with whatever needs immediate attention, won't you?"

"Twenty-five hundred won't go far if I have to pay a *handyman*," Celia said.

He shrugged. "Suit yourself. Probably a waste of time anyway. Ma, I figured you were here nosing around. Come on, let's go."

"You can pay John later," Ruby said, ignoring him. "After you've sold up. I'll keep tabs on his time. I do all John's billing."

"Celia — we can't lose," I said.

She looked cornered.

"Please, Mommy?" Ally said. "I've just started my bug collection. I can't leave *now*."

Celia looked at him and her face softened. "Well ... I'll give it a couple of weeks. If it looks like we're finally getting things done and *if* the store looks even feasible, we'll stay — but just until the end of August."

"Yay!" Jojo shouted.

I wanted to shout, too, but instead I just plastered a grin across my face so wide it hurt. She'd agreed to two weeks and maybe the rest of the summer. She smiled back at me then, and for that one second we connected.

Now, as the moon glanced off a row of jars on a small table I'd set up for Ally's bug collection, I wondered if Celia and I might actually be able to pull this off. I'd never seen Ally so happy. He'd still counted his pencils before bed, placed his clothes just so on the chair and turned the light on and off three times before he settled down, but he didn't seem as worked up about it. And this change had happened so quickly. The most important thing, for his and Jojo's sake, was to keep Celia here, sober and busy — and with luck, *maybe* by August, she wouldn't want to leave at all.

The excitement I'd felt in the kitchen — was it worth investing in? I just didn't know. What would have happened if I hadn't found Celia's wine stash? Would she have downed it all by now? Or would it still be in her hiding places? Why had she brought it, if not to drink? Yet, she hadn't tried to go to the liquor store in Stellar yet, either. Hope bobbed up and down like a yo-yo.

A large bird flew out of a nearby pine with a soft screeching hiss. I watched it float away into the night. If only I could fly, feel light as air. I fell back on my bed with a thud and lifted one pale arm. Not a single feather in sight.

Chapter Fifteen

*Life is like a good black-and-white
photograph, there's black, there's white,
and lots of shades in between.*

Karl Heiner, academic

It was growing light when I finally fell asleep. Jojo woke me by lifting my eyelids and peering in. I could smell toast on her breath.

"It's nine o'clock. Mommy says get up and start working or she'll ditch the place today!" She pressed a wet kiss on my cheek, and as I tried to grab her, she scuttled out of the room giggling.

Life would be much grayer without her annoying, never-ending cheerfulness.

I glanced across the room. Ally was already gone, his bed half made. Hey, he *was* loosening up a bit. Good. I dressed in khaki shorts and a black T-shirt, grabbed my camera, resting it in the small of my back and hooking the lens case to my belt.

I was searching for my sneakers when I saw a dead mouse in the trap under my bed. I snapped the other two traps by pushing them against the wall with a book, pulled out the loaded trap by the edges, ran to the hall and dropped the whole thing into the lined bin on the landing. The little body looked so tiny — and harmless. No more traps. I was not going to become a serial mouse killer. There had to be a better way.

Downstairs, Celia sat at the kitchen table, smoking and drinking coffee, while Jojo shoveled in cereal. I poured myself some coffee and debated breakfast but was too headachy and sick from lack of sleep.

Celia looked pale and on edge. Already regretting the plan? Probably.

"Ready to work, Bernie?"

"Yeah."

"Okay." Good. She wasn't backing out yet.

"Where's Ally?" I asked.

"Hunting for bugs, where else?" Celia let out a plume of smoke.

"Yoohoo!" came a voice from the store area.

"Oh *shit*. She's never going to leave us alone, is she?" Celia moaned. "Old busybody!"

"You said a bad word," Jojo announced.

"Sometimes adults use bad words. Sometimes it's necessary," Celia growled.

"And sometimes it's *not*," I whispered. "Besides, I like Ruby!"

Ruby walked in to confront one happy face and two glowering ones. She carried a wire cage and a plastic carry bag. Inside the cage was a small marmalade cat.

"I won't stay. I know you have a busy day ahead of you," she said. Her cheeks were bright pink. So, she'd heard Celia's flattering comments. *Jeez.*

She placed the plastic bag on the table. "In here I've got casserole dishes — lasagna and tuna noodle. They're frozen. You can thaw one for your dinner later."

Jojo was already on the floor crooning at the cat. Ruby said, "Bernice said something about too many mice, so she's not just a pet, Jojo. She'll soon rid the place of rodents. Don't let her out of the house or she'll be back at my place in less than a minute. I have her litter box in the truck. I'm parked at the gate."

"Wow, thanks, Ruby!" Jojo said, making clucking sounds at the cat.

"Yeah — thanks," I said. "What do we feed her?"

"Only milk. You might have to feed her in a week or so, but for now she'll dine on mice. Her mother works at my house and in my sheds. Get rid of any traps — and you didn't put down any mouse pellets, did you? A mouse full of that poison could kill her."

Celia shook her head. "None here — and I looked for it."

Ruby made for the door. "I'm not surprised. Charlotte couldn't abide poison."

"Thanks, Ruby. People always seem to be doing nice things for me," Celia said.

Ruby looked back, eyebrows raised. "The meals and that cat are for the kids. John will be by sometime this afternoon to do an assessment. I'll say good-bye now — don't want to outstay my welcome. Bernice, if you'll come to the truck, I've got three gallons of a light green paint you might use for the store walls and a gallon of cream for the trim. John doesn't need 'em."

I looked at Celia, who was frowning through a puff of smoke. I tried not to laugh. Celia thinks she can charm anyone. Not this time. I decided I liked Ruby Broom a lot.

I followed her to the truck. "Sorry."

"Not your fault, Bernice."

I began unloading the paint tins. "My mom — Celia — she's just really tired."

"Think she'll be up to the work?"

"Hope so."

We stacked the paint supplies and the litter box by the screen door. As I walked her back to the truck, I asked, "Why are you helping us? I mean it's nice, but —"

"I guess I'm really doing it for Charlotte. I think she'd like to see the place come alive again. I suggested to John that we buy it, but he was dead against that. Anyway, Charlotte would have been happy to see you here."

"Really? Celia says her mother didn't like Charlotte.

That Charlotte was jealous because she didn't have a family like Lydia."

Ruby stared at me. "Is that what Lydia told her? Well, that would be just like Lydia. Pretty as a picture with a tongue of pure acid. Lydia always had to be the little princess — the smartest, the prettiest, the funniest. Made Charlotte all the more gangly and awkward. But, you know, it was Charlotte who attracted people. She was so good with the guests. I loved that woman like a sister." She laughed. "Maybe I should rethink that, considering Lydia's kind of sistering. Oops, now it's my turn to apologize. Keep forgetting she's your grandma."

I shrugged. "I never met her. All I know is she and Charlotte hated each other."

"I don't know if *hate* is the right word, Bernice. But — well, that's all in the past."

"Did Aunt Charlotte cut herself off from people when she got older? Her later photographs seem to be all nature shots."

Ruby looked at me intently. "She did withdraw from most folks ... at one point. She was still a good hostess — yet more cool ... polite. After she closed the lodge, she withdrew even more. But she was pretty sick by then. Don't believe everything you hear, Bernice. Charlotte was a fine person."

"Did she stop getting close to people because of a young man?"

"Goodness, what makes you say that?"

"Pictures. His name was William."

"She kept pictures of William? Now that does surprise me."

"Who was he?"

Ruby's lips tightened. "Someone from a long time ago. Charlotte wouldn't like me gossiping. She was very private. I ... I'd better get going."

I watched the truck lumber slowly down the rutted drive. So Charlotte *had* been in love with William. Maybe if I dug through the darkroom, I'd find out what Ruby wouldn't tell me.

When I lugged in paint, brushes, rollers, turpentine and the cat's box, Celia was washing dishes. "Lucy called while you were outside."

"What did you tell her?"

"Not much. Just that the place is a dive, but we're fixing it up to sell. Why? You think I'd whine like a kid at camp who wants Mommy to come get her?"

"Yes."

She laughed. "She said she'd call you later. Listen, we should go and cash that check. After all —"

"No. We don't need money yet. We've got enough groceries, we haven't looked over Ruby's supply list yet, and I don't want to spend a single penny until we absolutely have to."

"Well, I'll go and cash it myself then."

"It's made out to me," I said. "And I'm not endorsing it. And you know *why*."

Celia pinched her lips and narrowed her cat eyes at me. I waited for the blast. But instead, she said, "Yeah. Okay. But you better keep it safe, until we can bank it. We've got to see that lawyer soon. Meanwhile ... see what cleaners we've got. I'm going to find some rags. The sooner we get going, the sooner we can sell this bloody place."

Why hadn't she argued? What was she up to?

"Bloody is a bad word, too, Mommy!" Jojo called. Celia let out a low screech as she left the room.

I found two buckets and dug out a big bottle of Mr. Clean and a giant package of green garbage bags. I opened the window in the store and turned on the lights. It was bad ... really bad. In some places, the dust looked like sheets of gray flannel.

"Remember, don't let the cat outside or you'll never see it again," I warned Jojo as I dragged the vacuum across the floor.

She nodded solemnly. "I'm going to call her Jack. She's got the same color hair as that funny boy that was here."

I hoped the funny boy would be honored. In a few minutes, Jack became Jackie. Better. When Jackie took off into the living room, Jojo followed with a squeal.

I wandered in after them. There was so much to do. Dust exploded as I uncovered overstuffed couches and chairs in knobby green fabric. Ugly took on a whole new meaning. While I was trying not to sneeze, a mouse ran right out of a cushion beside me. Jackie streaked after it like a marmalade bullet, Jojo shouting after them. Bloodthirsty little killers.

I looked around. What *was* I doing? One job at a time. I dumped the cloths, went back to the store and started clearing the shelves, grabbing crumbling cereal and rice boxes — empty now, with holes eaten right through them — and other containers so dimmed with age I couldn't be sure what they'd once been. I flattened the boxes and piled them near the cookstove.

I unloaded bottles of what might once have been syrup, jams and pickles into double garbage bags, then started on a row of murky-labeled tinned goods, packages of string (eaten into bits), fishing line (ditto) and candles (half eaten and half melted). I took a shot of some Swiss cheese soap bars just for fun. Mice eat soap? Do they foam at the mouth afterward? They must have the cleanest insides in the forest.

Celia came back loaded with rags. "We should do the living area first," she growled.

"Nope. The store."

We debated heatedly for a while, getting nowhere, until she held up her hands. "Okay, *you* work on the store. *I'm* going to clean the kitchen counters and at least get rid of the worst of the dust in that unlivable living area." She pulled her hair into pale spikes. "This place is a *nightmare!*"

She kept giving gruesome details from the other room, so I turned on the vacuum to drown her out. My head was feeling better, but my arms and legs ached. It was getting hotter and hotter in the shop. Luckily, Celia had found a rickety fan under the kitchen counter, and I put it in the doorway with the swivel on.

Just before noon, we dug out the thawed tuna casserole and ate a few bowls of it cold, hanging over our plates like a couple of vultures. I looked up at the same time she did. We both had bulging cheeks and mayonnaise-smeared mouths. For just one second a glimmer of laughter flickered in her eyes. I may even have smiled back. This smiling was getting out of hand. I frowned down at my plate.

She lowered hers into soapy water. "Back to the grindstone. Let's hope it's all worth it."

"It will be."

The kids came in, so I doled out more casserole, put the rest away for dinner and got back to work. About four thirty, Celia stomped into the store, threw a wet rag down on the floor with a splat, cried "Enough!" and stomped up the stairs.

I followed, dug out our bathing suits and called the kids. On our way out, Ally grabbed a basket of sand toys from the veranda and we walked to the docks, carrying thin striped towels I'd found in the linen closet. They smelled of cedar. Much better than mothballs.

When we got to the tiny beach, I took a quick shot of them. Ally smiled, showing his small white teeth. Jojo stuck out her tongue. I growled at her and she laughed. I sent them off to play, telling Ally he was in charge — and no swimming unless Celia or I were watching. He almost swaggered away, swinging the basket full of toys with a couple of bug bottles on top.

There was a ten-foot diving board attached to the end of the straightest dock. Seemed solid. I did a shallow dive, surfaced slowly, dove again — deeper this time. Gliding through the yellow-green, bubbles tickling my arms and legs, I surfaced again and flicked my wet bangs off my face.

Quitting the swim team last year had been hard. But Celia's drinking had made it impossible to practice. Looking over at Ally and Jojo digging in the sand, I realized I'd never resented them when things didn't work out for me. Just *her*. Just Celia.

Chapter Sixteen

If you can't make it better make it bigger.

Anonymous

———

I floated on my back, letting the heat sink into my above-water parts. Things hadn't turned out too bad. If Celia resented my control of the canoe money, she sure wasn't showing it. *Yet.* What was going on with her? Was it some kind of waiting game she was playing?

How long could she last before our money ended up at the local liquor store? My stomach tightened. I had to face facts. She'd do it eventually.

I was about to swim to shore when something hit the water beside me. Bubbles churned and a strong current swirled around my legs. I shrieked. Jack's head bobbed up like an orange beach ball right in front of me. I pushed it under. He stayed down. The water became very still. Where was he?

A surge of bubbles and strong hands wound around my ankles. I was under in a flash. The hands let go. I kicked hard and swam for the docks, laughing. I was about to heave myself out when Tony walked onto the diving dock. Loose khaki shorts and white T-shirt, carrying a drink. Celia trailed behind him — a glass in hand.

Pulling myself onto the dock in one swoop, I grabbed her glass before she could protest, smelled it — rum — and tossed the whole thing into the water. I grabbed my towel and camera and ran up to the house. Shocked silence followed me.

A newly opened bottle of dark rum stood on the kitchen table. So this was how long our truce had lasted. Celia could stand being a Real Person for only a few days. I poured the rum down the drain, but I was shaking so hard I dropped the bottle in the sink and broke it. Let her clean it up.

I pounded up the stairs to my room, stripped off my wet suit and dragged on shorts and a T-shirt. I looked out my window, expecting to see Celia charging up the path. But she was sitting on the dock talking to Tony, his hand on her shoulder. I bet she was loving *that*.

I grabbed my camera, ran downstairs and along the path toward the campers' road, rage bursting out of me in horrible dry gasps. "I hate her, I *hate* her. She ruins *everything*."

By the time I got to the Brooms' property, I was trembling like I had the flu. Mr. Broom's garden lay quiet and still. Heavy bees floated around the hollyhock blooms. A light breeze turned the tomato leaves and exposed greenish red fruit underneath. The pungent smells of plants and damp soil, the peace of the garden hit me with a pain in my chest. Nothing was going to change. *Ever.*

I continued down the middle of the road, until a van, bearing down, honked loud and long. The driver shouted something out his window. Beside him was the pretty red-haired woman. She sent me an apologetic smile as they roared by, kicking up dust and making me cough. Gave them the finger. Didn't care if the truck backed up and drove right over me. Hated this stupid place. Hated my life. I'd tell Celia to do whatever she wanted. Then *I'd* leave. For good. She could drink herself to death for all I cared.

Ten minutes later, I came to the campers' parking lot — about fifty dust-streaked cars lined up in uneven rows. Beyond were two loading docks and a number of marina bays. Half the mooring spaces were empty, a variety of boats — big covered ones, small aluminum and a couple of wood — were tied up in the others.

I slumped onto a rock beside the water. A brown duck and six fluffed ducklings swam up to me, quacking, then the mother paddled out a bit and bobbed around. Did she want me to feed them? Wasn't that her job?

"Get lost!" I shouted. "Stupid duck!"

What was I going to do? How could I control what was clearly uncontrollable? Lucy was due to visit soon. Could she help? Probably not, although it would be good to have her here. For the millionth time, I asked myself why Lucy stayed friends with Celia. Was it simply that they'd known each other since they were kids? Was it because Lucy didn't have a life? Would I ever have a life?

"Hey," a voice said behind me.

I sighed.

"Whoa! Sorry. I'll go if you want me to."

"Don't care."

Jack sat down on the grassy sand, wrapping his arms around his knees.

"That was pretty heavy," he said.

"It's between Celia and me, okay?"

"No, I mean that glass was *heavy*. I did, however, dive for it. It's back on the dock. Empty. You know, it missed me by a molecule. I'd be dead if your aim was better."

I stared at him. Then I laughed. "You're a dope." Lifted my camera and took a quick shot of him.

"You and that camera. It's like your third eye. Don't you ever want to put it down and *look* at things? It'd make you a better photographer."

"I'll tell you what. You go live the life I had in Winnipeg and then tell me if I need to see more, okay? What are you — the philosopher of Black Spruce?"

He shrugged. "Blame Charlotte for that advice. I think she meant that the more you *experience* life, the better you are at choosing things to photograph."

"This from a person who stopped taking pictures of people. From someone who obviously stopped *looking* at people after William?"

"Who's William?"

"I don't know. Someone she loved, I think."

"How do you know about this William guy?"

"His photos are in the darkroom. Didn't you see them?"

"I saw lots of people in those files. But, hey ... any guy whose photo was taken more than once must be someone Charlotte was in love with. That makes sense."

"I know what I *know*, okay?"

He looked at me assessingly. "You're very dramatic, you know that? You should take acting instead of photography."

"I don't *act*!"

"Well, that was an amazing scene on the dock. *Verrry* dramatic. I tried out for the lead in last year's play. They needed a tall, dark, handsome guy. Hey, that's me, I thought. Two of us tried out. The other guy was up to my shoulder, blond and weighed less than that camera you're carrying around. But apparently he could sing without breaking lightbulbs."

I pushed his shoulder with my foot and he fell over. *Very* dramatically.

I couldn't help laughing again. "It's *serious*!"

He sat up. "Parents can be a pain in the what's-it. At least your mother has some life to her. My dad's the strong silent type. It's like pulling teeth sometimes just to squeeze a few words out of him. He's a good dad, don't get me wrong, but Gran says he was positively chatty before Mom died. Nuts about her. But at least he's not a drinker like your mom, so I shouldn't complain."

"Celia isn't a drinker!"

"Right. That's why you threw her glass of booze in the lake. I get it, Bernie. You don't have to cover for her. If your mom had cancer would you be this mad at her?"

"That's different."

"Yeah? So, you think your mom *chose* to be an alcoholic?"

"What'd you do, study psychology after you finished philosophy?"

"Your mom didn't wake up one day and say, 'Hey, I think I'll become a drunk.'"

"Maybe not, but she can *choose* to quit!" I stood up. "I told her I'd have the kids taken away if she didn't. But look! The first drink she's offered, she takes! She doesn't *want* to stop! *That* makes it a choice!"

"She must have known you'd see her with booze. Maybe she was showing you she could resist —"

I laughed — a hard grating sound. "And cows fly and birds have lips and Earth is flat — and, yes, Celia *will not* drink alcohol again."

I turned and walked away.

Chapter Seventeen

*My favorite thing is to
go where I've never been.*

Diane Arbus, photographer

———

Tony was strolling toward the turnoff to his road. I tried to steer past him, but he moved with me and put his hands on my shoulders.

"Your mom says you guys have been fighting lately, and you were acting out."

I stared over his shoulder. "That's her story, is it?"

He put his finger under my chin. "I didn't know, Bernie. Or I wouldn't have brought over the bottle. I'll be careful from now on. I wouldn't ever want to upset you, you know that. Listen, if there's anything you want to talk about — anytime — I'm here for you."

"She —" I began.

A voice right behind us made me jump. "Sorry to interrupt. You seen Jack anywhere?" Mr. Broom stood in the shade, his eyes on Tony, Badger at his side.

Tony dropped his hands and walked away. "See you later, Bernie."

I gazed after him. He *pitied* Celia, and he liked me — *more* than liked me.

"I'd be careful there, Bernice."

I didn't answer. He could find Jack himself. Nosy Parker. I followed him to the lodge, though, glad we'd be arriving together. Celia couldn't act up with him there.

She and the kids were eating when we walked into the kitchen. "Oh ... hello, Mr. Broom."

"John."

"Yes, well ... John. Can I help you?"

She glanced at me and tried a smile. I wasn't falling for that. I dished out some tuna casserole for myself and sat beside Ally.

"Had dinner early," Mr. Broom said, "so thought I'd do some checking around. If it's okay with you, I'll look at the upstairs water tank first. I bet you have no hot water."

"You're right," Celia replied. "It would be heaven to take a decent bath. I'll come with you."

Mr. Broom held up his hand. "No need. I know the place. Problem with that?"

Celia's face tightened. "No — no problem."

When he was gone, I ate quickly, asking Ally and Jojo about their day and avoiding Celia's eyes. Ally went into great detail about the nest of carpenter bees he'd found and how they didn't sting, and I asked him the difference between carpenter ants and carpenter bees, and he told me he was just looking that bit up. By the time we were done and Jojo had told me about Jackie prowling the whole house — with her in hot pursuit — Celia was washing the dishes, and the kids ran off in search of cat and bugs.

I dropped my dish in the soapy water, expecting Celia to explode in my face. But she said, "I vacuumed and dusted the main room, so it's a bit more livable. But you're right. We need to get that store painted and loaded with supplies as soon as possible. You should be able to start on the painting soon."

"Whatever," I muttered, bewildered, but on full alert.

She cleared her throat. "Do you want to talk about it?"

"No."

"I didn't drink it, Bernie."

I shrugged.

"Tony asked and I said 'No, just a soft drink' — but he poured me the rum anyway. I didn't want to ... *explain*, so I took it. But I didn't drink it. Please believe me."

"Didn't give you the chance, did I?"

"That's true." She gave me the ghost of a smile. "It's not easy, Berns."

I didn't answer.

In a light voice she said, "Oh, that guy came by and chose one of the canoes."

"He did? That's good." I felt a leap of excitement, but tried not to let it show.

"Maybe if we'd held out, we could have gotten more for it."

"We did good."

"You're probably right. Why don't you take a break? Go out — maybe visit Ruby."

"Yeah ... maybe I'll take a canoe out for a bit."

As I was walking away, she said, "You owe Tony for that bottle of rum."

I didn't answer again.

"And wear a life jacket," she added.

We looked at each other. It was as if more important words hung between us, but neither of us could say them. She muttered something about asking John Broom if he could hook up the old TV to the aerial on the roof and left.

I went to the darkroom and looked around until I found a waterproof bag for my camera — just to be on the safe side. Canoes were touchy things.

As I walked to the front door, Jojo popped up from behind the couch, Jackie in her arms. "You goin' out, Bernie?"

"I won't be long."

"Where you goin'?"

"Out in the canoe for a bit."

"Can I come this time?"

"No. Sorry, Jo. I need time alone."

She pouted. "You never let me come with you anymore. I never been in a canoe."

I sighed. "We've only been here a couple of days, Jo. Next time. I promise."

"You better," she said. "I want to go in a canoe. Not fair." Then she ran to the stairway whimpering. I felt lousy, but didn't call her back.

Outside, the evening light had lost some of its heat and hung hazy over the water. A boat putted slowly past, three fishing lines stretching out behind. The red-haired woman and two of her kids. She must live nearby. The man wasn't with them. They all looked at me with interest and waved. I waved back, although I wasn't the least bit interested — and walked into the first boathouse.

The small red canoe was lighter than I expected. I turned it over and tipped it easily into the water. I dropped a smelly old life jacket in, lifted the wooden slat that held the doors in place and climbed into the canoe. I sat in the back, but the nose was too high in the water, so I crawled to the other seat, closer to the middle, and turned around. Better.

Working with my paddle, I managed to slide between the doors with only a few soft bangs. The woman and her kids were already in the far bay. Tiny mites floated in small clouds above the water weeds. The sun was low and warmed my shoulders. The distant shoreline was black, and just above it hung a layer of dark pewter clouds.

I was so busy trying to stay straight, I was in front of the Brooms' cottage before I knew it. Ruby and Jack were sitting on wooden lawn chairs on a wide dock, coffee cups in hand. Badger lay beside them, panting in the heat.

"Yoohoo!" Ruby called. "You be careful there, little one! You got a life jacket?"

I hauled the heavy thing up in the air then dropped it like a sack of flour.

Jack laughed. "That's about fifty years old! If you fall in, don't grab it or it'll drown you!"

"Get her one of ours — get one for each kid and she can take them home," Ruby commanded. "Paddle in, Bernice. I'm not having you on my conscience."

By the time I'd managed to get the canoe to the dock, Jack was back with three red jackets — so light, they whispered to the bottom of the canoe.

"She can swim like a mermaid, Gran."

"A bonk on the head with a heavy canoe and even a mermaid can drown," she said. "Go with her, Jack. Show her around the lake a bit."

I shook my head, but Jack was already telling me to turn around and face forward and he'd sit in the back. He grabbed a paddle from behind their chairs and hopped in. I clung to the sides of the rocking canoe.

"Don't worry, we won't tip," he said. "See you later, Gran."

Ruby ordered a pacing Badger to *sit* and *stay*, and waved us off before tipping her straw hat over her face.

"I just saw Badger at our place," I said.

"He's fast. Or else there's two of him. I can never figure out which."

We paddled in silence for a while. "Where are all the cottages?" I asked.

"This bay has only your place and ours. See how high the land is around here? Campers never want to build too far from the water. The rest of the lake is through those narrows ahead. The shoreline is much lower on the main lake."

Past the campers' docks, the ground rose to chunky battered cliffs.

"Good fishing along here." Jack pointed to the shifting black shadows below.

"My dream date. Catching slimy fish."

"We on a date?"

"You wish," I said, laughing.

As we moved alongside the cliffs, I saw they fell in a series of long shelves before dropping to a marsh cut in half by a narrow creek. Hidden in the pines were the burned-out remains of a small cabin. Three waterlogged stumps, sticking out just off shore, showed where a dock had once stood.

"Whose place was that?" I asked. "Did it burn recently?"

"I asked my Gran once, but she just said it had belonged to an artist — in the late fifties, early sixties. I guess he couldn't be bothered rebuilding."

An artist? Could it be William? Maybe he wasn't a guest at the lodge, but lived here. Did he die in the fire?

"Can we stop and look around?" I asked.

Jack nudged the canoe past one of the rotting posts, back paddling until we were parallel to a flat rock cloaked in green moss. I put my camera on a rocky spot and scrambled out of the canoe, but it kicked away from me, and I slid into waist-high water, dragging handfuls of moss with me. My feet sunk into soft goo up to my calves. Jack yelped and tried to steady the canoe, but then it tipped just enough to let the entire lake flood in. Life jackets floated in all directions. I managed to grab the three red ones, but the old one sank like a stone. Cursing loudly, Jack stood up, dragged the canoe to shore and flipped it over, water gushing everywhere.

"We're going to have to work on your dismount!"

I dragged myself out, losing one of my old sneakers. As I rinsed off my legs, mosquitoes swarmed us. I batted at them helplessly.

"Didn't you put on any repellent?"

"Of course I didn't. Let's get out of here."

"After all this, you don't even want to see the place? Hey, you've lost a sneaker. *Oh no* — that girly pleading look will not get me to dig for it. The primordial goo will keep it until an archaeologist digs it up in 3010." He rinsed off his sneakers and stuck them back on his feet. "City girl!"

"Okay, let's see the place," I muttered. "And there's nothing wrong with city girls."

"Except they don't know about bug spray or how to get out of a canoe."

Jack pulled a small plastic bottle out of his shorts pocket and gave it to me. I pumped the smelly stuff all over my arms. He sprayed the backs of my legs, then his hands and rubbed them through my hair and down the nape of my neck.

When I glanced up, dark eyes were looking at me with interest. I stepped back and picked up my camera, took it out of its waterproofing and walked quickly toward the remains of the old cottage, ignoring sharp prickles under my bare foot. He loped along behind, spraying himself and talking.

"Watch out for rusty nails. Listen, don't go in the place — hey — look! Rusty nail! Right there. Sticking straight up out of the ground. That roof is about to go. You should be wearing boots. Oh, and keep an eye out for snakes."

I yelped and backed away from the open door.

"Ha!" he hooted. "Knew something would stop you — just had to figure out what. You can look, but don't go in. Unless you've had a tetanus shot lately."

"You're very bossy, do you know that?"

"What some people call bossy, others call *helpful*," he said with a smile.

I pretended to sneer. Peering inside the cool, murky space, I spotted a metal bedstead, black with soot, leaning against one wall. Across from it, an old cookstove had fallen through rotted floorboards. A few straggling bushes had taken root inside a metal artist's easel. The dark gray odor of damp earth and moldering wood filled the air.

The silence was the buzzing-fly kind you get on hot summer days, but there was also a different kind of ... soundlessness under it. It was almost as if the ruined cottage had been holding its pathetic remains together, waiting for someone to come back. When I turned to go, a gust of dank air floated out of the open doorway and engulfed me in a sadness so intense my heart tightened in my chest.

I snapped the cap off my camera and took two shots.

"Not much to see," Jack said behind me.

"No," I said, frowning. "Not much."

Chapter Eighteen

*A photograph is a secret about a secret.
The more it tells you the less you know.*

Diane Arbus, photographer

We walked back to the canoe. The sun hovered above a wide pile of blue-black clouds. I fumbled with my camera to take a shot, but Jack said, "Hey, forget that! We gotta get a move on. Storm coming!"

I slid the camera into its case with a *tsk*. As we paddled away, the cottage sat in golden splinters of light and for just a moment seemed to come together, as it might have looked all those years ago. Did Charlotte take a boat or canoe to this place knowing William was waiting for her? I shook my head. Since when did I get so pathetically romantic?

The clouds rolled across the sky like a herd of stampeding bison, the evening's warmth torn away by a chilling wind that tried to shove the canoe back to shore. The cabin sank into shadows.

"Paddle on the other side and dig deep. We'll head to my place!" Jack shouted.

The wind pushed at us. A crack of lightning sprayed the inky shoreline.

"I have to get home!" I called back. "Ally's scared of storms."

"Forget it! He'll be fine. Your mom's there." I felt the canoe surge to the left, heading for his docks.

"She's no good with him! Ally needs *me*!"

"Just paddle, Bernie!"

"No, I want to go to my place!"

He bellowed, "I don't care! Either stop paddling or change sides!"

I kept trying to control the canoe, but Jack was much stronger and the nose kept its line toward shore. Finally, I changed sides and went with it.

The first heavy drops of rain were so cold on my back they took my breath away, but we were soon under the wide eaves of his boathouse after hauling the canoe onto the dock and turning it over. Another stab of lightning lit the sky, followed immediately by a clap of thunder that literally lifted me off my feet.

"Man, we coulda been hit," he growled. "You're one stubborn girl."

I looked at the gray wall of rain. "It was like the clouds were right on top of us."

"They *are* right on top of us," he said. He leaned into the open door behind him and pulled out two rain slickers. "I've got the life jackets. Come on, let's go to your place."

When we clattered onto our veranda a few minutes later, shaking rain off like a couple of stray dogs, we found Ally there with Mr. Broom, staring out through the screens. Thunder rumbled. Ally was pale but calm and giving John Broom sidelong glances. Being brave for him.

"Heard you were canoeing. Dangerous out there," Mr. Broom said, just as lightning forked and thunder blasted above. Ally leaned in closer to him.

"You okay?" I asked, and he nodded.

"He's doing great," John Broom said.

Ally added in a piping voice, "Mr. Broom says that after the rain stops we can go look at a big anthill in the old parking lot. He says we'll see them repairing their home. And soon we're gonna make a water bug pond in an aquarium."

Jack said, "Dad and I used to put tadpoles in it and watch them grow into frogs."

More thunder boomed, but Ally hardly flinched. "We did

that once in class, but the tadpoles died. Did yours die?"

"Heck no! My dad and me are experts at tadpoles. Right, Dad?"

Mr. Broom nodded, one corner of his mouth lifting.

Jack said, "Tell you what, Ally. We'll do it together, okay?"

I left them talking bugs and frogs and walked into the living room, prickly with irritation. Clearly, Ally couldn't care less that I was home, after all my worrying about him. Jojo was asleep on the couch, her head in Celia's lap, the cat in her arms. What was this — the Brady Bunch Goes to Camp?

Celia smiled sadly. "Jojo was *quite* upset when you went out and didn't let her come, too. She says you never let her tag along anymore. I explained to her that sometimes big sisters need time alone. But not *all* the time, Bernie."

Look who was accusing *me* of not paying Jojo attention. I pulled out my camera and clicked it, just as Jack and the others walked in. "Scene ten, act one thousand. Mother Dearest — Faking Concern for Youngest Child. Good take, Celia. Print it!" And I stalked out of the room.

Did she really think she was fooling me? Her lovey-dovey mother routine was big-time bull. She may have fooled Ally and Jojo, but no way would I get sucked in by that smiling, fake Celia. I knew the real Celia. The pathetic drunk I *hated*.

I sat on my bed for a long time, sagging like a balloon losing air. The next time I saw Jack, I bet he'd point out my overacting again. Couldn't blame him. I couldn't seem to control the Big Gesture.

I watched the rain slide down the window. The ledge was crammed with jam jars and quart sealers. The little table was covered with them, too. Insects in every one. Books were piled everywhere. Ally was taking over the room.

"Jeez, Ally, you've gone bug crazy," I muttered. "I hope

you're not going to start counting them every night before bed. You'll be up all night, for crying out loud."

Someone cleared his throat behind me. Mr. Broom stood in the doorway.

"Sorry," he said. "I was going to measure for shelves in the next room. Your mom thought you might like a few, too. But I can do the measuring here tomorrow. Oh — you've got hot water now. That tank just needed adjusting."

"Thanks. I'll leave so you can measure," I said, standing up.

"Stay. Won't take a minute."

He lined up his measuring tape along the wall behind my bed. He was so different from Jack, like one of those Christmas trees you see in sales lots in the city — branches pulled in tight with rough twine.

He looked at me over his shoulder. "You okay, Bernice?"

I tried to laugh as I swept my arm through the air. "Look at this room. Ally's taking up the whole space."

He smiled and his face softened. It threw me.

"Ally's a good kid," he said quietly, "but really tense — worried all the time. You, too, I think. I was wondering. Maybe you could help him by —"

Huh? What was he going on about? A Big Gesture bubbled up, and before he could say another word, I yelled, "Your whole family's just *full* of advice! You don't know anything about Ally and me! So why don't you take that advice you're about to come out with and stick it!" I ran out into the hall. Was there nowhere I could get away from these people?

"Bernice!"

I stopped halfway down the stairs. Mr. Broom stood above me, tape measure in hand. "I apologize, Bernice. I had no right ..."

I shook my head. "I didn't mean to get so mad. It's just —"

"No need to explain. My fault entirely."

And he walked away.

I stood, cheeks flaming. He'd tried to be nice and I'd yelled at him. I wasn't used to straight talk. As I walked down to the main floor, I could hear Celia yakking to the kids in the living room. Their voices came closer. Damn. The last thing I needed was to see *her* right now. I slid into Charlotte's darkroom, turned on the light and sat on the floor to wait it out.

I could hear them in the kitchen. Soon, a deeper voice and the smell of coffee filtered under the door. Was Mr. Broom having coffee with Celia? Poor guy.

To pass some time, I opened the filing cabinet and took out a pile of folders. Each was dated and stuffed with photos. The first was all about lodge life — people sitting on the lawn under big umbrellas, in boats with picnic baskets, diving or swimming or posing in oversized bathing suits and strange hats. In one, Charlotte stood with her arm around a woman with light-colored hair. Ruby Broom.

I riffled through more folders. Black-and-white pics of small and large groups of people flashed by. In one file, I spied William, sitting with a group picnicking in a grassy area. Actually, he was in most of the shots, and always with the same people — sketchbooks, easels, canvases and paint boxes littered around them. He must have been with a group of artists staying at the lodge. When they left, did he stay behind in that cabin in the bay?

I peered intently at the last picture. Was it? Yes. It was Charlotte! Sitting beside William. Her bangs covered her eyebrows — just like mine, her long hair falling past her shoulders. She wore an open-neck white shirt, loose-fitting slacks and bare feet. She didn't look like the miserable person Celia had described. She looked nice. And happy.

Intrigued, I searched the files for more pictures of William and Charlotte together, but no luck. I was right about one thing, though. Charlotte *had* stopped taking pictures of her guests — of any people — after those artists' photos were taken. Who could blame her? People were more work than they were worth. The rest of the folders were all nature shots except for one picture in its own envelope, dated five years ago — a skinny, dark-haired kid sitting at the kitchen table. Jack. He had a wide strap around his neck and the big camera attached to it rested on the tabletop. That strap was now around *my* neck. I felt a twinge of guilt. Had she promised it to him? If so, why didn't she leave it to him in her will?

The second-last folder was dated five years ago as well — a slim pile of dramatic color close-ups — the curved and fringed center of a water lily, an insect's bright green antennae, gray and purple moss, a pale yellow spider on a dark yellow petal. They were almost abstract paintings. I loved them. It was like she'd suddenly found a new way of looking at things. I put them aside, the spider on top to show Ally later.

The final folder had about twenty prints — all blurry and badly composed. At the bottom of the pile, in large scrawled printing was a note. "My eyes have gone. All out of focus, like my life."

How awful for Charlotte. If I couldn't have used a camera anymore, I didn't know what I'd do. Using it kept me from ... from what? ... I didn't know. I just knew I *had* to take pictures. Is that how she'd felt? It must have been devastating to have to stop. We weren't that different, it seemed. My life was definitely out of focus, too.

I put the files back in order, except the nature set. I wanted to frame them and hang them in the lodge. Funny — there were no photos anywhere on the walls.

Someone laughed on the other side of the door. Celia. This was followed by a man's rolling chuckle. I couldn't *imagine* John Broom laughing. Besides, I was sure he didn't even like her. The chuckle rang out again. *Tony*. She was making coffee for Tony.

I turned off the light with shaking fingers and slipped out of the darkroom and locked it. Tony smiled when he saw me. His skin was like caramel against his white shirt, his hair slicked back from his wide forehead. Mr. Broom was there, too, ball cap sitting on the table. He had a line of pale skin near his hairline, which made the rest of his face look like tanned leather. He gave me a quick nod.

Celia sat across from them, one foot resting on the seat of her chair, her arms wrapped around her knee, head tilted to one side, as if she'd been talking and I'd interrupted.

"So there you are," Tony said. "Is that another back door?"

I had no choice. "It's a darkroom." I gave Celia a defiant stare. "I'm gonna use it."

Celia shrugged. "I didn't know Charlotte was a photographer. But hey, I don't need a darkroom. However, we will need a stock room, Bernie, so I'll take the key."

"No. You'll have to find another place to put the stock."

"It's your idea to get this store up and running," she said. "So you'll have to —"

John Broom interrupted her. "It's not big enough for a stock room. Charlotte kept her store goods in the shed out back. I can revamp it. Put in a window air conditioner."

I gave him a grateful smile.

Celia shook her head. "More expense. Will it never end?"

"We were just talking about whether or not your mom should tear out the docks and build new ones or repair those," Tony said.

Mr. Broom pushed his chair back. "I've got to go. Let me know what you want to do. I can tear them out, but you'll regret it. Good docks are a selling point."

"One new dock is all we need," Celia said, her chin thrust out stubbornly. "Tony agrees with me."

"Won't need much work to fix three of the four, until you can replace the cribs with metal. Still ... up to you," Mr.

Broom said, shrugging. "The new owners will have to lay out good money to replace them. They're needed. Good selling point."

"For someone who doesn't seem to care what I do, you're very persistent," Celia said.

He grabbed his cap. "I don't need the work. Or the money. So I'll leave you to it." He walked out.

"Sheesh!" Celia grumbled. "What an *irritating* man!"

Tony laughed. "A bit of a yup-nope kind of yokel. Probably not too bright — but I hear he does good work."

Jack and Ally appeared in the doorway. Jack's face was dark red. "Dad's a hell of a lot smarter than you. If you ever say that again, I'll rearrange your face, you slimeball!" He swung around and was gone.

Tony laughed softly. "Oops. I'll apologize next time I see him. I guess I'll slink off to my cave. See you later, guys." He touched my arm with his fingertips as he walked by. An electric jolt went right through me. He ruffled Ally's hair, but Ally pushed his hand away. He'd already taken sides.

I wanted to go after Jack, but my arm still tingled. I couldn't take sides. Not yet.

Chapter Nineteen

*The senses heighten so that I am totally
immersed in what's happening at the moment.*

Keith Lazelle, photographer

I sat on my bed, unable to sleep. Until today, I'd thought
John Broom was a yup-nope kind of guy, too. But his apology to me earlier had changed that somehow. I felt bad about
what Tony'd said about him. Yet, even though it *appeared*
nasty, I was pretty sure he hadn't meant it.

Just thinking about Tony made me feel desperate. What
was the matter with me? Why couldn't I stop feeling so *out
of control*? I couldn't even pin down what he thought of me.
Sometimes he seemed really interested and other times, he
acted like I was a kid.

Why did I have to meet him? I'd gotten along just fine
taking care of Jojo and Ally, keeping my distance — especially at school, knowing I'd only lose any friends I made as
soon as we had to move again. I guess that made me a weird
loner. Like Ally. Like Charlotte.

I lay back on my pillows. Tony said he was a loner, too,
but I doubted that. He was so outgoing and easy to talk to.
Maybe he was just lonely — just needed someone to share
things with. Someone like me.

When I woke up, my first thought was, when will I see
him again? Probably not before hours of happy cleaning with
Celia. Leaving Ally sound asleep, I grabbed my camera, dressed in the bathroom, picked up a juice box and a couple of
muffins and walked along the lake path toward the Brooms'.

I'd noticed a big flat rock over the water. It would be a quiet spot to eat.

There was no mist, just a soft hazy light over the still water that gave everything a dreamy, secret feeling. I sat on the rock, focused my camera and took a couple of shots of the silence. The sun warmed me as I ate, relaxing my neck muscles, calming my knotted stomach. I stretched my legs. Now and again a big fish jumped about three yards away, flashing silvery black. No mosquitoes. Nice.

My deep, easy sigh was cut off when a voice said, "I want that fish. Been after him for weeks. You're on my casting rock."

Badger waggled up to me and slurped the side of my face. I pushed him away and lamented, "I never get any peace and quiet!"

Jack frowned from under the peak of his ball cap. "Hey. Relax, Bernice Dodd. We'll go."

"Never mind. You're here now, *Jack Broom*. Go ahead and cast. I'll watch."

"You'll have to sit close to my legs. So I won't catch you with my lure," he said. "Or move behind that tree, if getting close to me bothers you."

"Just get on the stupid rock," I snarled.

Badger backed off and ran away down the path. Smart dog. I sat close to Jack's blue-jeaned legs. He cast his line out with a soft whir.

"Probably won't bite," he muttered. "Lots of bugs on the water. But still, I like a good challenge."

He looked down at me and my cheeks grew warm. I wasn't going to blow things with Tony for some orange-haired guy who gave me advice every two seconds. I looked at the lake with great concentration.

I heard him snort. After a couple more casts, he said, "I better not see that creep Tony today. I may have to head-butt him. What a sleaze."

"He said he would say sorry the next time he saw you.
He —"

"Yeah, well, I doubt that. You know, my dad's the
smartest guy I know. He was studying architecture when my
mom died. Soon after, we moved back here. Gran says he
was too broken up to finish."

"I think Tony thought he was just being funny. He only
meant your dad doesn't say much." Suddenly I lied. "He felt
bad about it. Really."

Jack snorted again. "Whatever. Hey, you wanna go to
Stellar?"

"Today? Yes! Can you get your dad's truck?"

"No, Gran needs it. Got a motorcycle, though. Secondhand, but a beauty."

"I can cash the canoe check — open a bank account.
Maybe see the lawyer. Can we leave now?"

He glanced at his watch. "I haven't even had breakfast.
It'll take us about half an hour to get to the outskirts of
town. The bank doesn't open until ten. Some stores open
then, too. We'll drive around and I'll give you a tour. When
we're done, I'll take you to the chip truck for the world's
best hot dogs and fries. I'll pick you up in an hour — just
past eight thirty. Okay? But tell your mom where you're
going. She'll worry."

The Irrepressible Mr. Advice. I sniffed. "She won't
care."

"She'll think a bear got you or something. Let the kids
know, at least."

"Okay, Grandpa," I sneered. "I'll leave a note. But I'll be
at *your* place at eight — on the nose!" And I ran down the
path before he could argue.

When I got to our shore, Celia was taking an early-morning swim — heading out into the bay. I slipped along the
bushes, ran inside and put the check in my camera bag.
I found Ally and Jojo eating toast with cheese spread in

the kitchen and told them to let Celia know I was going out with Jack.

I walked quickly, only slowing down when I was out of sight of the lodge windows. As I got close to the end of Jack's driveway, a motor started up with a *rooomm-rooomm*, and in a few seconds, a bike and rider slid around the corner of his drive, kicking up stones. It ground to a halt beside me. Jack wore a helmet the color of his jean shirt. Reaching behind him, he grabbed a silver one and handed it to me.

"You ridden a bike before?"

"No."

"Okay. Here's the deal. Keep your feet up. Don't lean. Hang on tight. Don't shout directions."

"Aye, aye, captain!" As soon as my arms went around his waist, he gunned it and we were off, zipping over the dirt road, tearing down the sandy path, wet leaves slapping our helmets. I laughed out loud and he grinned back at me.

Soon we were roaring along the Trans-Canada. We passed lakes, rocky ridges and, in no time, gas stations, building supply stores and houses on stone outcrops. At the edge of town, we drove past a DQ and a giant pickerel sculpture as high as a two-story building, zipped over a few bridges — one with huge circles of floating logs below. On our right was Lake of the Woods — and just ahead, the sweeping entrance to the town, a giant water fountain in the bay, and in the distance a long horseshoe-shaped marina and parking lot. Tied in the curve of the enormous dock was a double-decker tourist boat. Jack slowed and turned up the town's main street.

We rumbled past book and clothing stores, restaurants and antique shops. He pointed out an old-fashioned store-front that said McGill's Hardware. He turned left at the Canadian Tire store across from the Stellar museum and dropped down a steep road to a place called the Arrow Head. "Gift shop!" he called. "Ice cream, too!" We swooped past the Safeway lot and straight up a steep residential street lined with old frame houses. For half an hour we drove through the curving roller-coaster streets, catching glimpses of water almost everywhere.

Finally, because I was poking him, he wove his way past a large frame house — Tea Shop and Museum — and wound back onto Main, turned left and stopped in front of the bank. I could hardly get off the bike, my bottom was so sore.

"You need a softer seat," I grumbled. "Or maybe I do."

"You're too young to be so old."

I walked into the bank, giving him the finger. I heard him laugh. It took a few minutes to convince the teller that I was sixteen and didn't need my mother's signature. I also pointed out that my mother already had an account at the bank. Finally she let me deposit the check. I took out a float of a hundred bucks in case the family needed anything. I still had the forty dollars Lucy had given me as spending money. Might as well use some of that today.

I was grinning when I got back to the bike.

"Where to now?" he asked. "You said a lawyer?"

I thought a minute. What would I ask the lawyer? We now had money to open the store on a small scale. Ruby would help Celia get a business license.

"Nah. No lawyers today. Need film, though. And a pair of cheap duck boots. I'm tired of having wet feet."

"Okey-dokey. Hop on."

We pulled out into traffic. An hour later, after buying film and boots for me, a big bug-collecting container with a magnifying glass on top for Ally, a sand-castle building set for Jojo and a jug of milk, we parked and walked down a side street that descended to the marina. To our right was the lake, to our left the backs of Main Street shops and restaurants with fluttering umbrellas on their patios. It was a pretty town. I took a shot of Jack with the tourist boat behind him.

The chip truck had a permanent spot on a short hill above the marina lot. A few tables with blue-and-white umbrellas were crammed onto a small concrete pad. It was only eleven fifteen, but the truck's side flap was open and the smell of oil, onions and salt flowed out. We ordered two dogs, loaded, double fries and colas. The fries were sizzling hot. I doused mine in white vinegar; Jack soaked his in brown malt. Snowing them with salt, we decided to share so we could enjoy both flavors.

The guy behind the counter knew Jack and leaned his elbows on the counter to chat from inside the van. When he saw my camera, he asked if he could look at it. Jack said, "Hey, Todd, how about taking a pic of Bernie and me?"

"Bernie? That's a guy's name." The boy, wrapped in a big white apron, stepped out of the trailer.

"She look like a boy?"

"Definitely not," Todd said, grinning, and asked how the camera worked. I checked the light, showed him the focus and said, "Just aim and shoot."

Todd told us to sit close together. I could feel Jack's breath on my cheek. Todd pretended to get hiccups and the camera bobbed all over the place.

"Take the picture or I'll throw my drink on your sneakers and you'll stick to the van floor all day," I said. Todd grinned and took the shot.

When a family approached the chip van, he handed me the camera and slid back to work. Jack and I wolfed down the hot dogs and fries. As we picked at the final few crunchy chips, a light breeze with a flush of heat wafted over us. Soon it would be really steaming. Our table overlooked a small charter plane company at the end of the marina. We talked — *he* talked — about the town. It was pretty interesting. Fur trading, wild taverns, logging and prospecting — two big Native reserves nearby and rich cottage owners everywhere — loads of history.

"You'll have to see the museum," Jack said. "We could bring Jojo and Ally. The Native collection is amazing, and you get a real sense of this whole area."

I nodded, but I was focused on a small red sports car parked nearby. "Wanna walk back to the bike?" he asked. "Or scout around for old lover boy."

"Huh?"

"Your eyes have been glued to his car for about five minutes. Good thing there's no written test on my last few fascinating historical details."

"I don't know whose car that is! And I don't care. Let's go!"

As we walked past restaurant patios, Jack said, "There he is."

I stopped dead. "Where?"

He pointed. "Looks like he's got himself a lunch date."

Sitting at one of the tables, Tony leaned over and kissed a woman in a big floppy straw hat.

Through dry lips, I said, "He told me he hardly knew anyone around here."

"Yeah, right," Jack sneered, then his expression softened. "Hey, maybe she's a real estate agent. I hear he's thinking of buying the place he's renting."

"You think so?" I asked, my heart lightening a bit. "Could be. He said he might buy a place. She looks like a real estate agent, doesn't she?"

Just then Tony glanced in our direction. I waved. He waved back. I took a step forward, but he turned abruptly with a quick final flap of the hand and leaned toward the woman again.

I felt as if I'd been hit in the stomach. Jack took my arm and steered me away. "They're probably discussing business. We don't want to interrupt."

I let him lead me toward Main Street, keeping up a running commentary about the town, but I wasn't listening.

"I gotta get home," I muttered. "Make sure the kids are okay."

Jack nodded. We didn't talk the rest of the way to the bike. I couldn't do anything but stand beside it, arms hanging limp. As he did up my helmet, he leaned down and looked into my eyes. I looked away, blinking hard.

He sighed. "You got it bad, huh? But ... remember, Bernice Dodd ..."

I stiffened, ready for a lecture.

He began to sing loudly, "... just call out for Jack, and you know wherever he is, he'll come runnin' ... 'cause you've got a friend. Oh yes, Bernie, you've got a friiieeend!"

People turned and smiled at him. A girl with long blond hair gave me a thumbs-up. I couldn't help laughing. "Put on your helmet and get on the damn bike!"

Chapter Twenty

Never boss people around.
It's more important to click with people
than to click the shutter.

Alfred Eisenstaedt, photographer

I let Celia blow off some steam, then I said, "When you get the license for the store and are ready to order, we can work out the money."

A tiny muscle under her eye twitched, a sign that tears were close. "First, you go to Stellar without telling me —"

"I told the kids to tell you."

She waved that aside. "And then you open your own bank account. Is *that* fair, Bernie? I'm the *mother*. I make the decisions on how this is going to play out, not you. I need that money. It's mine ... ours. It's not just yours."

I tried not to shout. "I'm protecting it. For *all* of us."

She took a deep breath. "Okay, Bernie. I know where this is coming from. I don't blame you. But I am trying. You *know* that."

I didn't know that, actually. So I said, "When we've got the place cleaned up, we'll get the money and buy supplies."

She looked away, chewing her lip. We sat in silence for at least one whole minute — a long time, if you've ever sat it out. Then she said, "Okay. We'll do it your way."

"What's that supposed to mean?"

"It means what it means."

"We'll do it *my* way? Since when? Until when?"

"Give it up, Bernie. I've agreed. Leave it there. Let's

get to work." With that, she began to clatter buckets and run water.

What the heck was she up to? She was no straight-talking John Broom, that was for sure. My small voice warned, *Don't trust her.*

Would I ever be able to convince her to stay permanently? Did I want to stay? Would Tony stay, too? Who was that woman? Why had he waved me away as if I was nobody? I turned the vacuum on to blast out the questions dusting up my head.

Celia and I didn't talk, except for pass-the-salt stuff, the rest of the afternoon. My exhausted brain had shut down by dinner. We all went to bed early. Upstairs, Ally asked me to look at one of the moth and butterfly books he'd found on Charlotte's shelves. I sat on his bed and we examined the colored plates. He showed me a moth that looked just like a hummingbird with tiny clear windows in its wings. At first I only half listened, but soon his excited voice cut through my numb brain.

"If we plant the right flowers out front next spring, Mr. Broom says we'd see one for sure. And he promised to take me to his place where these moths *and* real hummingbirds come all the time, *and* he's going to bring over two hummingbird feeders for us. Jack says he's got a couple of big aquariums that I can have and I can keep lots of common caterpillars in them and watch them eat leaves. And then ..."

I stared at him in wonderment — Mr. Broom said this and Jack said that. Sounded like the Brooms had taken him over. I wasn't sure I liked that one bit.

"... then I'll let them go," he continued, "'cause they can't be held prisoners for too long, but Mr. Broom says he'll show me the right leaves for each kinda caterpillar and soon they'll get ready to turn into butterflies and moths. Mr. Broom says that he used to do that when he was a kid. So did Jack. But you got to get the timing just right."

When he finally wore himself out and looked drowsy, I moved to a chair by the window to think. Odd to imagine John Broom ever being a kid. But as irritated as I was, I had to admit he'd turned my little brother from a white-faced frightened kid into a Super Junior Naturalist. I'd never seen Allister so excited. But, let's face it, men didn't stay around our family long. How soon would Mr. Broom be out of Ally's life? My kid brother seemed less afraid, less anxious, but it wouldn't take much to send him reeling back into his sad, obsessive little world.

"Ally?"

"Yeah?"

"You like Mr. Broom, eh?"

"Yeah. And Jack, too."

"What do you think of Tony?"

He shrugged, rolled over and faced the wall. Well, Tony hadn't had time to really *talk* to Ally yet.

"Bernie?" a little voice said from the door.

"Shhh, Ally's asleep. What are you doing up, Jojo? Didn't Mom tuck you in?"

"Yeah, but she read my story real fast 'cause she was tired. Now she's sleeping. I miss you guys. Can I come in here with you?"

"Got your pillow and blankie?"

She held them up triumphantly, scuttled across the room and slid under the covers of my narrow brass bed, grinning happily. The cat stretched out beside her.

I turned off the lights. In less than two minutes, the room was filled with stereophonic snorts and burbles. I leaned my head against the window and gazed out at the smoky blue lake. The putt-putt of a small boat sounded in the bay and a loon called mournfully in the distance. Suddenly, a shadow moved near the closest boathouse. I stared intently. Was it Tony? Coming to see me?

No such luck. Badger appeared first, then Jack, a fishing

rod in one hand and a stringer of fish in the other. To my surprise, I wasn't all that disappointed. I grabbed my camera and leaned close to the screen. I knew it probably wouldn't work, but I took a shot anyway. Jack looked up.

"I thought you were supposed to throw fingerlings back," I said through the screen.

He held up the fish. "Excuse me? These are *big* ones."

"What kind?"

"The best. Pickerel. Gran won't have jack fish in her kitchen."

"I don't like fish, remember?"

"You'll like these. I'll get Gran to invite you for a fry-up. If you're not too busy mooning over the Toothless Prince."

"Who?"

He hesitated, then said sharply, "Creep Lafferty with the fake white teeth."

"They're not fake," I snarled.

"Like you'd know. I think I know who he was with today."

"How? She had a huge hat and big sunglasses. You wouldn't recognize *Ruby* in that getup!"

"Fine, whatever. Hey, maybe the old coot will drive his MG to the school bus stop this fall, carry your books home for you. If he can drive without his bifocals."

"Jeez, what is your *problem*?"

He pointed at his chest and the fish slapped against his legs. "Me? I don't have a problem. I don't have a crush on some geezer with an out-of-date haircut and a painted-on tan."

"Yeah, well at least he knows how to coordinate his clothes — and doesn't look like he's glued a pumpkin on his head!"

Jack bowed, sweeping the ground with fish tails. Badger gave one a quick lick before they were swept into the air again. "I bow to your pure and unencumbered fashion sense.

Plain shorts, plain jeans, plain T-shirts, plain sneakers. One of the *multitude*. In *dress*, in *thinking*, and clearly in *spirit*. I worship at the feet of your mediocrity. I leave you to your lustful thoughts of aging gigolos and drunken mothers."

"Pig!"

Ally murmured sleepily, "Bernie? Who're you talking to?"

"No one!" I shut the window with a bang. "No one at all!"

Chapter Twenty-one

*If you saw a man drowning and
you could either save him or
photograph the event ... what kind
of film would you use?*

Anonymous

For the next week, neither Jack nor Tony came by — just
Ruby bringing more casseroles, and Mr. Broom, who was
building shelves in the bedrooms and store and repairing the
floors. He even put a new screen in the back door, so the cat
wouldn't escape when we aired out the paint fumes. I had-
n't actually gotten around to painting the store yet. Mr.
Broom kept replacing shelves and insisting I couldn't paint
until the walls and shelves were perfect. Might not say as
much, but he was as bossy as his son. Things had definitely
slowed down, except for cleaning, scrubbing and ... oh yeah,
more cleaning and scrubbing. But, hey, the longer it took,
the longer we'd stay. If you counted that as a good thing. I
wasn't sure anymore.

I was half relieved and half desperate that Tony and
Jack stayed away. Finally my pride kicked in. Life, I decided, was a lot less complicated without them. At least that's
what I told myself. About fifty times a day.

Lucy phoned often during that week. I spoke to her just
once, and it was obvious my dear mother had given her a
warped view of things, so I told her my version, leaving out
Tony, of course. Instead of instant support, what I got was
a deep, heartfelt sigh and, "Sounds like Celia's having a bit
of a rough time. Don't be too hard on her, Bernie."

"No harder than she is on me. That's fair."

"You two! Listen, sweetie, you and your mom want the same thing, remember that. To get that place ready for sale. And to get back on track."

"You mean we *had* a track once?"

"You know what I mean. I'd hoped you and Celia would —"

I stopped listening. When she ended with " ... don't you agree, Bernie?" I pretended the kids needed me and hung up.

She called again today, but I let Celia answer and made myself scarce. Celia said Lucy would be coming for a visit — next Saturday — a week tomorrow. Then Lucy would see for herself who really needed the lecture once she got here.

I went to bed feeling dragged out and exhausted, only to wake up in the middle of the night with a headache and a terrible thirst. My legs felt like dead weights, but I needed to go to the toilet badly. Afterward, I headed downstairs to get a couple of painkillers. I filled a glass with ice and water. There was a strong smell of coffee in the room — and the metal pot was warm. Looked like Celia had stayed up late.

I gulped down the pills, filled the glass again and ran up the stairs — until my right foot caught on the frayed carpet and I fell with a loud thud, ice cubes and water spraying everywhere.

"Shit!"

Celia flicked on the overhead light by her room. She was still dressed.

"What's going on, Bernie? Are you okay?"

I held up the glass. "Thirsty. Fell."

"Sure you're all right? You're limping." She took my arm.

"My toe hurts a bit, that's all. I —"

In the night's heat, the smell was unmistakable.

I yanked my arm away. "You've been drinking!"

"No! I haven't ... honest, Bernie. Honest!"

"I can smell it on you."

She stepped back and waved her hand in the air. "I went downstairs awhile ago. It was too hot to sleep. I thought I'd make a cool drink. I couldn't find the stupid lemonade mix, and while I was rummaging through the cupboards, Tony knocked on the door. He was out for a walk, saw the light on and checked to see if everything was okay. I offered him coffee."

"And he just happened to bring more booze."

"No. There were ... four bottles of wine at the back of the cupboard. Not mine, Bernie. Old ones. Tony said one was a very good year. While I was making the coffee, he opened it and poured us each a glass. I had a few sips. But that's *all*."

"Tony would never suggest you take a drink."

"Really? Why not?" She grabbed my arm. "What did you tell him?"

I shook my head. "Celia, people aren't stupid."

"It's because you threw that glass in the water."

"There was *rum* in that glass, Celia!"

"That was a misunderstanding. And so is this. I knew I was making a big mistake tonight and had coffee instead. Tony took the rest of the bottle home. I insisted, Bernie. I want you to know that. I *insisted* he take it."

"And the other bottles? Did you *insist* he take them too?"

She looked uncomfortable. "We may need them, for guests."

"*What* guests, Celia? No bed and breakfast, you said. *Remember*? Not to mention no liquor license."

"Those bottles will remain in the cupboard."

I laughed. "Oh, sure they will."

"I only had a couple of sips!" she cried.

"*Whatever*," I muttered, walking past her.

She grabbed my arm. "Why won't you believe me, dammit!"

"You're joking, right? The streets of Winnipeg are

littered with your promises. You won't ruin things for the kids again, Celia. I won't let you!"

"What's that supposed to mean? We had a deal, Bernie. We'll work on this place. We'll sell it. We'll get enough money to make our lives better. We'll —"

I shouted in her face. "Tell someone who *cares*! I'm going to bed!"

I left her standing there, locked the bedroom door behind me and sat in the dark. She'd crack soon. I had to be prepared. She'd lied about taking only a few sips ... but she wasn't drunk, either, I could see that. Probably planned to drink the other three on her own and had just put on a prim little act for Tony tonight. And why had he come to visit *her* so late when he hadn't seen me in a week?

A small voice cut through the darkness. "You and Mom were fighting again."

"Ally? Hey, I'm sorry we woke you up."

"I thought when we got here, maybe you guys wouldn't fight so much."

I growled, "Yeah ... well, she's pretending to make things better, but she's not. She says one thing and does another. She's a *liar*!"

"I wish you weren't so mad all the time, Bernie," he said sadly.

"What do you mean — mad? I'm not mad all the time."

"Most of the time, then."

"I'm never mad at you. Or Jojo."

He sighed and turned over. "It's okay, Bernie. 'Night."

The sun blasted straight into my eyes. Ally was up and gone. He'd been leaving his bed quite messy during the week, but this time it was made up like a soldier's cot ready for inspection. I frowned, then shrugged it off.

I picked up my camera. I still had a few shots left on this roll. I'd been so busy working and so tired, I hadn't taken any pictures all week. I'd have to check to see if the stuff I needed for making prints was in Charlotte's darkroom, then finish the roll. I hoped I remembered the steps in developing negatives. I was *almost* sorry I wasn't talking to Jack. He could have helped.

Celia was in the kitchen, wearing an apron and rubber gloves, her head in the oven. Too bad it wasn't *gas*.

Looking over her shoulder, she raised one eyebrow. "Thought I'd let you sleep in a bit. I've set you up for painting the store. John says it's ready. I'll finish in here first. Jojo's gone into town with Ruby, who's checking out that grocery distributor for us and getting some prices. John's going to look over the place again to decide what's the most urgent. And he's definitely fixing the dock soon. I figured it was the right way to go. Do you agree?"

Oh, so *that* was it. She was trying to trick me into feeling *involved*. I rolled my eyes. "Whatever."

"Get some breakfast," she said.

"I don't want breakfast. I'll paint. And by the way, there's no one here but you and me, Celia, so you can drop the motherly routine."

A tiny smile she'd been working on fell off her face into the bucket of dirty water beside her. She stuck her head back in the oven.

Ally walked in and opened the fridge. He looked pale and tired. "I'm thirsty."

"I made lemonade this morning, sweetie," Celia said. "Or there's iced tea. We're low on milk and juice until Ruby and Jojo get back."

He poured a glassful of lemonade and took it out of the room, not looking at either of us.

Celia frowned. "You think he's okay?"

I snapped. "He heard us fighting last night. How do you think he feels?!"

"I'll talk to him in a bit," she said, rinsing her sponge.

"Sure, you do that," I sneered. "Make him feel even better by telling him what you were up to."

"I wasn't up to anything. I explained what happened. Can't we just forget it?"

I didn't answer. Went into the store, grabbed a tin of paint and pried off the lid. Who did she think she was fooling? I stirred hard, slopping moss-green paint over the sides.

"Hey," said a deep voice.

"Hey," I growled, not turning around.

"So you're painting the store, huh?"

I poured the paint carefully into a roller tray and put the lid back on. "No, I'm icing a cake for a very unMerry unbirthday. For *me*."

"For you?" Jack asked.

"For me." I couldn't help smiling.

"I was an A-One absolute jerk," he said.

I nodded. "Yes."

"None of my stupid business."

"Yes."

"Really rude and stupid and idiotic."

"Yes."

"Should be shot?"

"Yes."

"Stop me when I've told myself off enough to satisfy you."

"Okay."

He made a face, hunched his shoulders. "I'm sorry, okay?"

"I *may* accept your apology," I said sternly.

"Do I really look like someone trying to be a pumpkin?"

"No. Your head isn't big enough. More like a neon golf ball."

"Ahh, that's better. I don't feel quite so hurt. Now about my fashion sense."

I laughed, feeling suddenly happy.

But it ended when Celia appeared, leaning around the door frame. "Oh, hello, Jack. I see you've worn some old clothes. Come to help your dad, have you? Or can we snag you to help Bernie?"

Jack looked with dismay at his patterned shorts and long purple shirt. "I'll have you know, Mrs. Dodd, that these are hot couture shorts."

She did her tinkly laugh. "As I look closer, I see they are. But I also see a color in them that matches the green paint exactly, so it won't show if you splash."

He grinned. "Painting it is, then!"

"Good-o!" Celia waved and went back to work in the kitchen.

"Jeez, whose side are you on?" I said.

"Side? What? Where?"

"We had a big fight last night. She —" I didn't want to admit that Tony had visited *her*, never mind the wine part.

"How the heck was I supposed to know that?"

Grudgingly, I said, "Yeah, okay, but from now on, just assume we've had a fight. You can't go wrong then."

He grimaced. "I'm really going to pay for that brainstorm under your window, aren't I?"

"Yes, but you can make it all better by helping me develop some film later on." I handed him a paintbrush. "However, your first punishment is that *you* get to do all those complicated shelves while I paint the nice flat walls with a nice big roller."

Chapter Twenty-two

When your mouth drops open,
click the shutter.

Harold Feinstein, photographer

___

We worked for almost three hours. Now and again, Mr. Broom would grab Jack to help him measure something, but Jack always came back. A lot of sawing and hammering was going on upstairs. I decided to be nice and help Jack. We completed the base coat and put Ally to work cleaning brushes and rollers after we carefully examined two new bugs in leaf-filled jam jars. I snapped a couple of shots of Ally and Jack holding up brushes dripping in paint, then took the last of Celia standing in the doorway, looking like she was about to fall in a heap.

She grimaced and said, "I have a headache. I need a swim and a glass of iced tea — in that order. Phew, it stinks in here."

For once she was right. The store was hot, the stench of paint nose-searing, and I had a nagging pain above my eyes.

"Bernie, you look awful. It's the fumes. Let's all take an hour off," she said. "You want me to make some lunch, Ally? We could have apples and cheese down by the lake."

"A picnic, like?"

"Sure, why not? We'll also take those peanut butter and cracker packages you like. And a couple of juice boxes."

Ally's face lit up in wonderment. "Really? Just you and me?" It twisted my heart.

Celia smiled down at him. "Yep. I'll get our picnic ready. You go grab your suit."

He scuttled from the room, thin arms pumping.

Celia looked at me, smiled at Jack, blinked a couple of times and headed for the kitchen. Over her shoulder she said, "Eat something, Bernie."

I made a face at her back.

"Boy, you guys are like two porcupines. All prickly and defensive," Jack said.

"Not without reason!" I snapped.

"Hey, just an observation. When did she start — you know —"

"Drinking? Been awhile. Not that she's a fall-down drunk every day. Celia's a binge alcoholic. She seems fine, sometimes for days — then wham! she's gone. Usually out every night for a week or so, doesn't come home on the weekend. Then when she does, she's got a massive hangover. Once she sobers up, we get back to some pathetic attempt at normal life. And then it starts all over again." I thought about last night's "sips" of wine. That binge was due anytime.

Jack said quietly, "Sounds tough, but she seems pretty normal now."

"Of course. That's what she's hoping people will think."

"Ally okay?"

"I'm not sure. He's had some problems the last few years."

"I know — Dad told me."

"Told you what?" I asked irritably.

"That he's easily upset, that's all. Your mom will help him relax over lunch. Maybe he's homesick."

"You need a *home* to feel homesick, don't you?" I said with a tight laugh. "Let's develop this film. I hope you're better at that than at analyzing my family."

As I followed Jack to the darkroom, he muttered something about mouthy girls. I gave him a shove inside and shut the door behind us.

"Don't hit me! I'm sorry," he whined, ducking behind his upraised arm.

"Oh shut up, you big wimp," I said, shoving him again. I looked around the little room. "Jeez, I don't even know if Aunt Charlotte has everything we need."

"There's lots of stuff. I was the last one to use it." He waved his hand toward the five portrait shots tacked along the corkboard.

"*You* took those faces? They're really good."

"Why, thank you, Miss Dodd," he said, looking pleased.

I pointed at two of them. "Are those —?"

Jack's breath sifted across my cheek as he leaned past me. "Yeah, Charlotte. I have quite a few shots of her at home. She had a really interesting face — like yours — a mix of open and closed, funny and sad. She could be a real pain, like — uh —"

"Me?"

"Yeah, that would be the one. But she still remembered everything there was to know about cameras, and her work was always really good. She asked me to burn her folders of prints and negatives when she died. But I didn't. I wanted to look them over first. I thought I might take a few. But my dad said they weren't mine to take — or to burn."

"Why would she want to burn her stuff?"

"I don't know. Maybe she thought her family — you guys — wouldn't be interested. Although she knew I liked her work. Especially her new nature studies. I got the idea of doing face close-ups from them."

I looked into my great-aunt's eyes. It made me sad to think I'd never meet her, never speak to her. Would she think that not meeting her sister's grandchildren was a loss? Maybe not. I got the feeling Charlotte was used to loss.

"When did you take this picture of her eyes? It's stunning."

"I developed those the day before she died. I came by the

next morning, and she was sitting on the veranda. Just sitting. I spoke to her. But she was ... gone. I think she was waiting for me to find her."

"Weren't you scared?"

"No. It was a shock, but I wasn't scared. We both knew she would die soon. Her breathing was getting really bad and her heart was tired. Gran tried to get her into Stellar, but Charlotte refused to leave the lodge. She said they'd put her in the hospital or drag her off to some sterile nursing home. Cold folks homes, she called them. She wanted to die here. She'd lost most of her eyesight and had nothing left, she said. She wasn't afraid to die. Just sad."

"I didn't think —" I cut myself off.

"What? You think I couldn't talk about death with an old woman I loved? You think I came by and told her knock-knock jokes every day?"

I blushed. "I'm just ... you knew her so well, that's all. I — I wish I'd ..."

"She would have ... *recognized* you. Like I said, I see a lot of her in you."

I felt a flush of pleasure. Jack moved around purposefully, setting things up. He'd really loved Charlotte. So had Ruby. Jack was lucky he'd had Charlotte to teach him. And Ruby — who made him gingersnap cookies and washed his clothes and fed him — and probably got him up in time to catch the school bus. And a dad who didn't drink, or shout, or act like a jerk, even if he was as stiff as wallboard. I had Lucy, sure ... sometimes ... but really, she was Celia's. And as for Celia and my father, well ... yeah.

"So how come you don't use this room anymore?" I asked.

"I have my own darkroom now — a small addition on the side of our place. Dad didn't want me here after Charlotte died. He said it didn't belong to us."

"But she left you the Leica."

"Yeah, that and the Pentax — a few months before she died, but her will left everything to her family. But she did give money to Gran, and to me — for university. The will didn't mention the cameras, so Dad made me bring them back. They're *yours* — well, your family's. I'm saving up for the best digital and a Pentax — or maybe a Leica if I can ever find one. With Charlotte's money I won't need any of Dad's savings."

"Hey, don't tell Celia you got money from Charlotte and she didn't, except for the parking fees. She'll go nuts." I unloaded the Leica and held it toward him. "Here. I want you to have it. It's yours. She meant for you to keep it."

He grinned. "As long as you're giving away cameras, I'd rather have the Pentax. It has a built-in light meter."

I laughed. "It's yours. Until I find out it works better than this one, and I take it back!"

"Deal. I'll tell you what, we'll share it. But I'll keep it at your place, okay?"

"Sounds good. That goes for the rest of them. I'll work with the Leica, but you can borrow it anytime."

"If I can rip your fingers off it."

"Exactly."

"Cool."

"So, let's get going here. You do it. I'll watch. Need to refresh my memory."

I watched him assemble everything, the mad scientist accent and all. "Ve shall cook up a brew zat vill curl your hair, frawwline," he crooned. "Vee vill bring forth all ze creechures from ze black lagoon, and ve vill *expose* zem for vat zay are! Expose them, get it?"

"Yah, I get it, Herr Lunatic," I said. "Hurry up, it's getting hot in here."

He took the Camera from me and put it beside a small processing reel and tank on the counter.

"Ready to drop into ze darkness — just for a moment, my frawwline?" He leered.

"Will you just get on with it!"

He leaned over and clicked off the light. I heard the camera snap open and knew he was putting the film onto the reel, and then into the processing tank. In a few minutes he turned the light back on and, with a bit more leering and cackling, he poured chemicals into the tank. He swished it around and poured out the liquid.

At the developer stage, he muttered, "Invert, invert, twist, twist, now bingadeebangbang!" After that came a musically accompanied acid stop bath, a chanted fixer and final wash and a surprisingly quiet drying stage. I watched his long fingers clip one end of the film to a makeshift clothesline above his head, then attach a bigger clip on the other end to weigh it down. He turned off the fan to keep down the dust.

"Yah!! Ze magic eye revealed!"

"Now we wait, right?"

He nodded. "Yep. I'm starving. What you got?"

"Baloney," I said. "That ought to suit you to a tee!"

We loaded paper plates with bologna sandwiches smothered in mustard and mayo, grabbed a couple of colas and sat on the grassy slope in the shade of a birch clump. Celia was on a lawn chair on the beach watching Ally collect things in a small net. His shoulders were up near his ears, which meant he was feeling tense. Someone else was in the water, swimming toward shore. My heart stopped. At the dock I could see the tip of a yellow canoe.

I heard Jack's voice in the distance. "You going to university after high school?"

I pulled out the light meter and took a reading. "No money."

"I'm going to try for photography in the fine arts program.

You need a portfolio. You could try for a bursary. Or if your store gets going, get paid for working there."

I didn't say anything, just focused on the swimmer.

"It says I have to bring a dozen eggs and a live turkey as part of my tuition."

"I am *listening*, you know."

"Oh good, because I thought you'd turned into a statue of Juliet in Love with Camera at the Ready. Yes, Juliet, that *is* aged Romeo. You should wear your glasses — you'd be able to see him better."

"I don't wear glasses," I snarled. "And I don't give a damn who that is!"

Jack put down his half-finished lunch. "*Sure* you don't. I've got to find Dad and make sure he eats. When he's working, he forgets. If you want to develop the prints later, let me know."

With that, he ran up the path and disappeared around the side of the house.

"Jeez," I said under my breath to his retreating back, "what is your *problem*!"

I couldn't pay attention to Jack's real reason for being so mad. I didn't *want* him to feel that way about me. Not as long as Tony was interested — if he *was*.

Celia was peering into Ally's net. His wet, skinny body was covered in goose bumps, his lips blue, chin shaking. He was explaining in a determined but patient tone that it wasn't a *stick*, it was a *b-b-bug*. I took a couple of close-ups of his intense face.

Celia touched it with her finger, jumped back and screeched. "It *is* a bug!"

"Yes, Mommy. That's what I t-t-told you," Ally said. "And he's made this little home out of p-p-pebbles and pieces of water plants."

Behind them, Tony sloshed out of the water, his blue Speedo stuck to his body, the water streaming down over his chest and arms and the long pale hairs on his legs. My stomach seized and my face grew hot. Like a robot, I lifted my camera, took a shot and sat on the sand away from Celia and Ally.

A shadow fell alongside mine. Mr. Broom — in gray T-shirt, jeans, work boots and regulation ball cap.

Tony was jabbing at the small creature in the net. "Quite the marine biologist, aren't you, son?"

He reached out to pat Ally's head, but Ally slipped out from under it and ran clumsily across the sand. "See, Mr. Broom? It's a caddis fly, right? Not a water scorpion, right?"

Ally seemed so eager for reassurance, it was heartbreaking. Mr. Broom immediately hunkered down so they could examine the bug. He talked quietly and Ally's face relaxed. Celia watched, an odd smile on her face. Tony plunked himself between us, but closer to me and slightly in front.

"I was so hot from paddling, I just had to have a swim," he said.

One hand came back, wrapped itself around my bare foot and squeezed it hard. I didn't move. Slowly his hand ran down my instep and one finger slid between my big toe and the next one. I couldn't breathe.

Mr. Broom stood up, eyes on Tony, who removed his hand and ran it through his thick blond hair, spraying sand across my legs.

John Broom said to Celia, "I came down to ask you to take a look at a few things. I've laid out some plans in order of importance. But I want to show you the fuse box on the side of the building first — I'd like to move it inside this fall. You need to know how it works."

Celia stood up, wrapping a big towel around her. They started toward the house. They were leaving. Perfect.

But Mr. Broom stopped and said, "Come on, Ally. You should know how things work around here, too, Bernie. And we should have your input on the plans."

Celia was about to argue with him, but something stopped her. She looked at me and Tony and her cat eyes narrowed. "Yes, Bernie. You should see these plans."

She was jealous. Too bad. I felt powerful, completely in control ... until Tony leaped to his feet, walked to the dock and lowered himself into his canoe.

"See you later," he called. "I've got to get a move on myself."

He'd just *arrived*. I walked onto the dock. "You don't have to go."

"I'm afraid I do, Bernie." He looked at me sadly.

"I could come by later," I said in a quiet voice.

His eyes flicked past me to Mr. Broom and Celia. "I'm having dinner with a friend — I'll see you, Bernie."

"The friend I saw you with in Stellar?"

He looked puzzled. "In Stellar?"

"Yeah. Someone in a big hat. At that café."

"Oh — *her*." He laughed. "No. Someone much more interesting."

He might as well have slapped me in front of everyone. I stared after his canoe as he paddled away.

"Come on, Bernie!" Celia called.

She and Mr. Broom walked up to the lodge with Ally, still looking at his stupid bug. I didn't know what to do, what to think. I straggled behind, hating John Broom with all my might. They walked along the side of the lodge toward a big gray box and had just reached it when two people appeared out of nowhere.

Lucy! A week early! Then my jaw dropped at the same time as Celia's. Right behind Lucy was none other than Mario Fonti.

Chapter Twenty-three

*Love involves a peculiar
unfathomable combination of
understanding and misunderstanding.*

Diane Arbus, photographer

———

"I told Mario I was coming," Lucy said. "He knew I was nervous about driving a rental car on the highway ... so he —"

Celia interrupted. "You're both welcome." With a quick little rush, she hugged Lucy, stood back and held out a hand to Mario, who wrapped it in both of his.

"I hope it's okay, Celia. Now, I'm only here to make sure Lucy's safe and sound, eh? I can head right back if —"

I lifted my camera and clicked off two shots. No one noticed me. I could stand back and still get ... well, in this case, a lot of strained smiles. I knew Celia was more upset than she was letting on. I mean, even I was still stunned. Now what?

I heard Celia say, "Don't be silly, Mario. Stay. *Please.* You'd only have to come back and pick up Lucy in a few days and it's too long a drive."

What she really wanted was for Mario to vanish off the face of the earth, but hey, Mario's a trusting sort of goof. After all, he thought she wanted to marry him. So he nodded and said, "As long as you're sure."

Lucy loped over and grabbed me in a bear hug. She hugged Ally next, asked where Jojo was and put her hand out to Mr. Broom.

"I'm Lucy Armitage."

He shook it. "John Broom."

She looked at him questioningly. Mario was eyeing him, too.

Celia said, "John's working for us. He's the handy—"

Mr. Broom's face hardened. "Builder. I live on the next property. That's my son, Jack." Jack gave them a wave from the back doorway. "Jack's been giving a hand this morning. Painting."

"I — I didn't mean —" Celia's cheeks flushed. "Bernie, can you get their things from the car? We're done for the day, Jack. Thanks for your help."

"I'll keep on working, if that's okay. Gran and Jojo are having a tea party at our place. I didn't want to interrupt. I eat too many of those little scones and Gran gets pretty nasty." He backed into the lodge.

Mr. Broom said he'd unlock the chain so Mario could drive through. "Meant to do that for you before," he said to Celia. "I can bring yours in closer, too, if you give me your keys."

"It's not that far, I prefer to leave it there — out of the way, thanks." She still looked like she'd been hit between the eyes.

Mario, Ally and Mr. Broom headed to the gate. Lucy chatted nonstop about her trip, her arm around me, until a big, sleek car crunched over the stones.

"That's quite a rental," Celia said, looking at the silver luxury ride.

"It's Mario's." Lucy laughed. "I've told him a million times to stop driving that stupid van everywhere. So after you and he — uh ... anyway, he bought this."

Celia gave it the once-over. When Mario opened the trunk and pointed at an overnight case, muttering, "That's mine," I knew, for sure, he'd planned all along to stay and win her back.

Thank goodness we had a couple of semi-clean rooms upstairs. Mario, Lucy and I loaded up with gear. Mr. Broom grabbed a large box and we all staggered into the lodge. Celia followed, saying something about making coffee.

Upstairs, I decided to put Lucy across from Celia, and Mario across from Ally and me, in a room with a single bed — at the far end of the hall from Celia. No point in making it easy for him. Besides, I wanted Lucy to have the best room. I put her suitcase on the double bed and was turning to leave when she slid through the door and leaned against it.

"Whew. She seems okay with him here. What do you think?"

"Who cares? I'm just glad *you're* here."

She smiled. "Are you? You seemed so touchy on the phone. It's the main reason I came earlier than I said — to make sure you and I were okay." She hugged me hard. "Oooh, but I've missed you. All of you, but especially you, Berns. It's been so *lonely* ..." She took a deep breath. "But it's so beautiful here! Look at that water!"

"Didn't you bring Mario for a reason?" I asked.

"Not to get them back together, if that's what you're thinking."

"Won't stop him from trying."

She pointed out the window. "Look — a loon — swimming in the bay!"

Okay, two can ignore the obvious.

"How long can you stay?" I asked.

"I don't have to go back 'til Tuesday night."

The muscles in my face sagged. "I thought — I was hoping —"

"I still have some time coming to me, Bernie. I'll come back when you open the store — give you and Celia a hand. When you really need me."

"We need you *all* the time, Luce. Everything is hanging by a thread — this place, Celia, *everything* ... Maybe I made a mistake. Maybe ..."

No. No tears. Let someone else raise the level of the lake. I swallowed them down.

Lucy hugged me, her chin resting on my head. "Big changes, sweetie. But you can do it, Bernie. And I'm not that far away." She held me at arm's length. "It's worth any risk, isn't it? You don't really want to come back to Winnipeg, do you?"

"No. I like it here. But it won't last. It can't."

"Well, I think it will. It's great for Ally. He's all brown and sandy. And you never know with Celia. She may like it and isn't telling you."

I raised my eyebrows.

She sighed. "How is she doing, really?"

I sat on the edge of the bed and told her everything. Except about me and Tony.

"So you still don't trust your mom to tell the truth about her drinking."

"There was rum in that glass, Lucy. And I smelled wine on her breath last night."

"Has she been drunk?"

"No, but —"

She nodded. "But you think it's only a matter of time."

"And I'll be right."

"Maybe she has a better sense of where she has to go now."

"Dream on, Luce!"

She chewed her lip, thinking, then nodded and muttered, "Okay. Here goes."

"Here goes what?"

"Bernie, let me tell you about the Celia I know. When we were kids, it was just her and her mom." She thought a moment. "I was about ten when I became Celia's friend. Her only friend. Later, I realized it was because she didn't want anyone to meet her mother. But I liked Celia a lot and I just kept calling for her — until one day she let me in the house. Her mother was lying on a chaise longue by a window overlooking the garden. She was small and very pretty like Celia, but dark. And haggard. She sent Celia to make Kool-Aid and then she talked to me nonstop. About how sick she was and how she'd never recovered from Celia's birth. Toxemia, I suspect. She drank from a glass of wine the whole time, the bottle within reach. As sick as she was, she said she intended to outlive that good-for-nothing husband of hers, wherever he was."

"Jeez," I muttered. "Another boozer."

Lucy nodded. "I didn't know it then, of course. All I knew was she treated Celia like a slave. Running errands, cleaning, cooking. Poor kid. But Celia and I got along really well — she had a warped sense of humor like mine, so we laughed a lot. I even got her to laugh about her mother. We called her the Queen of Hurts."

"What happened to Celia's dad?"

"No idea. Just walked out one day and never came back. I was so happy when Celia met your dad and could escape that toxic house. He seemed like such a nice guy."

"Not for long. He walked out, too."

"You're right, but at least you know where your dad is. And he does write now and again."

I snorted. "Two lame ducks get married and produce me and Ally — two *more* lame ducks. Then Celia turns into her mother."

"Don't be like that, Bernie. Celia's done a lot of growing up these past weeks. That car accident shocked her into it."

I sighed. What about the glass of rum on the dock? What about the wine on Celia's breath? "So how come you never told me about Lydia before?"

"I figured it was for Celia to tell, not me. I only hope she forgives me."

"I won't say anything."

"Not even during a fight, Berns."

"Not even then," I said, hoping I could keep that promise. "But, Lucy, if Celia saw what drinking did to her mother, why start?"

"Celia always swore she'd never be like her mother. But I think she drank to stay close to your dad — to hold on to the marriage. Often the partner of an alcoholic takes up drinking, too."

"Is that why she let Dad hurt her? To hold on to the marriage?"

"She didn't *let* him, honey. She didn't *ask* for it. In the end, he did the right thing, though. He withdrew."

I sneered. "What a hero, huh?"

"I know this is hard for you. I'm trying to help you understand your mom a bit better. She's had a lot of hurt in her life."

"She's not the only one," I murmured.

"I know, honey. Celia's hurt just goes back farther, that's all. Yet, you and Celia — you're a lot alike. You both keep things in for too long. You simmer until your anger explodes, but Celia's unhappiness turns inward. I think that's why she kept drinking."

I shook my head. "She's like her mother — self-pitying and manipulative —"

"Bernie —" she began, but I interrupted, "Forget it. I know what she is. So do you."

She patted my arm. "I didn't come here to upset you, honey. Just think about what I've told you, okay?"

I shrugged.

She stood up. "Enough. Time for some fun! Show me around!"

Chapter Twenty-four

*There are many photographs
which are full of life but
which are confusing ...*

Brassai, photographer

As Lucy and I came downstairs, I could hear Mario and Jack in the store. I didn't know where Celia was and didn't care. Didn't want to talk to Jack, either.

What Lucy said had shocked me. Pretty little Lydia had become a drunk. Is that what had ended things with Charlotte? But knowing about my grandmother didn't change things between Celia and me. I just felt more tangled up inside.

Lucy looked around the veranda. "Nice. The rattan chairs need some paint and new fabric, but it looks very comfortable."

I glanced uneasily at the chairs, knowing that Aunt Charlotte had died in one. I imagined her sitting there looking at us, camera at the ready. What would she see? A girl with a frown and hair like hers — and an untidy woman with a kind face. Or would she see herself as a young girl — standing off to one side, wondering where life was going to take her?

"You okay?" Lucy asked.

I nodded and followed her out onto the big stone steps.

"Wow. I love it!" she exclaimed.

A voice said gently behind her, "You'd like to run a place like this, Lucia?"

She nodded. "Absolutely, Mario. I'm so tired of the theater.

Too many egos and too many bosses." She looked at me and laughed. "That's all I talked about on the way here. But *this* would be something I'd really like to try. Being my own boss. Planning all the changes. Bringing the old place back to life."

"I'll sell it to you cheap," Celia said, appearing beside Mario. "So far, it hasn't been a whole lot of fun."

Mario frowned. "But if you don't like it here, Celia, why stay?"

Clear what *he* was after — Celia back in Winnipeg, where he could convince her to change her mind and marry him. The schmuck.

"We'll stay until we get a good price. And to be honest, the place *is* growing on me — a bit. I feel ... better here."

What was she up to now? Was this for Mario's benefit?

"I can see why!" Lucy cried, her face alight. "It's wonderful. Come on, Bernie. Give me a tour. Mario can come, too."

Mario held up a brush covered in green paint. "I felt sorry for the kid in the store, said I'd give him a hand."

"Isn't that just like you? You'd give the shirt off your back as a paint rag!" Lucy scolded, shaking her finger at him. "Never mind, I'll take you on a personal tour later." She ran down the steps and stopped halfway to the docks, looking around and smiling with delight.

"Can you help Mario and Jack, Bernie?" Celia asked. "Remind me to pay Jack for all his time. I'll take Lucy on the grand tour. See if I can extinguish a few of those stars in her eyes — she hasn't seen the docks or the boathouses."

Mario said, "You shouldn't throw water on Lucy's pleasure, Celia. She needs a weekend of fun."

"Yeah, Celia," I said, "go easy. She's been having a tough time at work."

"Really?" Celia scoffed. "Like we haven't? Lucy can go

home on Tuesday. We have to stay. Things are always *fun* when it's someone else's worry and work."

"So much for it *growing* on you," I said.

Mario shook his head and walked back into the house.

"I was only kidding, Bernie. Lucy —" She stopped, her attention caught by Mr. Broom walking toward Lucy, carrying a bucket. He held it out, leaned in to her and said something. She hooted and, for the first time, I heard John Broom laugh. His teeth were white in his dark face, his laugh a warm chuckle.

I lifted the camera and focused. "Hey, maybe Luce will have a summer romance with Mr. Broom. If she can make him laugh, she's halfway there." I clicked the shutter.

"Don't be ridiculous!" Celia snapped and strode down the path toward them.

She spoke sharply to Lucy, who looked around, surprised. Celia took her by the arm and led her away. I took another quick shot as Celia glanced back at Mr. Broom. His expression had returned to its unreadable mask. I watched him walk to the side of the house, swinging the pail. He glanced at me ... and smiled. His entire face changed, becoming mobile and alive, like Jack's. Before I knew it, I smiled back.

Celia was such a snob. Just because she saw Mr. Broom as *beneath* her, it didn't mean he and Lucy couldn't get on. Hey, maybe Lucy'd end up living right next door! Determined to make it happen, I went in to help Mario paint.

Jack was still there, his hair streaked with green paint. I glared at him, put my camera on the counter under a drop sheet, picked up a roller and got to work. He sidled up to me, gave me a lopsided grin and said, "So — *I'm* full of baloney — how about you?"

Of course I ignored him and started painting. He kept getting in my way with his paint roller. Mario was up on the ladder doing the trim, whistling through his teeth.

I pushed Jack with my elbow. "Give me some room, okay?"

"Huh? Oh ... okay, I'll move over here." He walked around, took up a position on my other side and began rollering with great concentration. I sighed and moved to another wall. Soon, he was right beside me. When his roller rammed into mine, I snarled, "Go away!"

He stumbled back and tripped over the roller tray; his roller hand shot out and smacked into Mario's backside. Mario looked down, shocked. Jack grabbed a rag and tried to wipe up the mess, which, of course, only smeared the paint.

"Oh no. Jeez, I'm sorry!" Jack moaned.

Mario patted Jack's shoulder. "Hey, it's only a bit of paint. These are old pants anyhow." He laughed. "Why don't you two take a break? I'll let the pants dry, then quit. Go on. You obviously did a lot today."

"Thanks," I said. Wiping my hands, I went into the kitchen to get the bottle of painkillers.

"Something wrong?" Jack asked, from the doorway.

I took a deep drink of water with the pills. "The paint gave me a headache — actually, two headaches. If you'd go away I'd be rid of *one*."

His laugh was so infectious I couldn't help joining in.

He crossed his arms. "Listen, I promise to try not to bug you about ... you know, *him*. Can't seem to help myself. But I'll really work on it. Friends?"

"Yeah, okay. Look, I gotta figure out dinner for two extra people. Celia will leave it until the kids are ratty and tired." I searched the freezer and pulled out a lone package of hamburger. "You want to develop that film later?"

"Sure. I told Mario I'd take him fishing after dinner. How about right after that?"

I waited, wondering if he'd ask me to go fishing, too. But he didn't.

"Okay," I said, oddly disappointed.

"I'll help Mario clean up and head home," he said. "See you later."

I was trying to thaw the hamburger in a bit of water in a huge frying pan and opening tins of tomatoes and kidney beans when Mario walked in, arms and hands covered in paint. "Now that's a great kid," he said as he washed up.

"He's okay. Some visit, huh?" I said, chopping a big white onion. "Hardly here two minutes and you're working."

He shrugged. "I don't relax easy. Working helps. But ... well, that could change soon." His dark eyes grew misty. This guy *really* wasn't going to give up.

I dumped the water out of the pan, broke up the meat, added oil and the onions and some chopped garlic and fried it all brown. Then the tomatoes. Mario sat at the table, a contented smile on his face. How dumb could one guy be? Celia was only going to chew him up and spit him out. I offered to make coffee — naturally, Celia hadn't bothered — explaining we didn't have beer or wine.

"Coffee? That's *my* specialty. I even brought espresso and my pot. And how about I whip up dessert?"

"I don't think we have much, but be my guest."

"Oh, you think I'd come without groceries?" He pointed under the table at a big plastic box and a cooler. He clattered around in the cupboards, then unloaded the cooler into the fridge. He peeled and sliced apples into a dish, mixed brown sugar, flour and butter. I couldn't very well ask him how he intended to win Celia back, but I knew how he felt. Tony's face slid across my vision, followed by his expression as he leaned over to kiss the woman in the big hat. I put my hand over a sharp pain in my chest and focused on Mario.

After sprinkling the brown sugar crumble over the apples, he put the dish in the oven. I was just dumping a load of chili powder into the frying pan when Lucy wandered in. She sniffed the air and pronounced it a perfect blend of coffee beans, apple and chili spice. She had a rosy glow on her face and a brighter glow on her nose. She looked ... pretty. I'd never thought of Lucy as pretty.

"Lucia!" Mario cried. "You've burned your face. You have to remember your cream tomorrow. You'll peel, I think."

She put her hands to her cheeks. "Celia and I sat on the dock and talked for ages. Oh, Mario, it's so lovely here."

Celia walked in behind her. She rolled her eyes. "Try as I might, I couldn't burst her bubble."

"A week ago she probably would have been more convincing," Lucy said, laughing. She cocked her head at Celia. "I think you *do* like it here. You didn't work *hard* enough at bursting my bubble."

Mario put his arm around Lucy. "No one should *try* to burst another person's bubble, especially one so sweet of soul."

Hadn't Celia burst *his* just a month ago? I guess everyone was thinking the same thing, because the room was suddenly thick with silence.

Celia broke it with "Hey, it smells like Bernie's chili. We used to have that at least once a week — and leftovers for *days*, eh, Berns?"

A dirty look from me.

She said, "Oh, Bernie, I didn't mean *that*. Your chili's great — I —"

Just then, Ruby and Jojo walked in. When Jojo spotted Mario, she let out a whoop and hugged his leg. He kissed her nose, muttering, "Bambina cara."

"You staying for good? You and Lucy gonna live with us?" she asked, looking up at him pleadingly. "Will we have a wedding? We got lotsa room!"

If possible, the silence this time was heavier.

I couldn't stand it. "No, Jojo, Lucy and Mario are just here until Tuesday."

"Oh." She stuck out her bottom lip in disappointment, then brightened. "But you have three whole days left, right?"

"Almost," Mario said, rumpling her hair.

I said, "Mrs. Broom — Ruby — these are friends from Winnipeg. Lucy and Mario."

She shook their hands, pretending not to have noticed Jojo's wedding comments. "I promised Jojo a picnic on the island tomorrow. Maybe you'd all like to come."

"I don't think so. Thanks anyway," Celia said quickly, but Lucy piped up, "An island? Where?"

"Just across the bay. We own it, actually. Real pretty. Nice sandy beach for swimming. A stone barbecue my husband built years ago."

"Ooh, Mommeee!" Jojo cried. "You *have* to come!"

Lucy said, "Mario? Bernie? How about it?"

"Sounds good," Mario said.

"Sure!" I added, just to bug Celia.

"Great," said Ruby. "I've got wieners and buns in my freezer. I'll bring those and cookies and fruit. If you want anything else, bring it along. Oh, and I have marshmallows. Ally made sure John and Jack'd come. So we'll be quite a gang. That's —"

Celia interrupted. "Well, I suppose if everyone's going, I'll have to."

"Yahooee!" Jojo danced around the room hugging everyone.

"Gee, Celia," I said, "you could stay here and finish the painting."

"Good one, Bernie."

Just for a split second, I think we may have smiled at each other again, but I grabbed a spoon and concentrated on the chili.

"That's settled then," Ruby said. "It'll be fun."

"Thank you, Ruby," Celia said. "It'll be a nice break from this work."

Ruby looked ready to say something vinegary, but her face softened and she nodded. "My pleasure. I'll be on my way. See you folks later. I got two hungry men to get dinner for." And she left with a cheerful wave.

Chapter Twenty-five

The thing that's important to know
is that you never know.
You're always sort of feeling your way.

Diane Arbus, photographer

When the screen door slapped shut, Jojo asked Mario, "*Will* we have a wedding? Will I get to wear my new dress?"

Mario shook his head. "No wedding, bambina. But I promise to take you all out to dinner when you come to Winnipeg. We'll go to a restaurant where you can wear your beee-utiful dress."

She looked sad, but just for a moment. She liked eating out. The rest of us looked at our fingernails or out the window.

"Okay, let's get dinner going here," Mario cried. "I'm starving."

After that, we worked on not allowing that awful silence to fall again, but it was tough going. When Ally ran in to show us a giant water beetle, our exclamations of amazement were positively operatic. When Ally said he'd go up and show the huge bug to Mr. Broom, who was working on shelves in our room, Jojo followed, and we were plunged back into Deafening Silence. Thankfully, Jojo came right back, holding up Jackie. Show-and-tell time again. Relief swept through the room.

The topic of Jackie's ability to kill mice killed a fair amount of time. Lucy set the table while Mario and Celia buttered and grilled focaccia bread.

Ally walked in and said, "Mr. Broom says good night. I'm hungry!"

Celia smiled at him. "He's such a strange man, very ... *distant.*"

"No, he's not," Ally said. "He just doesn't talk all the time. I like that."

She raised one eyebrow. "Come and eat. It's chili. You like Bernie's chili."

Mario said, "And you'll like dessert, too."

Mario *was* a nice guy. Maybe it would be okay if he and Celia got back together. I had to admit she looked great, legs and arms tanned, shoulders shiny from suntan oil.

When we sat down, Mario said, "Hey, you got that camera, Bernie. Why not take a picture of us at the table?"

Reluctantly I took some shots. Mario leaned toward Celia and then toward Lucy. Lucy said something in his ear and he guffawed. Celia looked surprised, her slanted eyes narrowing. I just kept clicking.

As we ate, Lucy and Mario chatted with the kids. Celia didn't eat much. She watched everyone, a small scowl creasing her forehead. Was she thinking about getting back with Mario? Or about vanishing for a while after they left? I hadn't even checked out the bars in Stellar. How would I ever find her? Suddenly, the image of Lydia sitting by her window, drinking wine and blaming young Celia for everything dropped into my mind like a slide into a projector, but I pushed it away. I rubbed my temples, digging the tips of my fingers deep.

Lucy said, "You're suddenly very pale under that tan, Bernie."

"Huh? Yeah. Headache. From the paint."

Celia got up, put two painkillers beside my glass of milk. She rested her hand on my head. I pulled away.

"I already had a couple." I pushed my chair back. "I'm going for a walk."

"No dessert?" Mario asked. "Apple crisp — Italian style."

"With oregano?" Celia teased.

"How *did* you know?"

Celia and Lucy laughed. A little too loudly.

"I'll have mine later," I said.

"But I brought mascarpone and cream because I know *someone* who loves it whipped together," Mario said. Lucy put a hand on his arm and he nodded. "Okay. I'll save some for you, Bernie."

"It'll taste even better later," I called, and escaped out the front door.

I lay back on the dock and let the sun warm me. I'd barely noticed what a beautiful blue-sky day it had been. Too busy auto-focusing on my stupid life. I opened up to the warmth and the sounds around me. My muscles slowly relaxed. Under the boards of the dock came the hollow echo of water.

A low thunk of wood against wood, and I turned my head. At eye level was a piece of black-and-white flannel and a brown hand holding a paddle. The searing light made my eyes ache.

"Hiya, mermaid," Tony said. As he leaned over, the sun flamed around his head. "My friend didn't show for dinner, so I came home and burned some eggs. Came over to see what you're up to."

Now was my chance to make sure I saw him tomorrow. I told him about the picnic.

"You wanna come?" I asked.

He smiled. "Sounds like fun. Sure, why not?"

If this was a movie, I'd have heard music all around us. But only the dock shook as someone moved across it.

"Why, hello there." Lucy's voice was warm.

As I sat up, the knots in my back tightened again.

Tony peered up at her. "Hi, yourself. Tony Lafferty. And who might you be?"

"Friend of the family. Here for a few days. Lucy Armitage." She put out her hand.

He reached over me and took it in his. Another heavier

tread hit the dock. I groaned. Tony gave me a sympathetic wink.

"And this is Mario Fonti. Another friend from Winnipeg," Lucy said. "Bernie, we've done the dishes. And Jack is on his way over to take Mario fishing. How about you and I go for a canoe ride?"

Now we just needed Celia to round off our happy little gang.

"Well, I'll be moving along," Tony said, his smile enveloping just me.

"You don't have to go yet," I said quickly, but he pushed languidly off the dock, dug his paddle deep and sliced through the water, his open shirt billowing in the breeze.

"Fancies himself, doesn't he?" Mario muttered.

"That's because he has something to actually *fancy*," I said.

His face fell. God, I'd hurt his feelings. "Sorry," I mumbled. "He's really very nice."

He patted my shoulder. "You're probably right." But he still looked sad. *Darn.* My big mouth.

Lucy said, "He *is* good looking, but he reminds me of actors I've known — all gesture, no substance. Celia better be careful there."

I snorted. "Oh, he's got *Celia's* number, all right. It's Tony who has to be careful."

She lifted my chin with one finger, her brown eyes searching ... speculative. I looked away, so she couldn't see what was in mine.

She sighed. "How about that canoe ride?"

As we walked back to the lodge, I suggested she put on slacks. And lots of bug spray. While she did that, I changed into jeans and a long-sleeved shirt and stuffed my camera into my waterproof bag. When we got back to the dock, Mario and Jack were setting off in the aluminum boat, Mario all in khaki, including a wide-brimmed hat. Sahara Mario.

When Jack pulled off his baseball cap to wave, I almost fell in the water. His short hair was glossy black.

"What have you done?" I squealed.

"The green paint came off in the shower, but it turned the red a weird blue. I didn't want you to confuse me with Bozo the Clown."

"No chance. Bozo's much cuter!" It wasn't true. Jack's eyes looked even blacker, his face older and more angular — like his dad's.

"Hey, Mario! I won't wish you luck," I called, "because I *hate* fish."

"Oh, you haven't had fish the —"

I held up my hand. "I know, I *know* — the Italian way!"

Lucy chuckled and Mario wiggled his eyebrows. "You just wait," he said. "I'll get you eating fish and *loving* it!"

"Good luck," Lucy cried, waving like they were off to hunt tigers.

"Have fun, Lucia," he called back. "Be careful in the canoe."

"Good-bye! Good-bye! We'll miss you!" Jack cried, waving like an idiot. Then he gunned the motor and took off.

"What a cutie that Jack is," Lucy said, watching the wake of the boat. "Imagine a boy that cute right next door. And funny, too."

I stiffened. "We're friends, Luce. That's all."

She pursed her lips. "Too bad. 'Cause he's a looker. Oh well, who knows what one person sees in another? So, let's go canoeing. If I get good at it, we can paddle to the island tomorrow."

As we drifted into open water, I tried to get the canoe going in one direction. I discovered if I held the paddle against the side of the canoe after each stroke and gave it a twist, it would keep a steadier course. Lucy chatted and oohed and aahed, paddling lightly on one side.

When we passed by our docks, Celia was sitting on the

diving board, bare legs hanging over the end. She looked small.

"You wanna join us?" Lucy called. "You could sit in the middle and we could drive you around."

Celia laughed. "Where? In circles? No, it's okay. Can't leave the kids."

Since when? I almost called out, but I had to admit — grudgingly — that she *had*, in fact, been looking after them since we got here. Showing off, mainly, but even so ...

"I can come ashore and you could go for a ride," Lucy offered, but Celia got to her feet and waved us off. "Don't be silly. I've got lots of time to go for canoe rides with my daughter. Right, Berns?" She quickly turned and walked toward the house.

"Sure," I muttered. "Like *that* will happen."

"Okay," Lucy said over her shoulder, "let's get this train on the tracks!"

Before we knew it, we were skimming past the Brooms' place and along the wall of rock leading to the painter's cabin.

"Oh look!" Lucy said. "What a pretty spot. You wanna take a closer look?"

I described my last visit — and how I'd dumped the canoe. "I don't think we'd do much better."

"Too bad. I wonder what happened to the place? Who lived there?"

"Jack says an artist — maybe in the early sixties, but no one knows what happened to him or who owns it now."

She gazed at it in the lowering sunlight. "I feel a deep sorrow coming from it."

A tingle went up my arms. "You do? Because when I walked up to it, I got a feeling of sadness, too."

"Well, someone must remember the guy who lived there. I bet Ruby Broom knew him. Maybe he died in the fire."

"I wondered about that, too."

The cabin had to have been owned by William. Maybe this was where Charlotte took the beautiful moody portrait of him. If he *had* died, it might explain why she'd stayed single. Ruby *had* to know what happened. I'd pin her down as soon as I could.

Chapter Twenty-six

*... to photograph becomes a magical act, and slowly
other more suggestive images begin to appear
behind the visible image, for which the
photographer cannot be held responsible.*

Robert Doisneau, photographer

"Hey, you guys! Get a gander at these!" Mario was showing off a string of flapping fish. I caught his proud stance on film with Jack holding up two fingers behind his head like antennae.

"I'll kill you, Jack!" I cried. "I told you I hate fish."

He bowed, trailing his cap over the ground. "My lord and master demanded fish and fish he got."

When Lucy and I guided the canoe into the boathouse, Jack was waiting. As he helped Lucy out, she said, "Remember what we talked about earlier, Bernie. Try and be nicer to you-know-who at the picnic tomorrow, okay? Please?"

"Nicer to who? Me?" Jack asked.

Lucy said, "I'm sure she's *always* nice to you, Jack."

"Ha! Dream on!"

Lucy laughed. I didn't. He made a face at me, like a starlet in love, so of course, I couldn't help smiling. He leaned forward to give me a hand, but I waved him away.

"I can do it," I said.

He grabbed my arm when the toe of my sneaker got caught under the gunwale.

"I keep telling you, you gotta work on that landing of

yours. You're all toes." His hand slid toward mine but I pretended to fuss with my paddle. He was confusing me again. I didn't *want* to be confused.

Lucy and Mario led the way to the lodge, Mario waving his arms around, describing his Big Fish adventure. Jack and I straggled behind, slapping mosquitoes. The kids were on the beach, Mr. Broom and Celia, coffee mugs in hand, watching them. Didn't Mario see Celia and John? Wasn't he jealous? I glared at them on his behalf.

"You wanna bother developing those negatives?" Jack asked, his voice cool.

"Of course I do," I said, "if you're still up for it."

He shrugged.

"Hey, don't do me any favors."

"I said I'd help. What do you want, *blood*? The mosquitoes are getting enough as it is."

What was his problem now? When we got to the kitchen, Mario was laying out newspapers for gutting the fish. Lucy put coffee in the machine they'd brought Celia as a housewarming gift. "I'll go see if John and Celia want some fresh stuff."

When she left, I said to Mario, "We've got a film to develop — that room behind us is a darkroom."

"It is? Hey, that's great for you, Bernie. Sure, sure, you go ahead. I won't let anyone disturb you."

We left him to his fish and closed the door behind us. Then I locked it.

"Okay, let's get started," Jack said, all business. "How big do you want these pictures?"

I didn't bother making nice. He was mad at *me*. For no reason. I tried to ignore the voice in my head that said, *Oh, really? Think about it.*

"We have lots of paper," I said. "I'd prefer eight by ten. I can do it."

Again a shrug. "Whatever. I'll get the trays organized, you cut the negatives."

I carefully sliced the negatives into strips of four or five while he set up the developing trays and Charlotte's enlarger, adjusted contrast paper on the easel so the light would cover the surface, placing a clean sheet of glass over it. He put the first strip of negatives into the enlarger.

"You know how to develop?" he asked.

"Yes," I snapped. "Just keep them coming — but not too fast."

I made sure there were plastic clips set up along the string above our heads and got ready for the first print. I was eager to see how the old camera worked. Or not.

He turned on the safe light and got to work. After he'd exposed the first image, he handed me the contrast paper and I put it in the developer tray, emulsion side up. Slowly it turned into a black-and-white picture. Celia came up out of the solution, hands on hips, hair wild around a contorted, slightly blurred face. The Black Spruce witch — just after she'd warned me not to take the car into Stellar. I quickly put it in the stop tray, the fixative bath and then a rinse.

The second one was also of Celia. Not bad. Her face was sharp and clear, with deeply etched lines around her eyes. I hadn't noticed those lines before. Yet that wasn't anger in her eyes. What was it? *Fear*? Of what?

The next one was the Brooms' garden, followed by one of Mr. Broom walking between the rows of corn. He hadn't seen me yet. There was a relaxed peacefulness about him. Until he'd laughed with Lucy, I would have bet he didn't know *how* to relax — or laugh. Maybe the only thing I really knew about him was that he liked giving unwanted advice, like his son.

Next were three amazing shots of the swallows. The walls of the boathouse were hard and clear, contrasting with the blurred swoosh of the birds. I could almost hear their chattering and the snapping of wings.

Next came Ally, holding up his spider jar. His face was smudged with dirt, his eyes bright, but now I recognized the familiar signs of anxiety in his shoulders and the way he was gripping the jar. Hadn't seen that at the time. But, still, he looked better, didn't he? I hung up the print, vowing to keep a closer watch on him.

Jack handed me the next three shots with a tight expression. I saw why. Tony. Working on his laptop. My heart rate went up, but I tried to look cool and only slightly interested. The light was perfect. I'd been sure at the time that Tony hadn't noticed me taking them, but in the third, his eyes were looking right at me, a secret smile on his face. That smile sent a quiver straight to my fingertips.

As I quickly hung all three prints to dry, I looked over at Jack, but he was setting up the next negative, lost in concentration, his long hands deft and sure. Lucy was right, he *was* good looking. Suddenly I wanted to touch his crisp black hair. But something stopped me.

At that moment, he glanced over and I covered my confusion by growling, "Can't you move any faster?" He growled right back. What the heck was the matter with me? Didn't I *want* a friend?

The next few prints were the "Swiss cheese" soap on the shop shelf, the kids on the little strand of beach and the one of Jack at the campers' dock, which was pretty good — arms wrapped around his knees, one side of his mouth turned up in a half smile, eyes full of interest. I quickly dipped the next sheet into the bath.

It, and the next one, were of the burned cabin — curiously pale, as if I'd shot them through a filter. They shouldn't have been that overexposed. Slashed through each print was a diagonal foggy patch. The cottage was a dark shape behind — a lurking shadow. If I didn't know better, I'd say someone had passed their hand across the lens the moment I touched the shutter release. Whatever it was, it had ruined my shots.

The picture of Jojo and Celia on the couch in the living

room made my stomach tighten. Celia was looking straight into the camera with a worried frown, as if trying to look beyond the lens ... to what? *Me?* I hastily hung it up and turned away.

Suddenly Lucy's voice was in my head, telling me what Celia had been through: controlling alcoholic mother, vanishing father — not to mention two lousy relationships. Disappointment in the way life had turned out. Disappointment in herself. Maybe I should try to be nicer, try to make things better between us.

No. I'd tried too many times.

"I'll believe it when I see it — ten times in a row!" I murmured.

"What?" Jack asked.

"Nothing."

The next one — taken out of my bedroom window — of Jack holding the string of fish, was blurry. I threw it away. Just as well. Didn't want to remember our fight that night.

The next four were at the Stellar marina — Jack in front of the tourist boat, the row of cafés, the plane service and the one Todd, the chip guy, had taken. In that one, our heads were close together, me looking at Todd and laughing — Jack looking at me in a way that made a flush start in my neck and rush to my cheeks. I glanced over at him before pinning it up, but once again he was busy. Thank goodness.

As I hung the final two — Ally and Jack holding paint-brushes and Celia standing in the kitchen doorway looking worn out from work — Jack suddenly broke the silence. "So who was Lucy telling you to be nicer to in the boathouse? Your mom?"

I was surprised. "What? Yeah. But I don't like being given advice, especially about Celia."

"No kidding. Not even *good* advice."

"You don't know anything about it."

He took my arm and dragged me over to the three shots

of Celia. "Look at her. Are these images of a mean, self-centered person?"

Why was he goading me all of a sudden? I pulled my arm away. "Yes! As a matter of fact, I see a person only interested in herself. That's what I see because that's what I know!"

"Come on, Bernie. Really look at her. Isn't that just a person trying to work things out the best way she can? It's in all three shots. I can see it."

"Well, I *don't* see it!"

"You mean you *won't*. All you do is whine about her — but you don't do anything to fix it."

"She's the one who needs to fix things. She had a chance to make things better for us after our dad left — and after Seb left, and she blew it both times. Even chickened out of the wedding!"

"What wedding?"

I took a deep breath and told him the whole pathetic story, trying, I think, to get that smug look off his face as much as anything.

It worked. "Really? Mario? And then she ran away here."

"No. I *made* her come."

"How'd you manage that?"

"I made her a deal she couldn't refuse."

"Sounds scary —"

"Hidden depths. That's me," I sneered.

"Well, looks like, in spite of your attempts to have her fail, she's doing pretty good — and now Mario's come to get her back."

I snapped. "I didn't plan this to fail! I don't want her drinking again! And she has no intention of going back to Mario. It's all an act to impress anyone who's watching. You fell for it, didn't you?"

He shrugged. "Well, if you want to stay and if you want *her* to agree to stay —"

"Just let it *alone*! Be a photographer, not a shrink. I

never see you with a camera, but you're loaded with 24/7 advice."

He growled, "You're not with me 24/7, are you? Unlike you, I have a life besides photography. You should try it."

"Fine. Whatever. Thanks for the help with the film. See you."

"So, what's this? Thanks for the help, now hit the road, Jack?"

"I said thanks. What more do you want?"

He crossed his arms. "Well, there's one thing about you, Bernice Dodd. One always knows where one stands with you — in the doghouse or hovering near its door about to get kicked in the backside."

"Oh, *does* one?" I hissed.

"Yes, *one* does." He moved closer.

"Well, *one* better watch it, or that kick will send one flying all the way to Lake of the Woods."

"Just you try it," he said, face close to mine.

"I will."

"No, you won't. Girls can't kick worth a damn. Especially city girls."

I gave his leg a kick with the side of my foot.

"Hey, no need to get violent." He winced and rubbed his leg dramatically. "Okay, maybe you can kick — but only *halfway* to Stellar."

I snorted. He grinned. I aimed another blow, which he dodged, only to bang into the table holding the enlarger. He feigned great injury.

I laughed. "Dope."

As we put the solutions and paper away, he said, "So, tell me, what goes on in that head of yours, Bernie? Seriously. Are you ever just plain happy?"

I pointed at the picture of Celia with Jojo curled up against her. "That would have been me ten years ago. I think I used to be happy all the time."

"So what happened?"

"Well ... one day the Spirits of Bad Vibes looked down and said, 'Hey. That kid's too damn happy. Let's *get* her!'"

He laughed. "What happened to your dad? And who's Seb?"

He got the condensed version of my father's desertion and Seb's short duration as Father of the Year.

"Jojo seems happy. How did that happen?"

"Weird, eh? Things just seem to roll off her back. Jojo wasn't around for my dad and was too young to miss her own, but I think all those things hurt something really deep inside Ally."

I told him more about Ally's strange habits and Sean the bully.

"His teacher tried to talk to Celia, but she just said Ally was high-strung. All the time he was getting sicker. I tried my best. But it was never enough."

He laid his hand on my shoulder and squeezed it.

"I knew Sean would never stop bullying him," I said, my voice thick. "So after the wedding was canceled, I told Celia I'd have the kids taken in by Social Services if she didn't come here."

He chuckled softly. "You are one tough cookie. Like I said ... scary."

I smiled. "I don't scare you."

"Oh yes, you do!"

"Do not."

"Do, too."

"Not."

"Too."

His hand lifted from my shoulder and gently pulled my earlobe. For some reason, I leaned into his hand. He pulled me forward and our faces met, then our lips.

He pulled away first, just a little.

When I opened my eyes and saw him so close, I stepped back. "Jeez, look at the time. Eleven o'clock." I stumbled to the door and opened it a crack. All was silent.

"You want a cola?" I asked, my voice a little high.

"Sure."

I poured us each a glass and sat down at the table. He sat beside me, one arm on the back of my chair. I looked around the room, trying to think of something to say. This was bad. Not that I minded the kiss. Not that I'd mind it happening again. It was just that I wasn't sure *how* I felt. And, besides, there was Tony.

Jack was looking intently into his glass. His skin was dark and smooth, his lashes long and black, and there was a small crease near his mouth.

"Have *you* ever been just plain happy?" I asked.

A rueful smile flickered across his mouth. "Sometimes. Not always," he said softly. "Listen, Bernie ..."

A burst of laughter came from the veranda — Mario's voice, teasing someone. Celia whooped. I made a face at Jack, who shook his head sadly and looked back down into his glass. I couldn't stop myself. "That man is pathetic! Celia won't change her mind. I mean, what is he *thinking*? My mother only has room in her head for *herself*!" I fell back against my chair, swamped with disgust.

He removed his arm. "And you only have room in your head for your anger."

"What's *that* supposed to mean?"

"You're angry all the time, Bernie, even when you're *not* angry. Look, you're a good person. You have a great sense of humor. I like you. But your fury at your mom stomps around, growling at *everyone*."

"That's not true! Prove it!"

"Okay, how's this? I think you only like that creep Tony because he's interested in your mom. And you want to screw it up."

"He doesn't care about her. You're just jealous!"

"All right, so I'm jealous." He stood up. "But he's a total jerk and is using you."

"He is not! *You're* the jerk!"

Jack shook his head wearily. "You know what? I don't think we're really friends, Bernie. You can't handle having a friend. You say your mom only thinks about herself. What about you? You're so full of anger you can't see past it."

Something tore inside me. "Past *what*? This perfect life I was given? I have a mother who's a drunk and a sister and brother I'm totally responsible for — a brother who will never be healthy if we leave here. It's not just about me! I can't bear the idea of things going back to the way they were — and I can't *bear* waiting for her to fall apart again!"

"If you want this to work, Bernie, you've got to help her not to fall apart. I think your mom is trying."

"I don't need your *stupid* advice — you're worse than your father!"

His face, by now, was dark red. "I'll take that as a compliment. You know, Bernice Dodd, you're so damn angry you can't see that things are actually going pretty *well*. When you don't stir them up, that is."

"Hey, yeah!" I slapped my forehead. "I'm so happy, I just can't wait 'til my darling mother goes AWOL and I finally have to leave here! What's to lose? Your friendship? Some loss!"

Jack said nothing. Just walked out the back door.

Chapter Twenty-seven

I am sometimes accused by my peers
of printing my pictures too dark.

Don McCullin, photographer

I sat by the bedroom window, my knees under my chin. No way would I get to sleep now. The moon was full with a green hazy glow around it. A faint whiff off the water freshened the air, but I felt sick to my stomach. Jack'd never come back now. He was wrong about Celia, but I could have told him that without kicking him out of my life.

After a long time staring at the glimmering water, I heard the others coming upstairs. Mario called out good night. Celia and Lucy called back. Lucy's light came on, creating a pale square on the ragged grass below. There was to-ing and fro-ing as everyone took turns in the bathroom, followed by a soft knock on my door. I groaned, but opened it cautiously.

Lucy held up a pair of my underwear. "Found these in the bathroom," she said in a loud whisper.

"Oops." I grimaced.

She peered into the room and chuckled at the bottles on the table, the windowsill and along the floor.

I told her how Ally's new hobby had exploded all over the room.

"This place really has done wonders for him," she whispered, sidling into the room, "but he's still stressed, Bernie, don't you think? I guess it will take time. As for Jojo, she's quite taken with that cat, and with Ruby, huh? I like that woman — and her son. Down-to-earth. Direct. No nonsense.

And you know ... I think this place is doing Celia a lot of good, too. But *you* ... well, I'm not so sure about you, Bernie."

I bristled. Not *more* unwanted advice. "I'm fine."

She sat on my bed. "You said you belonged here, but actually you seem to be the one most at odds with it. Celia's adjusting. So are Jojo and Ally, but —"

"Celia adjusting? What's wrong with *that* picture?"

She continued. "Give her a chance. You're so angry, Berns. It isn't healthy."

I snorted. "Jeez, you and the rest of the world."

"What do you mean?"

"Nothing. I'm tired, Lucy."

"I just want you to be happy, Bernie."

She kissed me quickly and left the room, closing the door quietly behind her. I stared out the window. Happy? I wanted me to be happy, too. But it wasn't going to happen anytime soon. And then there was the picnic tomorrow. I had to go — Tony said he'd be there. Would Jack stay home? Would he ever speak to me again? Would apologizing do it? But he'd said some lousy things — and was always taking Celia's side. Maybe *he* should apologize, not me. I was fighting a war here. If no one understood that, then tough.

I crawled into bed and tried to forget the whole miserable evening. It took awhile, but finally my brain slowed down. I drifted off, only to suddenly wake up with a jolt, as if I'd been about to trip off a cliff. Where was I? Safe in the little bedroom. It was one in the morning. I sighed, turned over and tried to get back to sleep.

But a little voice wouldn't let me. *Why did Jack say you were angry even when you* weren't *angry? And Ally and Lucy say you're angry all the time, too.*

"Oh shut up," I growled.

I heard voices murmuring down the hall. Was something wrong? I turned on the hall light. Mario, in pajamas and housecoat, stood in front of Celia's door, looking as if he'd been caught smoking in the boys' locker room. Her door opened and she stepped out, tying her robe.

I called out, "Hey, Mario! You lost? The bathroom is next door to *your* room."

Mario pushed his hands into his housecoat pockets and looked sheepish.

I said, "Oooh, maybe you're *not* lost, huh? Celia, you are too much. Can't you leave the poor guy alone? And with Jojo in there? Jeez!"

"Shut up, Bernie. You don't know what you're talking about," Celia snapped.

"If you'd let me explain —" Mario offered, but Celia interrupted. "You don't owe her an explanation, Mario. Go to bed, Bernice!"

"You two are just plain *sick*!" I shouted and slammed the bedroom door behind me.

Ally was sitting up. "What happened? Why are you yelling again?"

"Why didn't she just marry him when she was supposed to? Now she's got him sneaking around and she'll only dump him again. She's such a *bitch*!"

Ally gasped. "She is not!" His face was pale, hands trembling.

"She *is* a bitch! Here we are, trying to make a home and now she —"

"No!" he cried. "She's not a ... what you say she is. Stop saying that!"

"You're just a kid, Ally. You'll soon learn." I kicked one of my sneakers across the room. It knocked over a jar on the floor.

Ally scrambled out of bed. "That's my luna moth caterpillar!" He looked into the jar. "They're rare — you coulda killed him, Bernie!"

"I'm sorry, Ally. It was an accident." We both peered

into the leaves and twigs. "He's okay, isn't he?"

"He seems okay," he said, putting the jar carefully on his bedside table. His bottom lip quivered. "I was only keeping him until tomorrow. I'm going to sleep now. Don't yell anymore, Bernie."

Shocked, I hugged his stiff little body. "I'll try, Ally. Honest."

After he slid into bed, I sat on the floor wondering how soon I'd be forced to break that promise.

The next morning I woke up with such a bad headache I knew I'd throw up if I moved. I lay on the lumpy mattress and tried to ignore the early-morning voices drifting into my room along with the smell of coffee. When my stomach felt more stable, I sat up slowly, clutching my head to keep my brain from sloshing around in my skull. My watch said eight o'clock. The picnic was at eleven. Would I make it? Ally's head popped around the door frame.

"Hi, Bernie. You not up yet?"

"No," I murmured, brushing my dry lips with my tongue.

"You sick, Bernie? Was it my fault? I didn't mean to get so mad last night."

I smiled and croaked, "Not your fault. All mine."

"You having one of those bad headaches? You gonna throw up?"

"Both, Ally."

"I'll get a glass of water and Mom's sick kit."

I held up my finger and thumb in the OK sign. When he returned, he knelt on the floor and carefully dug through the small medical box.

"Here — two extra-strength pills and one of those pills for barfing."

I drank them down all at once. He plumped up my pillows and I slowly lowered myself back onto them, letting out a dry sob. He patted my arm. "I'll get Mom."

"No! Ally, just tell them I'm sleeping in for a bit and to leave me alone. I'll canoe over to the picnic when I get up, okay? Close the curtains, please?"

He pulled the old curtains across the window. Dust filled the air, but at least the sun was blocked. I had a sense he might be working himself up to say something, but he just sighed and I heard his footsteps leave the room — and return. A cold cloth was draped over my forehead.

"Thanks, Ally. You're a peach," I muttered. "I'm just sleeping in for a bit. I don't want anyone fussing."

"I promise," he said, adding firmly, "I'll put my foot *down*." He stamped his sneaker to make his point.

When he left, shutting the door, I laughed, holding my head to keep it from exploding. He was looking after *me* now.

As soon as I closed my eyes, Jack's hurt face appeared. I pushed the image away, took a deep shuddering breath, let the pills take over — and fell into dark silence.

I didn't wake up until someone knocked on the door. I ignored it, but it creaked open anyway, and Celia's voice said, "It's almost ten o'clock. You can't hide out forever. Lucy won't be here very long."

"Go away," I muttered.

"We need to talk about last night."

I squeezed my eyes tight against a throb of pain pumping across my temple.

"Wait a second," she said, "you don't look so good."

"I have a migraine, okay? I can handle it. Don't need fake concern right now, thanks."

She said quietly, "You would think that camera would show you things as they *are*. But you're so busy trying to catch a shot of me as Bad Mother, you can't see what's in front of you."

"Jeez. The third in-house shrink in a row. I already know you're a bad mother. Don't need a photo to tell me *that*." A flicker of shame hit me, but I ignored it.

"Well, come when and if you feel better," she said, closing the door quietly behind her.

Great. Now I really was Jack's version of the Loser.

When I woke up an hour later, the headache had eased quite a lot. I sat up shakily. I had to get to the picnic. At least Tony wouldn't nag me. I grabbed my bathing suit, shuffled over to my duffel bag and took out shorts and a crumpled T-shirt, then picked up the camera bag, stuck my feet in rubber sandals and slopped down the hall to the bathroom just as Mario emerged in a cloud of steam. He was dressed in shorts, short-sleeved shirt and sandals, his nightclothes over his arm.

"Aaah, Bernie," he began, "I was talking to Lucy and she —"

"Not now, okay?" I said. "You'll be gone soon, so forget it."

I pushed past him. The shower was barely tepid. When it went suddenly icy cold, I gritted my teeth and cursed every living being in the place. Shivering, I toweled dry, dressed and headed down the stairs. Damn. Lucy was in the kitchen, screwing caps on water bottles.

"I thought you'd all be out of here by now," I said.

"Everyone's at the dock. Ruby and the Broom men are getting canoes and boats sorted. You coming?"

Looking at her round, kind face, I blurted out, "How can you *stand* it, Lucy?"

"Stand what?"

"Watching Celia mess around with Mario's head. Knowing you'll have to drive home with him all heartbroken and beaten down again. I mean, what do you *see* in her?"

Lucy pushed a muffin in front of me. "Celia's helped me in ways you'll never know, Bernie, including the death of my parents when I wasn't much older than you. Will you desert Jojo if she has stuff to go through later in life? Well, your mom's had bad stuff to go through. I won't desert her."

"Huh!" I said, tearing the muffin into little pieces. "Makes you a better person than me. You're a perfect friend and I'm a lousy daughter, I guess."

Lucy's voice was icy. "This self-pity crap is getting very tedious, Bernie. You've been wallowing long enough. Crawl back out if you really want to make things better."

Stung, I cried, "*Better?* What do you think I've been trying to do? Tell *her* to make it better."

"She's *trying* and you know it. And she's not going to hurt Mario. Don't worry about that."

"Lucy! I saw him coming out of her room last night."

She looked at me, as if trying to decide something, then said, "No, you didn't."

"I *saw* him!"

"Mario was coming out of *my* room last night, Bernie."

"What?"

"After you guys left Winnipeg, Mario and I saw each other every night. We went to movies, out to dinner, for long walks. We were filling in the loneliness at first. We've always been sympatico — best friends — but one day, well, we suddenly realized we loved each other."

I gaped at her. "You've *got* to be joking."

"No, Bernie. I'm not joking."

"You and Mario? Isn't that called a rebound? He was going to marry Celia just a few weeks ago, for crying out loud!"

Her face tightened. "Well, now we're together."

"Does Celia know?"

"Yes, we told her yesterday. She's happy for us."

I shook my head. "Lucy, he's going to hurt you."

"No, he won't, Bernie. I love Mario. He loves me."

"How *can* he? I mean, not that someone couldn't love

you, they *could*, but he's still crazy about Celia. I think John Broom is interested in you, Lucy. Couldn't you be interested in him? Then it wouldn't be so ..."

Lucy tried to smile, but she was struggling. I pretended not to notice. Mario didn't love her. He would leave her the way Celia had left him.

She filled her arms with water bottles and said firmly, "I don't want to hear any more of your opinions today, Bernie. If you're coming to the picnic, come. If not, I'll see you later."

Chapter Twenty-eight

Photographs are moments
eternally flabbergasted.

Shayna Bauchner, photographer

Me and my gargantuan mouth. Another Big Gesture that failed. I only wanted to keep Lucy from being hurt and now she'd hate me forever — like Jack. I loved her. I had just said those things to keep her safe.

My heart jumped when I spotted Jack loading our fishing boat with supplies. This was getting worse by the second. Ruby was already putt-putting away from the dock in a small wooden boat with a pile of water toys and Jojo, lost inside a life jacket, huddled in the nose and happily waving at everyone on the shore. Badger sat quietly, bright-eyed and alert, beside her.

Celia bobbed around in *my* red canoe near shore. No way would I get in *that* with her. And no way was I going to ask Jack for help getting one of the bigger canoes down, either.

Ally sat on the floor of a big blue canoe, white-knuckling the sides, his pale face hovering above the bright life jacket. To my surprise, Mario stepped from the shallow water into the back of Celia's ride. Lucy, in a long peasant skirt and bulky preserver, was trying to get into the blue one from the dock. Jack gave her a hand while his dad held the canoe steady. John Broom was soon aboard, and carefully pushed off from the dock.

That left me, Jack and the aluminum boat. Great. Absolutely *no way*.

Celia called, "Oh, there you are, Bernie. Go with Jack."

"Tony's not here yet," I called. "I'll go with him."

Jack didn't look at me, but Celia said, "We're not waiting for him."

"I'll wait."

"No, you won't," she rapped out. "If Tony is coming, he'll go straight to the island — and we won't come back for you. Now get in the boat!"

I stalked to the dock, got into the little fishing boat and faced toward the nose. If Tony went straight to the island and I ended up here alone, I'd look even stupider than I did now.

Mario called out, "If Celia and I get into trouble, you'll rescue us, eh, Jack?"

"In a flash," Jack answered. "I'll give you a good lead."

The sun was warming and the morning breeze wafted the last trace of coolness over my bare arms. Jack clattered into the boat. I watched Celia and Mario tack this way and that across the bay toward the island, Celia laughing all the way. I shook my head in disgust.

Ruby's red boat was already nearing the island. Lucy, with Mr. Broom and Ally, was waving her arms about and pointing, then nodding. She and John Broom were perfect together. Even Ruby liked Lucy. *Way* better than Celia. Lucy was making a *huge* mistake with Mario.

When Mario and Celia were a third of the way across, Jack started the little motor and we cruised slowly after them. As the sun glanced off the ripples, I spotted a yellow canoe coming out of the glare to our left and my heart lifted. Tony stopped paddling and waved. I answered with great sweeps of my arm.

I said, "Go over there. I'll go with him."

Jack just kept moving slowly toward the island.

"Did you hear me?" I said. "I want to go with Tony."

"It's dangerous to board a canoe from a boat in open water," Jack said tersely. "You'll have to wait until we get to the island to fall all over him."

"Jerk!"

He veered the boat to the left and roared into high speed. We swooped around the canoe and it dipped and rolled over the waves. Tony had to grip it with both hands. "Hey! You trying to swamp me? What's the deal!"

"Your girlfriend wants to go with you," Jack called. I stared at him, horrified. Tony shouted, "Out here? No! You know better than that, Jack!"

Jack waved, gunned the motor and we took off, leaving a foamy wake — and Tony struggling red-faced to keep from tipping.

I hated Jack Broom with all my being.

He slowed and made a wide circle around Celia and Mario's canoe, then revved the motor until I was sure we were going to ram the island's sandy shore, but then he cut it, reversed for a few seconds and we slid neatly onto the sand. Lucy, Ally and Mr. Broom were just climbing out of their canoe. Ruby was already piling kindling into a tall horseshoe of stones. A rusty grill lay nearby. Badger ran off into the woods, tail swooping in happy circles.

"I'm off, Dad," Jack called as I climbed out. "See you later."

His dad said, "Off where?"

"I arranged with a couple of friends that I'd meet up with them."

I frowned. He wasn't staying? Something sank inside me. It wouldn't be any fun without ... oh, yeah ... that's right. I hated him, didn't I? The jerk.

Mr. Broom said, "Jack, go help your Gran get that fire going. I'll keep an eye on Mario and Celia." He looked worried. "They seem to be doing okay, but I don't like the way the canoe dips every time he takes a stroke."

"Bernie can help Gran. I've gotta go, Dad."

"We need that boat, Jack. One two-horse-power boat and two canoes isn't enough in an emergency."

"But —"

"No buts, kid."

Jack glared at his father's back. I felt a sudden shift of spirits, which surprised me, considering he'd just been so horrible. Tony was still paddling toward the island, so he couldn't have been that upset by what Jack said. Maybe it would be okay after all.

"We need some nice straight sticks cut for hot dogs," Ruby said as she set up a folding table. "Bernice, you and Jack can do that."

Jack vanished into the wood behind the campsite. When I found him, he was slicing off willow branches with a sharp knife.

"You don't need to help me. I've done this a thousand times," he said.

I pulled leaves from a couple of sturdy twigs. "Are these safe to put food on to?"

When I only got silence, I looked up to find him watching me, his face blank. At that moment, I had a terrible sense of losing something important. I opened my mouth to say something — anything — that might change things, but instead I ran away.

Tony was just beaching his canoe. Mario, his life jacket still on — did he think the island was going to sink? — was helping him tie it to a nearby tree. When Mario wandered off, I ran up to Tony.

"I'm sorry, Tony. Jack's an idiot." I felt a stab of guilt but didn't take it back.

I expected a smile, but got a low growl. "Did you have to tell him I was your boyfriend? What were you thinking, Bernie?"

"I didn't! He's just jealous that I — that —"

"Yeah, well, use your head, okay? I don't need lectures from your mother's friends."

"Did Mario say something?" I asked, my voice rising.

"Shhh. Just a look and a few well-placed words about my bringing a woman friend next time."

"Mario has no right to say that to you!"

"Keep your voice down. Look, forget it. I've got to go play with the old folks. I'll talk to you later."

Sitting on the sand beside a fallen log, I seethed with resentment. All I'd wanted to do was paddle to the island with Tony. What was so wrong with that? Now he was mad at me, thanks to Jack's stupid, juvenile behavior.

I watched Jack prop a pile of hot dog sticks against the table before stripping down to his bathing suit and running into the water. He did a shallow dive, then swam rapidly away from the island. He was a strong swimmer, his long arms cutting the surface with a smooth, regular rhythm. Lucy followed, doing a sedate side stroke. Mario inched his way in, shoulders up — as if he was heading into arctic waters.

Jojo set up toys on the sand, while Ally used his bug net in the shallow water. Celia sat on a rock by the shore, Tony beside her, chatting and smiling. Who cared anymore? Not me.

Mr. Broom was getting a pail of water to set near the fire. And, of course, Celia just had to speak to *him* as he went by. Whatever it was made him laugh. Celia grinned after him, adjusting her ball cap. Utterly sick-making.

I gazed unblinking into the hazy blue sky. The shoreline in the distance was blurred, the sun making everything waver and shift. Yeah. Like my head. Everything in there was still pretty much out of focus, too.

Chapter Twenty-nine

I have been a witness, and these pictures are my testimony. The events I have recorded should not be forgotten and must not be repeated.

James Nachtwey, photographer

When Ruby's fire died down a bit, she pronounced it perfect for cooking wieners. I knew I'd gag on whatever I put in my mouth, so I leaned back against the log and tried to ignore everyone. No one seemed to notice, anyway. They all gathered around the makeshift BBQ pit, poking their wieners into ideal roasting places, pretending to push anyone away if their spot was threatened. Lots of laughter. Fake laughter, if you'd asked me. Tony was the loudest and seemed to be having the most fun. I looked at my feet and swallowed hard. When I looked up, Jack was sitting on a grassy sandbank facing the lake, quietly eating.

A plate was thrust under my nose. "I made you one. You still got a headache?"

Ally had burned a wiener, put it in a bun with mustard and relish and piled a small amount of potato salad and two cookies beside it. He held up a can of orange soda.

I took the plate. "Mostly gone. Thanks, Ally. This looks perfect. I'm just not —"

"I know — you can't eat much after you're sick. But maybe a bit?"

He sat beside me. I put my arm around his shoulders. "You okay?"

He nodded and said solemnly, "This is the *best* place on

earth. I never want to leave. I'm gonna be a pilot like Mr. Broom one day. And build cabins like him. But ... Bernie — are you listening?" He turned my head to look at him.

"Yes. I am."

"I have to tell you something, okay?"

I smiled. "Okay. Shoot."

"Mr. Broom and I looked at a room two down from ours. He's gonna put in shelves."

"For what?"

"So I can have my own room."

My first reaction was a silent *Yes!* He must be feeling better. This was great.

"Hey, that's good, Ally. You need more room, that's for sure."

He nodded. "Yeah. And I want a room that's quiet. Just mine. Don't be upset, Bernie. It's just that you're so ... mad all the time ... and when you yell at Mom, it makes me all jumpy inside. So I ... I wanted to ..."

"— get away from me?" I tried to sound light and funny, but felt like I'd been hit in the stomach.

"Don't be mad, Bernie," he said, the spot between his brows tight. "But you don't laugh anymore. You never tell jokes. Coming here was supposed to make us happy, but you're not. Please don't be mad at me."

Well, I'd heard that before. I looked him straight in the eyes. "I'm not mad at you, Ally. Not even a bit. You should have your own room."

"Thanks, Bernie." He suddenly smiled. "I'm gonna have tons of shelves for my bugs!"

Jojo shouted, "Come on, Ally! You said we'd eat with Mommy!"

Ally said, "Okay with you, Berns?"

I smiled. "Take off, kiddo. Thanks for lunch."

I watched him kicking up sand toward Celia and Jojo, sitting in the shade. Celia handed him a plastic glass of something. I sat back against the log and tried not to cry.

Half an hour later, Ruby called out, "I'm going to pick berries. John and Lucy are coming."

"I'd like to get enough to make Mario a pie," Lucy called.

Jojo shouted from shore, "Can I come? Please?"

"Not this time, honey. It's too hot and buggy."

Jojo moaned, but went back to sifting sand through a plastic sieve. Mario, Tony and Celia, joking and giggling like kids, got ready to hit the water. Jack scowled at them before walking down the shore and disappearing behind the wide branches of a balsam.

Celia ran into the water carrying an air mattress. She sat on it and shouted to me, "I'm going into deeper water, Bernie. Watch the kids!"

I grabbed a couple of foam noodles. "Can't. I'm going down the shore a bit."

"Bernie, watch the kids!"

"Watch them yourself."

I walked over rocks, sticks, stranded water weeds and sandy patches until I came to a small beach. I sat for a while, soaking up the sun, then stripped to my suit, walked out to my waist and floated on the noodles. It was quiet. The water was warm.

As I lazily drifted, the sun suddenly dipped behind scudding white clouds and the wind picked up. Soon, crisp waves broke against the noodles. My legs grew tired from fighting to stay near shore — and the breeze turned icy on my wet arms. When a huge horsefly began to dive-bomb me, I gave up and dragged the noodles to shore.

Tony was sitting by my clothes, forearms on knees, a beer held loosely in his hand. I walked over, half pissed off and half excited, trying not to show either.

"You mad at me?" he asked.

I shrugged.

"We have to be discreet, that's all," he said. "That kid Jack could ruin it."

I sat down. "Nothing to ruin, really, is there?"

"You've gone off me, have you?"

He put one hand on my back. I tried to grab a handful of breath, but couldn't do it. My heart stopped as his fingers moved slowly down my spine. At that moment, a loud shriek cut through the air, followed by alarmed voices.

"Something's wrong," I said, struggling to my feet.

"They're just having fun. Relax."

He tried to pull me back down, but I yanked free and ran toward the sounds. I made it just as Mr. Broom ran out of the woods with Lucy. Mario was trying to swim toward Celia, dragging his air mattress behind him. Celia struggled in deep water, letting out pathetic squeals. Her air mattress swirled toward shore in the stiff breeze.

Mr. Broom bellowed, "What is it?"

"Jojo," she cried, then dove, coming up with Jojo, choking and gasping.

"No!" I shrieked, and ran to help.

But Mr. Broom was already there, carrying Jojo to shore, red-faced and coughing. "She's okay. She's okay. But what happened!" he asked.

"I was trying to catch minnows," Ally said, "and Jojo said she wanted to use the flutter board and go out to Mom and I said no, so I went after the minnow and then I heard a big splash and Jojo was way far away and going under the water so I called Mom — but I don't think she heard, so I shouted louder and then she came."

Celia sobbed. "I heard Ally ... shout and then I saw Jojo's head go under. Thank God she's safe!" She leaned against Mr. Broom and hugged Jojo. Lucy handed them a big towel and they wrapped Jojo in it, rubbing her arms and legs.

Frightened by all the fierce attention, she began to wail.

Mr. Broom patted her leg. "You're fine, Jojo. Just a bad scare."

"Where the hell were you, Bernie?" Celia cried, suddenly turning on me.

"I told you I was going down the shore. You were right here!"

Lucy was talking urgently to Mario, but he was trying to explain things to Ruby, and Ally was trying to explain things to Jack, who'd also come running — and Celia just kept shouting accusations at me and I shouted right back. Jojo wailed louder.

"Enough!" John Broom bellowed. Shocked silence fell. Jojo sniffled into his neck. "There are eight adults on this island. We are *all* responsible."

"No, you're not. She's not your kid," I cried. "She's Celia's kid!"

"And your sister!" Celia cried.

I tried to lift Jojo from Mr. Broom, but she twisted away, arms out to Celia.

"Yeah, you're right, Celia," I said. "I should've known better than to leave her with *you*! I should've known you'd be too interested in putting on a show to pay attention. So blame me for almost drowning Jojo. Why not? You blame me for everything else!"

"That's not true! If anything, you blame —"

"Give it *up*!" I shouted. "It was *my* fault. Happy now? Just leave me alone!"

I ran to the aluminum boat and sat on the middle seat, staring furiously over the choppy water. I heard voices coming closer. I wasn't staying around to hear any more. I pushed the boat out and pulled the cord. How did this stupid thing start? The boat drifted sideways to the shore in the growing wind. I pulled furiously, but nothing happened.

Someone grabbed the side of the boat, forced the back

end to move toward the bay and pushed off, climbing into the bow.

"Move!" Jack shouted.

I edged past him to the front seat and wrapped my arms around my stomach, my head down. In a few seconds he had it backing into the growing waves, the propeller burbling. His father shouted something. Jack nodded and waved. Then he swung the boat around and turned up the throttle.

Halfway across the bay, it dawned on me. Tony hadn't been in the huddle around Jojo. Where was he?

Chapter Thirty

*If you are not willing to see
more than is visible, you
won't see anything.*

Ruth Bernhard, photographer

A frigid spray of water hit my face every time the boat's nose smacked into the waves. By the time we reached the docks, I was soaked.

Battling the wind, Jack pulled up beside the smaller boathouse. I scrambled out, ran to the lodge and up to my room.

Out the window, I could see the bay was really choppy now, whitecaps dancing in the sun. Jack was heading back to the island. I changed into some clothes and sat on the bed staring at my feet until I heard the motor returning — probably bringing them back in shifts because of the wind.

I lay down on my bed and pulled a blanket over me. I tried to tell myself Jojo was safe, but the terror wouldn't leave me. *Was* it my fault? I was sure Celia had heard me say I was going for a walk along the shore. Didn't she see me leave the beach?

What if Jojo had died? A wild surge of panic gripped me, and I started to shake.

Even after she was safe, I'd made a complete fool of myself — but the thing that hurt most was how Jojo twisted away from me and turned to Celia for comfort. How could she? And Ally — he'd told me twice in two days that I wasn't any fun to be around — or I was so mad it made him worried and anxious. *Me* — who'd tried to make him feel safe his whole life. How could he desert me just like that?

A soft knock on my door and the rattle of the doorknob made me lie very still, not breathing.

Lucy's voice came through. "Celia, leave her for now. Give her some time alone."

"But I need to talk to her," Celia answered in a high voice.

Lucy was firm. "Later. When she comes out. *Leave* her."

I fell asleep almost immediately afterward, wrapped in the old blanket. When I woke up, it was dark, and the room was stifling. I pulled my window higher. The wind had died and the slight breeze was warm. I could hear voices on the veranda. Ally's bed was empty. I unlocked my door and looked into the bedroom two down from mine. Ally was asleep in the second one, his brown hair sticking above the covers. So that was that. It hurt, but even I knew it would be good for him.

I continued on to Celia's room. Jojo was on her cot by Celia's bed, her head thrown back, her legs twisted around a light cotton sheet. Beside her was a small pile of picture books. A little fan hummed on the dresser. The cat, lying on her pillow, gazed at me quietly with yellow eyes. I lifted the books away, straightened Jojo's legs and tucked her in. She'd changed so much since we'd got here. More active now, she'd grown thinner, her round face less pudgy, her skin smooth and brown as taffy. I lifted one small hand. The nails were a pearly pink. Some of the edges had peeled. Celia must have painted them for her.

And me? I'd hardly thought about her for days. She was just ... *there*, cheerfully shouting through each day. How many times had she asked me if she could tag along and I'd refused, always promising *next* time? If Ally hadn't been watching out for her, she wouldn't *be* here, snoring gently in the fan's breeze. A swell of grief froze me, my mind and body stupefied by shame and horror.

To try and distract myself, I looked around. I hadn't been in this room since Celia had fixed it up. It was spare and clean, a smooth white bedspread over white sheets, an old knitted afghan tossed over the pine footboard. The air smelled of her perfume — a light spicy scent that made me feel horribly sad. The mom I used to know wore that perfume, too — the mom who took me to the secondhand bookstore when I was a kid and let me buy as many books as I could carry and then read to me until we'd worked through every single one. The past few days, I'd seen flashes of that mom, but that just made things worse.

I tossed and turned the rest of the night, but the next morning I decided to face ... whatever came. I walked boldly into the kitchen, my knees a bit trembly, but with luck, no one could see them. Mario and Lucy were washing up their breakfast dishes.

Lucy nudged him. He looked confused for a second, then said, "I'm gonna go for a walk, Lucia. Ate too many hot dogs yesterday. Indigestion. See you later, Bernie."

As he walked by, he reached out to touch my shoulder, but I stepped away.

"That wasn't very nice," Lucy said tersely.

"I don't like him anymore."

She sighed. "Oh, Bernie. Wasn't yesterday enough? Jojo's fine. Everything's okay."

"She could've drowned."

"But she didn't."

"Yeah, well, Celia blames me. So do you and Mario. And you're right. It was my fault."

"Celia was upset. No one blames you, certainly not Mario or me. We were all responsible for watching Jojo."

"*I* should have been watching her."

"It was an accident. It's over. Life will go on."

I threw up my hands. "But what *kind* of life? No one's

acting the way they should anymore. Everything's all mixed up."

"How?"

"You're crazy about the guy who was supposed to be crazy about my mother. Jack hates me half of every day and the other half he's even weirder, and Celia has been pretending to be sober *and* the world's greatest mother. She hasn't been any fun the past few years, but at least I knew where I *stood*. I knew my *job*! But now —"

She opened her mouth to speak, but I cut in.

"Are you going to marry him, Lucy?"

"Mario?"

"No, Darth Vadar! Of course, Mario!"

"Not right now. Maybe one day."

"Why?"

"Oh, Bernie, don't start —"

"I really want to know."

She sighed. "Because I love Mario. We've been friends forever. I tried to set him up with my girlfriends a few times. When I introduced him to Celia, I never in a million years thought they'd ... he'd — you know — that either would consider the other. But Celia and you kids — I guess he saw a ready-made family, one that needed him. I think he fell in love with a dream. And, of course, it wasn't until later that I realized ..."

"What?"

"That I loved him. And that he loved me."

I shook my head. "Lucy ... he saw — what? — a ready-made family and decided to *buy* us with a house and food? Then Celia dumped him — and now he loves you? Please!"

"You have *some* way of putting things, Bernie. He cares about all of you, but he was having serious doubts. He knew he and Celia weren't compatible. I suspect your mom sensed his change of heart — and that's why she backed out. She knew he was too kind to do it himself."

I rolled my eyes. "And he told you that *after* we left, I suppose?"

"The week before they were supposed to get married, actually. He also told me he's been interested in me for years, but didn't think I cared for him that way."

I stared, not sure whether to believe her. "But I thought you liked Mr. Broom. He likes *you*."

"Grow up, Bernie! I don't even know John Broom. Besides, he likes someone else."

"What is this, high school? There *is* no one else. He's practically a recluse."

"He likes your mom. If you were paying attention —"

"No way!" I cried, shocked to the core. "He couldn't. He knows what *she* is."

"And what is that, Bernie?" a voice behind me said.

"You know what! This is all your fault, Celia!" I shouted. "Lucy's probably going to marry Mario even knowing that you came *first*. You always come first, Celia, even before your own kids. You were so busy flirting and acting like a teenager yesterday that Jojo —"

Celia's face went bright red. "Be quiet, Bernice! I'm sick and tired of you berating me — when you're not taking photos or moping over Tony. I spend more time with the kids than *you* do, for all your talk! And as for yesterday, we both thought the other was watching the kids."

I snorted loudly. "Congratulations, Celia. You've just won the Black Spruce Passing-the-Buck prize. In fact, you've won everything, even turned the kids against me. Lucy's on your side. Everyone's mad at me. Perfect score."

"Don't be such a spoiled child! You can be as sarcastic as you want, Bernie, but whether you like it or not, we're in this together. And I would never turn Jojo and Ally against you!"

"You wanna know what, Celia?" I leaned into her face. "You can't stand the fact that for almost four years I've been the only real mother those kids have had. They're in love with you again, sure — but soon you'll decide it's all too much hassle and disappear. And this time I won't track you down. You can just leave and never come back. Like Dad, you know? Like your father? Take off — then turn left to *pathetic*! You don't have the guts to —"

I didn't feel the slap across my face for a second or two. I stared at Celia's open palm as it swung back up, but it stopped halfway. She gaped at it, then at me, her mouth opening and closing like a jack fish on a stringer.

I ran out the kitchen door.

"Bernie. Wait!"

I stopped, my cheek burning.

"I — I'm sorry, Bernie." Celia's face was gray. "I won't — I've never hit you before."

"It's not ever going to change between you and me. I used to hope. But it never will. Will it, Celia?"

When she held her hands out, I stepped back and she twisted her fingers together. "I can only promise to try, Bernie. I've arranged to go to AA in Stellar. I *have* been trying. I won't let you down, no matter how much you think I will."

I sneered. "You might stay sober long enough to sell this place, but back in the city, you'll go right out —"

"But that's just it, Bernie. I don't think we *should* sell it. I think we should do what you said — run it as a business. See how we do. People have already heard that the store will be opening soon. John has offered to take me to get supplies. I've ordered a secondhand freezer from a friend of Ruby's who's closing her store in Red Lake. She also has an almost new glassed-in fridge for milk and dairy stuff. Mario says that's more than enough to start up such a small shop. We'll use John's truck to haul them here. We need to get that money out of the bank, Bernie. I'll only use it for the store. I promise. This time, I won't let you down."

Every lousy memory of the past few years flooded into my head. "It's not fair to promise anymore, Celia. It's just not *fair*!" And I ran around the far side of the house through the bushes and straight to the boathouses.

Chapter Thirty-one

*She glances at the photo, and the pilot
light of memory flickers in her eyes.*

Frank Deford, writer

I sat on the wooden walkway of the smaller boathouse. I'd
loused everything up. And a big part of me knew I deserved
whatever I got. I'd hurt Lucy — the one adult I never, *ever*
wanted to hurt. I'd more or less told her that Mario didn't
love her. I'd less than more, I hoped, told her she wasn't
lovable. And deep down, I knew anyone watching Celia and
me would say Celia was the one who deserved a break. But,
after four years of riding that alcohol-powered roller-coaster
with her, I just couldn't let go of the certainty she'd take off
soon.

As for Jack, what did I expect? All I did was snarl at him,
whine about Celia and more or less be a pain in the backside.
The thought of losing him hurt in ways that really surprised
me. The kiss. The hurt in his eyes. His infectious laugh.

I shook them away. I needed to sort out my head.

I climbed into the little red canoe, pulled in a life jacket
and a paddle. I'd forgotten my camera, but wasn't going
back for it. As I pushed out of the boathouse, I glanced
toward Tony's bay. He'd be there for me — he'd said so. I
needed to see him, talk to him ... touch him. Celia only called
him a creep because she was jealous. *But where was he when
everyone was so worried about Jojo?* Probably gone for a walk
and didn't hear us. Yeah, that had to be it. I aimed the canoe
toward the long finger of birch and dense foliage that sepa-
rated our bay from his.

As I approached the point, a small boat putt-putted around it toward me. Damn! Ruby was sitting in the bow, wearing huge white-rimmed sunglasses, fishing rod in hand. Jack was driving, his line stringing out, beaded with water. I tried to look invisible and paddled nonchalantly, but they soon caught up.

Jack said something under the sound of the motor, and Ruby swiveled in her seat and waved. She said something back to him. He shrugged and aimed the boat at me and cut the engine as they came alongside.

"Catch anything?" I asked feebly.

Ruby shook her head. "Not a nibble. But we've only just started."

Jack was reeling in his line, a drift of weeds dragging along with it. Another day, I would have made a crack about the fish he *didn't* catch, but his stiff back told me I'd be wasting my breath.

Suddenly he looked right at me. "Goin' to see Tony? He's sunning on his dock. He'll be happy to see *you*, I bet." He examined the debris on his hook.

"How's everything at the lodge, Bernice?" Ruby said. "Jojo okay?"

"Yeah. I think she's fine."

"Good. A scare like that keeps everyone on their toes. It won't happen again, that's for sure. You've got some nice friends visiting, don't you? I like Lucy and Mario. Must be fun having them here."

"I guess."

"Nice to see the place coming alive again," she continued. "After all of the unhappiness it's been through, it needs good people in it."

"It'll have to wait for the next group then."

Ruby's eyebrows lifted above her sunglasses. "Oh? I thought everything was perking along pretty good — well, until yesterday, but everyone was upset — and foolish things were said. Those two kids are sweet as can be, and your mom is certainly working hard, I'll give her that —"

"Gran," growled Jack, "better stay away from happy family talk where Bernie's concerned."

Ruby took off her glasses and gazed at the lodge. As if talking to herself, she said, "I used to think it was that place that did it. But it's *people*. People make things much harder than they need to be. Look at poor Charlotte and her William. That Lydia —"

I leaned over and grabbed hold of the boat's gunwale. "Lydia? Lydia messed things up between Charlotte and William? How? What happened?"

Ruby looked surprised. "No point in keeping it a secret, I suppose. Charlotte and William were in love. So, what did Lydia do? Well, *she* married William. Uh-oh. I forgot. That makes him your grandfather, Bernice. I'm *sorry*. I shouldn't have said anything."

I stared at her. "My grandfather? The artist? But — but you said William loved Aunt Charlotte."

Jack, almost despite himself, asked, "So how come he married Lydia?"

Ruby shook her head sadly. "Because Lydia decided she wanted him and set out to get him. Lydia was a very ... determined young woman. Charlotte was running this place — her parents were slowing down by then — and, well ..."

"Didn't Lydia work for her parents, too?" I asked.

She laughed. "Work? Huh! Lydia was no Cinderella, that's for sure. Wherever William was, she popped up. I warned Charlotte, but she trusted William. Lydia told her she was too old for marriage, that a young outgoing wife would further William's career, and I'm sure she flattered him silly — teasing, flirting."

"He couldn't have loved Charlotte all that much if he left her for Lydia," I said.

"I believe he truly loved Charlotte. But she was

independent and hard to get close to. Lydia was all over him. And one day, out of the blue, William and Lydia were gone. She sent a postcard from Niagara Falls: they were married and a baby was on the way."

"And that baby was Celia," I said. "Poor Charlotte."

Ruby nodded. "Yes. Poor Charlotte, but she wouldn't thank us for saying that. The night after she got the postcard, she went to William's cabin, piled his paintings — mostly of her — outside the cabin, put the postcard on top, doused everything in gasoline and torched the lot. It was a windy night. Sparks and burning bits of canvas blew into the cabin. The place had half burned down by the time the rain came and put it out.

"It was just a week later that her parents drowned. Lydia and William came for the funeral. Charlotte asked me to tell them they weren't welcome. Lydia didn't care. She stayed in a hotel in Stellar and demanded Charlotte buy out her half of the lodge. She and William were going to live in Winnipeg. Charlotte arranged a mortgage, paid them off and went on with her life as best she could. I don't believe she ever saw Lydia again."

"William left Lydia when Celia was little. Do you know where he went?" I asked.

"He came back here."

"Back to Charlotte?" I squeaked.

"Wanted her to go away with him. But Charlotte told him to return to his wife and baby. He'd betrayed her — she would never take him back."

"Do you know where he ended up?"

"In Stellar. Worked at an art supply store and gave private art lessons, retired in his seventies. Died in a nursing home a few weeks before Charlotte."

"Did she know he was so close all that time?"

"She must have, but she never admitted it. He never came by, I know that."

"Does Celia know?"

Ruby shook her head. "I doubt it."

"Charlotte didn't tell me any of this," Jack said.

"She didn't want to hurt anymore — or remember," Ruby said.

"But she kept his photos," I said, "so she chose to remember some of it."

"People can sure screw up their lives," Jack said in disgust.

I looked at him, but his glance only grazed my face as he reached around and tugged the motor's cord. The engine sputtered. He pushed in the choke and it began to purr. Over his shoulder, he said, "See you around — or not." Then he gunned it and they left me behind in a confusion of waves.

What had happened to Charlotte and William was mind-numbing, but there was a terrible ache in my chest watching Jack's dark head and gray T-shirt move across the bay. He was never going to be my friend again. I'd pushed him away with my anger. As Charlotte had driven William away with hers.

I wanted to cry. Instead, I thumped the canoe's gunwale with the flat of my paddle. I needed to talk to Tony more than ever now. I paddled hard and rounded the point. He wouldn't laugh at me. He'd comfort me. And there was something much deeper we needed to explore.

My heart lifted when I spotted his blue bathing suit. He was lying on a wide dock. Good. He hadn't seen me. I decided to keep close to the shore so I could surprise him.

Suddenly, a woman walked out of his cabin. The red-haired woman I'd seen in the van, and later fishing with a boatload of kids. She ran past Tony, dropped her wrap and dived into the water. He went in after her. They came up close together ... *kissing*. It couldn't be. She was married. She had kids. Tons of them.

I tried to back away, but the breeze caught the nose and

spun me around. I guess they heard my thrashing paddle because they suddenly pulled apart. Tony turned and stared at me. I think he said, "I'll get rid of her," and swam quickly toward me. I tried to back away again, but the wind just pushed me closer. A hand grabbed the side of the canoe and Tony's wet face appeared.

"What are you up to?" he growled. "You can't keep sneaking up on me, Bernie!"

"I — I wasn't sneaking up on you. I was coming over to talk to you and —"

The woman was climbing the short wooden ladder onto the dock. She grabbed her wrap and a big cloth bag, jumped into the front seat of an inboard boat, backed out, gunned the engine and roared away.

Tony pounded the gunwale of my canoe with his fist. "*Damn it!*"

"Doesn't she have a husband and kids?"

"It's none of your business, Bernie. She's a friend."

It hurt my throat to say it. "Looked like more than just a friend."

"She's *just* a friend. You tell that to anyone who asks."

"Why would I tell? Who would ask? No one cares! Least of all me!" I tried to paddle away, but his weight held the canoe like an anchor.

"Let go."

"Now that she's gone, come for a swim," he said. "I've got some coolers on ice, going to waste. You can tell me what you wanted to talk to me about."

"No. I'm going home."

His hand grabbed mine. "Hey, Bernie, don't be mad. I never get to see you without that crew around." His eyes were bright with something that set off alarm bells in my head.

"Let go!" I said through my teeth, but he grinned and

leaned harder on the gunwale. Water slopped over the side. He was going to tip me!

I swung wildly with my paddle, catching him on the shoulder. He tried to grab for it, but I swung it again. This time he ducked under the water, letting go of the canoe. I back paddled hard and fast, putting a boat-length of water between us. When he broke the surface, I knew he was going to swim after me. I swung the canoe around, dug deep and managed to outdistance him.

"Fine. Go home to your drunk of a mother, you silly bitch! You're not worth the effort. Go on. *Get lost!*"

Chapter Thirty-two

You may see and be affected by
other people's ways, you may even
use them to find your own, but
you will have eventually to free yourself of them.

Paul Strand, photographer

As the canoe banged against the wooden walk on the far side of the big boathouse, laughter rang out from the beach. They were all there. I avoided them by going in through the veranda door and stared out the screen.

There was Mario putting suntan lotion on Lucy's nose, a blissful smile on his face. John was sitting beside Celia. She was talking and he was listening intently. He laid his hand briefly on her shoulder and nodded. When did all this *happen*? I'd been taking pictures since I got here. Hadn't that camera been practically glued to my eye until yesterday? How had I missed so much? Was I that stupid? That clued out?

I went to the kitchen and stood there, clenching my hands to stop them from shaking. Everyone would be in here soon, laughing, making lunch and asking me questions — or trying *not* to. My brain was going to explode. Hey, remember Bernice Dodd? She blew up in her kitchen. Bits of her everywhere. Had to scrape her off the ceiling.

I took two of the old wine bottles from the back of the cupboard, grabbed an opener and went into the darkroom. I locked the door and slid onto my backside, closing my eyes and trying to take long deep breaths — but when I opened

them again, there was Jack's picture on the drying line looking down at me with that quizzical smile.

"Yeah, okay, you were right." I held up the bottles. "I *am*
the Loser. And Tony is the Total Creep. Okay? Happy now?
A toast to Bernie — the Loser of all Losers."

I opened a bottle and took a deep swallow. I'd never had
wine before. It was warm and tasted like dark fruit. It filled
my nose with heavy fumes. No wonder Celia liked it. I took
another swig.

How long would it take for this stuff to numb my brain
and calm the shakes? I couldn't get Tony's sneering face out
of my head. There had been something dark and obscene in
his look. My bones contracted with disgust. How had I not
seen who he really was? He thought he was God's gift —
who could turn *him* down? I bet he'd barely waited until that
red-haired woman's husband went back to the city before he
moved in on her, making her feel like she was the only one
in the world. Was she the woman he'd met in Stellar? Or was
that another one he'd fooled. I took a couple more swigs of
wine. When would I start forgetting?

I stared at the picture of Jack and me at the chip van.
How could he look at me like that? As if he really liked me.
What was there to like? I must have been pathetic at the
picnic.

I filled my mouth with wine again and swallowed, letting
the fumes fill my nose and gazing at the prints we'd done
together. I stood up ... *whoa* ... waited for the room to steady,
then grabbed the pictures of Tony, tore them to bits and
dropped them on the floor. I picked up the Leica and took a
shot of them lying there.

"Bye-bye, Geriatric Romeo ... Bye-bye, suntanned flabby
loser. Hope Red's husband catches you ... hope he knocks
you right out of your ... out of your famous blue bathing suit
... you gig ... you giga ... you two-timing gigolo!"

With a loud burp, I drank the rest of the bottle, then slid onto the floor, where I lay flat on my back. I held the camera up and panned the ceiling. Nothing but nothingness, so I clicked the shutter. Then I scoped to the other bottle of wine. How did it get way up there on the counter? I couldn't seem to see the opener. Wasn't sure I remembered how it worked. So I just stayed where I was, camera on my stomach — not thinking. *Finally.*

I don't know how long I lay there. I may have slept. But then someone knocked on the door. I held my breath and tried to be as quiet as a dead mouse. They banged the door again. I hitched myself up, lolling against the wall. Ooph. My stomach felt very full and my head was orbiting the room ... no, the room was orbiting my head — I tried to shout, Go *away!* but the muscles around my mouth had dissolved. The doorknob rattled.

"Bernie. It's me. Lucy. Let me in."

I tried to find my feet.

"Bernie, let me in!"

I managed to stand up and turn the lock. Lucy'd understand. She was my friend. The door swung open. Celia stood on the other side. "Oh crap," I muttered, and tried to close the door on her, but she grabbed my arm and steered me back into the room, almost tripping over the bottle. I giggled. She shut the door and stared down.

"No. Oh, Bernie. *No.*"

"Oh, Bernie, yezzz," I said. "Oh, Celia, yezzz. Like mother ... like dauder ... like dauder like ... grand ... mother — or something along those —" I belched. The heaviness in my stomach rose so fast, I barely had time to stagger to the sink. The retching seemed to go on forever.

As I panted over the mess, mouth open, Celia ran a cold cloth across my face.

"Rinse," she demanded, handing me a glass. I could barely grab hold of it, so she held it to my lips.

After I rinsed, I grabbed on to the sink with shaking hands and said, "You can go now. I'm okay." I let out a hollow burp and grimaced at the foul taste.

She turned me toward her, held my face between her hands and looked me right in the eye. Her mouth was trembling. "Bernie, why did you do this?"

She was too close — out of focus. "Dunno."

"Oh, Berns. You *do* know I love you?"

"Do you? I forgot."

Tears rolled down her cheeks. "Well, I do. Very much. Don't do this. *Please*."

I wanted to say, "It works for you, why not me?" but it came out, "He doesn't love me anymore."

"Who doesn't love you?"

"Tony ... Jack."

"Tony is a —"

"Creep," I said firmly.

"Yes. But Jack —"

"Jack isn't," I muttered. "And J-Jack is never going to ... talk to me again."

"Yes, he will."

"No. No, he won't ever. And I almost drowned Jojo."

"No, you didn't. She's my child, Bernie. I've left that responsibility on you for too long. It was my fault."

"Both faults," I insisted.

"It was an accident, but we'll make sure nothing like that ever happens again. Okay?"

I wanted to go back to the old arguments, but my mouth had other ideas. "Nothing working the way I planned. We should leave."

"Don't you like it here?"

"No! Yes. I don't *know*!"

"Come on, sit on the floor," she said, helping me down. "How are you feeling? Less drunk?"

"A bit. Don't like being drunk."

"Good." She sat cross-legged beside me.

"You've been drunk lots of times," I said.

She nodded. "Yes. I have. But no more."

I shook my head, but had to stop to let the room go level again. "Can't trust you, Celia," I said sadly.

"I know, Bernie. I can only stay sober one day at a time. Will you give me one day at a time?"

"But what if you go away again?" Tears burned my eyes. I tried to hold them back, but they were in a conspiracy with my mouth. "And what if you don't come back? I always figured one day you wouldn't come back. Like Dad." Tears streamed down my face and out my nose.

"I would never leave you!" she cried. "*Never.*"

"But how do I know that? You go away for *days*." I was crying with loud gulps of air. "And ... and every time, I'm sure you'll never come back."

"I will *never* leave you, Bernie." She held my shoulders. "I'll go to AA. Faithfully. But I'll need your support, honey."

"But who'll support *me*, Celia? I can't get anything right anymore."

She hugged me tightly. "Oh, Bernsie. *I'll* support you. I'll take care of you and the kids. Will you let me try? Please?" She pressed her forehead to mine and cried. And I cried, too, but my hands remained in my lap.

"I didn't have a mom I could rely on, either, Bernie. Oh, mine was home every day, but drinking herself into a stupor. I always blamed myself for the way she became. Same with your dad — I thought it was my fault he wasn't happy. But I now know they both needed someone else to blame for them giving up on life. My mother used to yell that it was all my fault my father walked out, that if she hadn't got pregnant, he wouldn't have felt trapped, and —"

I muttered, "would've married her for love. I doubt it, though, don't you?"

She looked at me, surprised, so I added, "Ruby told me some stuff."

"When I met your dad I thought I'd found someone who would make my world ... well, better. As a kid, I always felt ... so ... inadequate. But your dad couldn't help me — only *I* can help me. He couldn't even help himself, as it turned out. As for Seb ... well, except for the lovely fact that we all got Jojo out of it ... well, we won't go there."

I looked at her through swollen eyes. "If you saw what happened to your mother and then to Dad, why did *you* drink?"

She shrugged. "Why did you drink today?"

"To get my mind to stop remembering, I think."

"Sounds familiar. But after the car accident, I realized I've been blaming others for my behavior for years — my mother, your dad, Seb. And I realized I was like my father. I *did* leave you — maybe not physically for long, but I ran away to alcohol. I wasn't *there* for you. I will work this out. I want to be Mom again, not Celia the alcoholic."

I gulped down a sob. She handed me a tissue, and while we were sniffling and dabbing, she whispered, "Will you help me?"

I looked up at Charlotte's eyes, at the sadness in them. What if she had forgiven William? Made her peace with Lydia? Would she have had a happier life? Who knew? She never tried.

I had to. So I nodded, and whispered, "Yes."

Chapter Thirty-three

Everything went together perfectly, and this is what I mean by knowing. I didn't have to analyze anything. I just recognized what was in front of me.

Wynn Bullock, photographer

As we sat on the floor talking, Celia insisted I drink lots of water. "If you don't, you'll have a terrible hangover," she said. "See? There's *one* advantage to having a drunk for a mother."

I sputtered into my glass. She made me laugh a few times more and we cried a bit, too. She looked at my photos hanging on the line.

"These are *really* good, Bernie. You've got talent."

We talked about photography — and then about Dad, about the kids, about Lucy and Mario, and finally I decided to tell her everything I'd learned about William, Lydia and Charlotte. I showed her photos of them. She studied them for a long time.

"Did I do right to tell you?" I asked. "I've been making lots of stupid decisions lately."

"Oh yes, you did right." She pointed to William and Charlotte, sitting side by side. "So they loved each other, huh?" Then she said sadly, "He never tried to contact me."

"Would Lydia have told you if he tried?"

She looked surprised. "No, I don't suppose she would. I'll never know now, will I?"

"Maybe he figured he'd done enough damage."

"Maybe. But it hurts. It's always hurt." Her eyes filled

with tears. "But I can't fix that, can I? And I won't do what he and my mother did — or Charlotte. I won't throw everything away."

"Man, we've had our share, huh?"

She laughed softly. "Yeah. But we've still got each other. We won't throw that away, will we?"

"No. I hope not."

She gave me a smile. "You'll be watching me, right?"

"If you watch *me*."

"Deal. Are you hungry now?"

I nodded. "A bit. But I don't want to talk to anyone. I know Lucy goes home the day after tomorrow, but —"

She opened the door quietly and peeked out. "No one there. Why don't you go up to your room and I'll bring you some toast and a drink. Then you can sleep it off."

"No black coffee. I've seen what that can do."

"Tea it is," she said and grabbed me in a hard hug.

A few minutes later, I slid under the blanket on my bed thinking how everything had changed in one short day. Tony had proved to be the Slime of the Century, and Celia had proved to be ... a real person again, not just someone who drank too much.

But some things hadn't changed. How was I supposed to know how much I'd miss Jack's lean, snub-nosed face, his silly grin? How was I supposed to know that my heart would hurt whenever I thought about his expression in the photo in front of the chip van? I thought about Lydia and William and what a mess they'd made of things. I thought about little Celia caught in the middle. I thought about Charlotte and the terrible hurt she must have felt at their betrayal.

I'd screwed things up with Lucy, too. Someone I'd loved all my life. Celia wasn't the only one with things to fix. So I'd better get fixing. But first, I needed to close my eyes. Just for a moment.

The early morning sun drifted through my window, touched lightly on my feet and lay warm on my face. I blinked in surprise. Had I really slept all afternoon and all night? I had a vague sense of Celia coming into my room with a tray. A small plate had toast crumbs scattered over it and beside it, a mug with a skim of grayish liquid on the bottom. I remembered stumbling to the bathroom at least once in the night. Now, my eyes burned and my mouth tasted like I'd swallowed glue, but my head only felt the size of a head and a half — not a basketball full of wine fumes anymore.

I expected the usual tepid shower, but was amazed to find the water actually hot. My head slowly shrunk to its normal pin size. I put on some makeup and blew my hair dry to arm myself for the job ahead. I crept down the stairs, like a trained sniper. Nervous. Watchful. Ready to die.

I was taking the lid off the coffee can when Lucy came in, followed by Mario. Oh no. Please, not this soon.

"Uh, you want some coffee?" I asked, not making eye contact.

"Sure. Wanna beat some eggs up, too?" she asked.

Mario stretched and yawned widely. "I brought some bacon. You start that, Lucia, and I'll put on the coffee."

I hunched over the bowl, breaking and whisking eggs, wanting to say I was sorry, but the words stuck in my throat.

Lucy put her frying pan next to mine, carefully laying thick slices of bacon into it. When I glanced over, she was looking right at me.

I croaked out, "Luce, I'm ... I was awful ... I shouldn't ... I —"

She wrapped one arm around my shoulder and shook me gently. "You said it because you love me and were worried about me. But I know what's right for me."

Tears hovered, then slid down my cheeks. Hey, *look*,

everyone — tough, never-cry Bernie can't seem to stop crying, for crying out loud.

"But I do think you owe Mario an apology for thinking that Tony was prettier than him. I mean, look at my guy — he's gorgeous!"

Mario shrugged, palms up. "She's crazy. What can I say?"

"I'm sorry, Mario," I said. "Lucy's right. You're not only better looking than that preening, conceited creep, but you're a million times nicer."

He gaped at me. "A million? Is that all?"

We laughed way more than was called for. Surely it couldn't be this easy. I didn't deserve easy. As for Mario, I had to have faith that he would be good to Lucy and would never hurt her. I must have been staring at them, looking pretty bereft, because Lucy grabbed me again. "Oh, Berns, it will be okay. Really!"

"I don't deserve you, Luce," I said, my voice wavering. "I deserve a kick in the backside. I deserve to be fried in that bacon fat. I deserve a sock on the nose. I deserve —"

She pretended to sock me on the nose but turned it into a gentle tap. "There. Done."

"Let's eat!" Mario shouted.

Chapter Thirty-four

*Sometimes it's a really good idea to put
down your camera and take time to see
what's going on in your own life.*

Bernice Dodd, photographer

Later in the afternoon, while everyone was sitting on the
shore, John Broom arrived. Ally ran straight to him, waving
a bug jar in the air. Mr. Broom lifted him up with one arm
and took him over to Celia. She watched them approach, a
strange, baffled look on her face, as if seeing the sun for the
first time.

I casually started off along the shore. I had one last
thing to do. I came to a halt at the flat rock between our
houses. I *knew* it. Jack couldn't be out in the boat or in
Stellar on an errand. Oh *no*, he had to be right here — *right
now*. *Damn*. He was lying on his back, jean-clad legs
stretched out, ankles crossed. One arm rested over his eyes.
His fishing rod lay beside him. I wished I had my camera
with me.

Should I warn him I was there? Should I sneak back
home? Should I sit beside him? Should I clear my throat?
The decision was made for me — Badger leaped out of a
bush and threw himself at me, knocking me sideways.

"Badger! Get off!" I cried as he slobbered all over my
face. "Get off, you idiot!"

"Badger. Come!" Jack was on his feet, hands on hips, a
growl on his face. As Badger bounded back to him, he said,
"You calling my dog an idiot?"

"I'm sorry — I —"

He picked up his rod and began to cast. "Never mind. You can go about your business now. He won't bother you."

Badger sat in the shade, grinning around a tongue that practically stretched to the ground.

I said through dry lips, "Well, actually, *you're* my business."

He cast deep. "Not anymore, remember?"

"I — I just wanted to say sorry," I muttered.

This apology wasn't going to be as easy as Lucy's and Mario's.

He glanced over his shoulder, shrugged, reeled in and cast again, the line singing. As he began to reel in, he said, "Doesn't matter. I'll see you around, Bernie. I'm busy right now."

Suddenly his line went taut and began to move back and forth.

"You've caught something," I cried.

Badger sprang to his feet and danced around Jack, who almost lost his footing. "Pull him away or I'll trip and drop the rod," he cried.

Suddenly the fish lifted out of the water with a spray of foam. I dragged Badger to one side and we watched Jack reel in the line. His rod was bent almost double by the time he eased the monster into his net. I caught the glare of a glassy eye the color of wet tobacco.

"I got him! A huge jack, and what a beaut! What a fight! Of all the times to get him. In the afternoon, for Pete's sake!" Soaked to the skin, he leaned over and carefully worked the hook from the gaping mouth. Grinning with joy, he held the dazed fish up, its head in one hand, tail in the other, belly hanging between, vulnerable and pale. What a shot that would make. At the same time, it must have dawned on Jack who he was showing it off to because his broad smile instantly vanished. He stepped onto a low shelf of rock, knelt down and lowered the fish into the water, moving it back and forth.

"Why are you doing that?"

He didn't answer at first, then muttered, "To get a flow of water and oxygen into his gills and —" He jumped back with a laugh as the big fish flapped his tail and took off, sliding through the amber water like a bladed shadow.

"So long, buddy."

"You didn't keep him."

"You don't keep the ones you wait for."

"Will you try and catch him again?"

"Nah. We've met. That's all I wanted." He stared over the still water.

I said, "Fishing is weird. You keep some and eat them and you throw others back for no reason."

"Kind of like you."

"What?"

"Well, you dragged me onto the shore, let me flap around for a while, then threw me back for a bigger fish."

"Yeah. You're right ... a nasty one that attacked first chance it got."

"What does that mean?"

I tried to laugh, but it came out a dry choked sound. "He's working most of the women on this lake, I think, and when I interrupted one of his tête-à-têtes, he —"

Jack leaned forward and touched my arm. "He *what*?"

I told him what happened, but not about the wine or about Mom. *Mom?* That stopped me. I'd just called her Mom. Not Celia.

"But you know what?" I said. "I was glad he acted like a jerk. Deep down I knew that's what he was, but I think I wanted to prove something — that I was grown up? To Celia ... or myself. I don't know. Anyway, looks like we're going to stay at the lodge. Celia — Mom has promised to go to AA.

We'll give it a chance." I tried not to look at him, but his gaze was so intense I had to. "So ... I came to find you — to say I was sorry."

"Sorry? For what?" he said, his eyes never leaving my face.

"For saying that I wouldn't miss our friendship if I left. I would. I did."

"You *actually* missed me?"

I nodded.

"Yes?"

I flushed. "Okay. *Yes!* But before I said I wouldn't miss you, you said you didn't think we *had* a friendship anyway. So it wasn't like I just said it out of the blue."

"I said that we didn't have a friendship anymore? I said *that*?"

"You said I was angry, even when I wasn't angry. *You* called *me* a loser."

He sat down on the rock. "I did? No ... I didn't."

I sat beside him. "Yes, you did."

"No, I didn't."

"You *did*."

"Hey, I thought you came to apologize to me."

We sat for a moment before I said, "I did. I *am* sorry."

"Well ... I *may* have said something along the lines of our friendship not working. Maybe we're almost even," he said.

I took a chance. Maybe he'd pull away, but I did it anyway. I leaned my head against his shoulder. "Yeah, you did. Since you're so bossy, I guess you'll always tell me what I need to hear, right?"

"You don't want that," he said, one arm sliding behind my back, pulling me closer. Prickles went up my arms and for a moment I couldn't breathe for the happiness filling my chest.

I whispered, "Okay, maybe I don't. But keep it in mind — just for future arguments."

Chapter Thirty-five

*When we care, we will not forget. The picture
in our head or the vivid printed picture will remind us.
Without care, we would not remember, only see.*

Anonymous

Sometimes I wish Charlotte could be here with us. I've framed all her amazing color photos, and after taking down all the dead wildlife, Mom and I hung the pictures around the living room. I picked black-and-white ones for my own room — including the one of Charlotte and William.

I keep hoping she found some happiness after William, that maybe her cameras and her home gave her some peace. Sometimes I imagine William and Charlotte bumping into each other in Stellar and realizing they could still be friends. Maybe meet for dinner now and again. Did it happen? I don't know. But among her office papers, I found a small newspaper clipping advertising his art classes. Another mystery that will never have an answer, but that small piece of paper taught me not to waste my chance to be happy, to learn to forgive ... even myself. Maybe Charlotte did some forgiving near the end. After all, she left the lodge to Lydia and William's child.

It's fall now and the leaves are turning. Here in northwestern Ontario, the poplars and birch are like low stretches of sunshine even on rainy days. And there's quite a lot of sunshine in my life at the moment. It's not perfect, but it's pretty nice. The store has been open for almost three months and we've made enough money to squeak through the winter. We're not starving — Ruby offers an endless supply of casseroles when we're not actually eating at the Broom house, which happens more often than not.

Mom is going to Alcoholics Anonymous and hasn't had a drink since the car accident. As for her and John, I'm not sure what's going on. According to Mom, it's best for an alcoholic not to rush into a new relationship — she's giving herself a year of staying sober first. Meanwhile, they go to movies and John takes her shopping, but they always have Ally or Jojo with them. Or Ruby. But they seem happy in each other's company. John Broom actually smiles quite often now.

As for Ally, he's doing a lot better. Once every two weeks, John and Mom take him into Winnipeg so he can talk to a child psychologist, spend the night with Lucy and Mario and return home the next day. I think I have a lot to thank John for.

Lucy and Mario come to visit almost every second weekend — and Mario has been a huge help planning the store. They're getting married next summer at the lodge. Jojo and I are bridesmaids. Mom is matron of honor.

And Jack. What can I say? When he walks into a room, the hair on the back of my neck stands up. That didn't even happen with Tony. He makes me laugh a lot. And he thinks I'm pretty funny, too — even my resurrected knock-knock jokes. I hardly growl at all anymore.

Jack and I have a whole school year together — he's in grade twelve, I'm in eleven — before he goes to university in Winnipeg. He's going to stay with Lucy and Mario. I hate the thought of him leaving for a whole winter, but it's only a four-hour bus ride. And lots of times he'll be here with Lucy and Mario. They bought a big house and I'll stay there, too, when I go to university, also majoring in — you guessed it. I only hope I remember to put my camera down often enough to keep things in focus. But no doubt Jack will be there to remind me.